The Theoretical Foot

The Theoretical Foot

A NOVEL

M.F.K. Fisher

COUNTERPOINT
BERKELEY

Library of Congress Cataloging-in-Publication Data

Names: Fisher, M. F. K. (Mary Frances Kennedy), 1908-1992.
Title: The theoretical foot / M. F. K. Fisher.
Description: Berkeley : Counterpoint, 2016. | "2015
Identifiers: LCCN 2015036016 | ISBN 9781619026148 (hardcover)
Subjects: LCSH: Americans--Europe--Fiction. | Voyages and travels--Fiction. | Man-woman relationships--Fiction. | Europe--Social life and custums--1918-1945--Fiction. | BISAC: FICTION / Literary. | GSAFD: Autobiographical fiction.
Classification: LCC PS3511.I7428 T48 2016 | DDC 813/.54--dc23
LC record available at http://lccn.loc.gov/2015036016

Cover design by Jarrod Taylor
Interior design by Domini Dragoone

COUNTERPOINT
2560 Ninth Street, Suite 318
Berkeley, CA 94710
www.counterpointpress.com

Printed in the United States of America
Distributed by Publishers Group West

10 9 8 7 6 5 4 3 2 1

All characters and places in this story
are fictious, except perhaps Geneva, Switzerland.

[Handwritten notation: "1988"]

1

He ran quickly up the stairs. At the first landing he stopped and waited with a strange expression on his fine goat-like face while his left leg seemed to yawn, as if it were breathless.

He leaned his forehead against the cool plastered wall, and while he reached with one hand to turn off the lights, he felt the breath come back to his leg. He waited a moment longer then stepped lightly, making his way upward to his high room. His feet knew every crack and led him willy-nilly to his love. But when he found the large bed empty and heard a quiet singing and the sound of water in the bathroom, he was glad—his leg no longer yawned, but now hurt like a cramp, like hollowed-out muscles. He lay down along one side of the bed.

A minute later he began to moan, to his own embarrassment. The woman came out, with water shining in the hair around her face, and looked stolidly at him, her heart leaping like a wounded rabbit against her ribs.

In five more minutes he was near insanity. He made strange barking noises and pulled at his hair until it stiffened with his pulling and his sweat into fantastic points above his incredibly tortured face.

A doctor came, and a nurse, and he thrust his bared arms at them as a thirsty animal thrusts forth its tongue for water. Oaoh oaoooh, he jabbered when they pressed the needles into him. More, more, he said. They could not keep ahead of the pain, though. It raced opiates and won, and all night long he howled and tore at himself, slippery with sweat, pinned to the wide bed of love by a leg that had turned cold and pure in color, a peg with five toes, shapely and hideous like a Greek carving in a glacier. Oaoh, oaoh, he clattered and held out his straining arms. There, there, more! He pointed wildly at the soft veins to show them where his blood thirsted for the opiate strong enough to slake the pain. But there was none and in his agony he forgot the needles that had been emptied there and was now filled with a cruel certainty that no earthly thing could succor him. He hated the doctor, and the monkish nurse, and the pinched flat face of his beloved, and he now knew he was alone.

i

On the morning of August 31, Susan Harper stood looking at herself in the murky mirror of a third-class station hotel in Veytaux, Switzerland.

It must be hitchhiking from Munich that didn't agree with her—she'd been so well all summer and she knew she'd looked well too. But now her head ached and her eyes hurt and she was convinced that she looked not just awful, but *awful.*

She pulled irritably at her smooth bleached hair and rolled it into a hard little knot on the top of her head. It was now so white and faded, her face looked dark as a Mediterranean. Her gray eyes, in contrast, seemed almost colorless now within their rings of thick black lashes as they stared out from under the startling black wings of her brows, undoubtedly her best feature. Eyes and brows? She never hesitated to use them, with outrageous infinitesimal winks and candid stares, but this morning everything about her looked flat and dull.

She sniffed as she stood peering coldly at herself. Who could look decent after four days on the road? She stuck a tiny green bow in the hollow of her washerwoman's knot and sniffed again.

Well, what *shall* I wear, then? she asked silently. Which gown from my extensive wardrobe? What would the famous Sara Porter appreciate? What's correct for a girl to wear to a Swiss casino at ten thirty in the morning, coming to see an older woman known as much for her smooth chic as for her snobbishness?

How could I—how could *anyone*—keep up her self-respect after three months of tramping over Europe with nothing more than a collapsible zipper bag for luggage? A bag that for years had been just big enough to carry her father's dirty slipovers and stockings home from the golf club every Saturday night? She was startled now to have thought of Father and of his pleasantly high-balled breath when he came in from a good game, how he'd then solemnly split his winnings with her.

What would Father think if he knew where she was now?

My green tweed skirt, she decided. Oh, that, by all means, since it is the only skirt I have. And my yellow sweater instead of the white, or shall I wear both at once to show her I really do have two? And my yellow socks instead of the white. I'll be a vision, but a *vision*!

It was all Joe Kelly's fault, of course, giving our last cent almost to every pathetic refugee who looks at us! And what good does it really do? No country wants its poor; there were such vast numbers of refugees suddenly and it occurred to Sue that helping them was only keeping them alive and this meant they'd live on longer in abject misery.

Then she, of course, instantly felt ashamed of herself for thinking such a thing, but her exasperation was again mounting as she looked at Joe Kelly. He was lying in bed on his back, his great hairy body spread-eagled; his heavy hand lolled darkly toward her. Still asleep! she thought. Still taking up the whole bed as he did even when she was in it.

Though she didn't need the light over the washstand to dress, she snapped it on in a vicious way, thinking, Well, maybe *this* will wake him.

Joe stirred, sighed once, murmurred *Sweet Sue* and was asleep again.

Susan watched him with her mouth pinched tightly against her fine, large white teeth. Suddenly all her crossness vanished and she was filled with such great tenderness and yearning for Joe, seeing his unprotected infant face as he lay there, that she felt almost dizzy, almost ill at ease, to have this great coarse and ultimately so mysterious man completely in her power, to have him lying there so innocently, as defenseless before her as a snail without its shell.

She leaned against the cool enamel basin—the cold burned into the soft flesh of her abdomen until she forgot about and now thought of how much she loved him. She wanted to draw him into her arms, to enfold him forever with her passion. Could she? Would she be able to stay with him? What if her boat back to the States should sail without her? What if she should simply appear, show up having followed Joe to Oxford? Then he would *have* to keep her with him! It wouldn't be decent of her to force him, and anyway—she clenched her teeth as the question arose in her brain—did he really want her?

She sniffed, shook her head to clear it. There is no use going over all this again and again. It had been decided, hadn't it? Maybe Sara Porter could help her. She was older. She'd done a lot.

Sue scowled at herself in the cheap wavy glass. Her nose dripped. She sniffed again.

Her white net panties were finally dry, thank God. Of course, there was the extra pair, pale green, rolled up like a stocking in the pocket of her father's golf bag. But for so long now she had washed the white ones every night in the sink of the next of their cheap hotels and hostels—she'd washed them out in a brook one time. She'd hung them up and would find them dry the next morning. Now it had become almost a point of honor to keep the green ones fresh, as if getting down to her last panties would be admitting that this strange life of theirs had become too hard.

She shook the panties out with one deft quiet flap, then stepped into them.

Sue was so small that even when she stood on tiptoes the mirror showed only her head and neck. She padded barefoot into the center of the room looking down at her thin and tiny panties, little more to them than a G-string, she thought with a great degree of complacency. The fabric shone white against her dark brown body.

How *beautiful*! she thought, to be so brown! Even the midsummer fog and mizzle of these last ten days in Germany had not faded her and she was glad. She felt again, as she looked down at herself, the steady, exhausting, exciting heat of those forty days with Joe on the beach near Cros-de-Tallas-Cagnes and the cool voluptuous water that slipped up over her body like milk. Perhaps now she'd never fade. Perhaps this satin darkness was as permanent as the other changes that had come over her.

She smiled, thinking of the envy of her school friends, of all the girls in her sorority house, when she showed them how brown she was. *And she's dark all over too!* Sue could hear their squeals.

But no, of course she couldn't show them as she wouldn't be in college at all this coming winter. Joe said he wanted her with him in England this year. He'd swore to it. Would she have to go back home?

She shook her head again, as if to doggedly clear it, then looked down at her thin brown body. She really was too thin now. She'd stood on a peasant market-woman's scales in Berne the day before: forty-one kilos, under a hundred pounds.

But she wasn't hungry anymore. It seemed to her that they'd been eating nothing but cheap sausages and heavy cheeses and thick, mud-colored bread for longer than she could remember. Joe was always glad to eat her portion or give part to the quiet refugee child, starving and half hidden in some dark Munich alley.

Their eyes haunted her.

Suddenly she brightened. Yes, it was true then, that making love made your breasts fuller. She peered downward. Yes, there was no doubt about it, her two little warm brown breasts were definitely rounder. She cupped her hands over them delightedly—they were firm as apples.

"Come here, self-worshiper," Joe said. "You're my own particular and peculiar little pervert."

At the soft sound of Joe's voice from the bed, she stared foolishly. His eyes, half-closed with sleep, gleamed in the light she now turned on.

"Your master speaks," he said. "Come here, woman!"

She pulled her hands away from the warm places where they'd rested and walked quickly toward the enormous armoire where her one skirt hung primly in the darkness next to Joe's hung-up slacks.

"No," Sue told him.

Joe's smile spread from his eyes to his mouth and he whispered almost menacingly: "Shall I have to make you, then?" He then shook one foot free from the covers as if to get up.

"No, no, don't," Sue said. Though she felt deliciously nervous she made her voice sound cool and sensible. "It's late. You know we told Mrs. Porter we'd meet her at the casino at ten thirty and it's almost ten now. And you still have to shave."

"Come here," he said again.

She moved almost timidly toward him. He stretched out one arm, dark with black hair and sunburn, drawing her into its curve. She sat stiffly on the edge of the bed, scowling at him from under her wide, thick, dark brows.

He drew his other hand, warm and limp with sleep, from beneath the covers and watched as he seriously cupped one large hand under both breasts, having room to spare. Then he squinted at her as Sue burst into an unwilling laugh, throwing herself across his enormous chest.

"Oh, Joe! Joe!" she cried. "You're so damned big!"

"The better to love you with, my dear."

"No," she said, "we *can't.* There's your Mrs. Porter?"

"*My* Mrs. Porter?" Joe asked. "Are you jealous of her? Sara's the—why, you little fool—I've known Sara—oh, Sue, sweet Sue, my lady, my tiny lewd and beautiful love . . ."

ii

It was almost an hour later that Joe Kelly stood slapping water hard against his hastily shaven chin, then snapped off the light above the washbasin. Drying his face, he turned to look blinkingly at Susan.

She lay, light and fragile as a Tanagra figurine, upon the tousled bed. Her face was flushed and her sleeping mouth smiled voluptuously. The little bow had slipped from her knot of hair. Joe picked it off the sheet and tucked it gently into her shell-like navel. Then he bent and kissed her.

"Sue! My Susan, you must wake. Come on, wake up. Hurry. Get into your clothes and find your way to the casino. We're late, damn you, woman, and it is all your fault, you do realize?"

He laughed at her sleepy, black-browed scowl, then ran out of the room and down the dark stairs and out of the ratty hotel.

The station square in the hot morning sunlight was just as hard looking and as unattractive. He stood for a moment blinking in the doorway, then hurried down the public stairway to the lower street. There seemed to be a new system of parking since he was last here, and a fancily uniformed policeman—with unaccustomed lordliness—waved white gloves at the bewildered motorists.

Veytaux's getting ideas, he thought. Silly business to take away all the charm this damn place ever had. No amount of boxes of geraniums on the lampposts can cut down the glare of that bobby's white helmet. What does he think he is, a bloody copper? And Sara will be sore at me—and with reason. Christ! It's already after eleven! "*Monsieur, wo ist*, I mean, *ou est le casino? Bitte? S'il vous plait*, I mean."

He pegged rapidly along the hot crooked streets, following as well as he could the politely proffered directions. How could he have forgotten his French so quickly? Well, give Joe time and he'd have it back better than ever. Maybe after Sue left, he thought. Then he began to worry about when this might happen.

He stopped suddenly and peered at the box of swollen mushrooms and a sheet of flour-dusted ravioli that lay coolly on a white marble slab in a store window. Would she leave? He'd pray if he could, would pray for twenty years, if she'd just now just please gather the guts to leave him. Then he could spend the last three weeks of his vacation in Paris or maybe go down to Beaune. But would she? Did he want her to go? How *was* he going to live without her? Joe was caught. He needed to talk to Sara Porter about it. Sara wasn't much of a one for confidences but this was different.

Almost directly above his head, a bell struck two quarters. "Damn it!" he swore aloud. Half past eleven! Then he hurried down the street to the marketplace and now, almost running, crossed by moving swiftly toward the looming bleak bulk of the casino, then on into its gardens where it was cool and green.

Joe paused, wiped his wet forehead and his upper lip with the back of his hand—he never knew whether to kiss Sara or not, but he did believe he needed to be prepared for it—and went up onto the terrace.

He'd hoped she'd be late herself but there Sara was, sitting in her cool and impersonal way, half in shade, half in sunlight, with amber burning in the glass of beer before her. Would she be furious with him?

She looked up, smiled at him, so that was all right, then. At least she was glad to see him.

"Hello, Sara!" he said. "God, I'm glad to see you!" His voice almost trembled in relief. "And God, I hope you can forgive me! I'll never forgive myself for being so late, your having to wait . . . ?"

Sara smiled again, then put her cool lips against his cheek for an instant before she drew away.

"Oh no, don't kiss *me*!" she said quickly. "You're hot, you're damp. Sit down, Joe, and get your breath. You want a beer, don't you? I can't drink alone. Jean!" she said to the waiter who was flicking white linen tablecloths over the checked ones on the terrace tables. "Please bring another beer, no, two. You need more than one to begin with, Joe, and I'll take some of it too."

"But . . . ?" and here Sara stopped talking and looked completely puzzled for a few seconds before her face changed expressions and she demanded quickly, "But Susan? I almost forgot—this is the first time you've turned up with anyone else, you know? Where's Susan? Didn't you tell me last night on the telephone that she's with you? Is she not well?"

"She'll be right along," Joe said. "She said to tell you she's terribly sorry to be late. But Sara, about Sue . . . ?" And he'd begun then to ask her about what had been on his mind, then immediately thought better. "Well, *you're* looking absolutely swell, you know?" Her dark hair, with its smooth precision, was twisted into a low knot at the back of her head, light streaks striping back from either temple. He stared at her thin peaked brows, her red mouth, so small and sensual.

Sara smiled vaguely under his affectionate scrutiny.

"Terribly busy lately," she said, "but work agrees with me. But what was it you were just thinking, Joe?"

"Oh," he said, "only that Sue's afraid of you."

"Is that what's made her more than an hour late?" Sara asked. "No, really, Joe, I got rather cross, not with Susan but with you, and not for the first time either."

Joe groaned audibly. "I know. God, I know. I'm terrible and you and Tim, too, are always so damned nice about it. But there was first one thing, then another, then we got sort of balled up and . . . ?"

He stopped, grinning faintly at his private joke. Or *was* it private? He glanced furtively at Sara; he never knew with her. Her face remained polite and aloof.

"But she'll be along in a minute," he finished lamely, feeling crude and collegiate.

"That's good. It's really nice to see you here again. Tim will be so glad to see you too. Now drink up, Joe."

Joe paused, the glass on its way to his open and thirsty mouth to say, "How *is* Tim?"

"Oh, fine as ever . . . a little pooped now and then. He gets upset, little things that he doesn't like to talk about. It's been a funny summer, what with this and that. But he'll be really, really glad when *you* get there."

Joe felt once more the uncertainty he so often had with Sara Porter. Was she really cold, really pushing all the world from her in a thousand subtle ways, or was she the warm hospitable woman he believed he knew? He shook his head slightly. Why worry? Most of the time, except when he remembered how long he had known her, yet how little he knew her, he felt all right about her and that it might not really matter.

They clinked glasses, and then sat for a minute without talking, watched the green light flicker over their table, listened to children playing lazily on the quay by the boat landing. Joe finished his glass and then poured half a second one solemnly into Sara's before he drank from it.

"God, that's good," he said, wiping the foam from his full wide lips, then smiling. "You know the beer in Munich isn't as good as it used to be, Sara. It tastes thin, somehow."

"What?"

"I said the Munich beer tastes thin, different from the old days."

"You know you speak more softly all the time, Joe. Whenever you blow into town I always go through a few hours of wondering if I'm becoming deaf."

"*Blow in* is right! Hell! And I promised you, last time, that I'd let you know in advance of my coming, didn't I?"

"Oh, don't brood. But yes, it *is* more convenient to know at least a few hours before, but I suppose you got all balled up again or something."

Joe peered at her suspiciously, but her eyes were as bland as the rest of her face and betrayed nothing.

"What I'm afraid," she went right on, "is that this time we can't put you up." She then stopped speaking to laugh at his pained and horror-struck face.

"Oh Christ, no," Joe said in protest. "And after all I've told Sue about La Prairie and your cooking? And how we've walked all the way from Munich just to get to you."

"You walked?" Sara asked. "Do you mean to tell me, Joseph Kelly, that you made Sue hitchhike? That tiny dainty little thing? No wonder you're late. It's a wonder you didn't kill her."

"Nothing of the kind! She actually loved it. It was the first time in her life she'd ever done anything so daring. And anyway, her size has nothing to do with it—that girl is as strong as a horse.

"But, Sara," Joe asked, "is it because you're sore that I didn't tell you when we'd land?"

"Of course not. As a matter of fact, we just got in last night ourselves from a jaunt up to Dijon. But the truth is the place is more full than it's ever been, but wait, here she is!"

Susan Harper stood for a moment on the edge of the terrace looking at Joe and his friend. If she didn't feel so awful, she thought, she'd be hurt at the free and easy expression in her lover's dark and undeveloped face, the new relaxation in his huge shoulders. But she *did* happen to feel so sick. Her head felt as if it were full of old feathers and she knew with a chill and a dreadful certainty that somewhere between Munich and Veytaux she had caught a prize cold. She sniffed angrily.

Then, as if it had been held at bay by space alone, shyness swept over her. She began to tremble inside and pray to God that her head and her voice would not quake and betray how her stomach was shaking as she began to totter across the miles of terrace that separated her from them.

She was wondering as she went along how this woman managed to scare her so thoroughly. The several times she'd seen Sara before, in America, she'd been quiet and kind and—in her own detached way—seemed honestly interested in what Susan was doing and what and where she was studying. Sue and Joe had gone to her house twice for dinner and had eaten and drunk and talked well into the night; rather *Joe* had. Sue still remembered the agonies of her own shyness that had almost conquered her before each visit and the awkwardness that conspired to make her clumsily drop glasses and trip over rugs and stutter as she never had since grammar school.

Was all that to start again? she wondered. She was grown up now, no longer the foolish virgin. In fact, Susan was only a few years younger than Sara was herself. And Sara hadn't needed these four years of living in Europe to make her polished, as she'd already been so smart and so cool.

Sue surreptitiously wiped a little tear of perspiration from the hollow of her upper lip, then stretched to make the most of her fifty-nine inches, pulled her skirt smoother over her tight little buttocks, and walked as haughtily as she could manage across the terrace.

"Good morning, Mrs. Porter," she said without smiling. "It's wonderful to see you again after so long. I hope you will excuse my being late."

Oh dear God, Sue thought as she sat down and remained stiffly posed on the hard café chair. She was wondering what had happened to her. At home she was one of those who had *social poise*, as it was called, one of the more valuable helps during rushing at the sorority house, necessary to impress the timid freshwomen with her sophistication.

Where, she thought, was all that now?

Sue frowned, suddenly hating Joe for bringing her here, all the while trying not to sniff. Sara's voice came to her as if through a dense fog.

"I'm glad to see you here, Susan. And Tim will be too. He's anxious to meet you. And of course it's all right about being late. I did a lot of marketing and then came back here because I didn't know which hotel you were staying at. I'm so terribly sorry not to have been able to put you up last night—we'd just got in from

Dijon. You want some beer, don't you? Jean, three beers. And then . . ." Sara looked at her watch and smiled at Sue and Joe before she turned to the waiter, ". . . and then in exactly seven minutes, three more, please."

Susan stirred herself to protest, permitting herself a quiet, rather unsatisfactory sniff, the sound covered, she hoped, by Joe's laughter.

"We haven't seen anyone order beers in such a lordly way for weeks, have we, Sue?"

"Maybe the beer in Munich tasted thin because of your politics, Joe, you don't suppose?"

"Well, no," he said. "Not even the political rape and treason that we've witnessed there could spoil my fine appreciative taste for beer. I swear, Sara, even *French* beer tastes better than that stuff in Germany now! And the food? Do you know that if you order butter in a restaurant . . ."

Susan listened to their voices flowing on wordlessly. She raised her glass as they did theirs, then sat sipping at it, wishing it was water. How could a thin woman like Sara hold her liquor so well? Wasn't beer bad for your figure? Maybe Sue should drink more of it before Joe began to think she was too skinny. But now there were only a few days more. Or would she be going home?

She looked with sudden spectulation in her enormous dark eyes at Sara Porter's face. Would Sara be able to help her? Why was it that in spite of her inexplicable shyness, Sue felt that this older woman—almost unknown to her—could tell her what was good and right to do? Maybe it was because Joe liked Sara so well—Joe, who had never really had a home or parents and few real friends like Sara and herself.

Sue sat watching Sara talk with him. They leaned back in their chairs, their voices murmurred. Sara had a light, soft way of saying words, her tone faintly pedantic, perhaps because of her crisp enunciation. Sara sounded all her *r*s. She didn't have a typical Western accent.

Sara was thirty but her face looked very young to Sue, perhaps because it was round in shape, the skin very smooth beneath the severely drawn-back hair. Sara wore a rather crumpled green linen dress and white cotton gloves obviously darned. How in hell was it that Sara—with her rumpled dress and her holey white cotton gloves—always succeeded in making other women feel dowdy?

Sue started, surprised to realize that Sara was now speaking to her. She flushed painfully when she understood that she had no idea of what had gone before. She gulped her beer, wiped one splashed drop off her cheek with unhurried dignity.

"Sorry! I'm really terribly sorry, Mrs. Porter, but I was looking at the lake through the trees and wasn't paying close attention."

"Poor Sue," she said. "I don't blame you. You must be absolutely worn out. Joe told me you've walked here from Munich."

"Oh no, I'm not a bit tired from that," Sue hurried to defend her beloved from what might be criticism. "It's the sun, I think. But what were you saying, please?"

She looked calmly from Sara to Joe, then was horrified to hear herself erupt in a loud sneeze that pounced on her with snarling suddenness. She sneezed so violently it rocked the little table upon which a beer glass spilled. She reached wildly for the handkerchief Joe was now offering her. Through her stinging eyes she saw Sara move away from the flooding path of beer before looking at Sue compassionately.

"God bless you," she said. "*Gesundheit*! Poor child, I think you're catching cold. Here, Jean, mop up a bit, will you? And tell me what I owe you. We'll have more beer at La Prairie—it's time I get there and start lunch."

By the time the bill was paid and Sue had given her nose a thorough—and delightful—blow, she felt almost human again. She stood watching Sara pull on her disreputable gloves.

"I'm sorry, Sue, I've forgotten to finish what I was saying. I've told Joe that I couldn't put you up, much as I might wish to, and then you came along and I forgot to explain."

Sara stopped and then looked abstractedly off toward an old man outside the terrace who stood in the garden of the casino delicately pricking his fingers on the sharp needles of a giant cactus.

"The house is full," she then went on, "but even if I had a room for you, I'd ask you to go up to the village inn this time."

For a moment there was silence, then Joe spoke. "Because Sue and I aren't married?" he asked, incredulously.

Sue felt her throat close. This was the woman she'd thought might help her! It had never occurred to her that perhaps Sara might disapprove of her. She looked miserably at Joe, who reached over and touched her hand.

"Oh dear," Sara said. "Now don't you two make me feel embarrassed. It's not me, nor is it Tim. You ought to know that, Joe."

"Of course," he said.

"It's because we have a rather queer household just now. There's Tim's sister Nan and my young brother and sister—they're all right—but there's also a friend of Nan's, Lucy Pendleton. *She's* the trouble, through no fault of her own, really. It's bad enough to have one illicit affair, as I am afraid Lucy does describe it, without flaunting another."

"What illicit affair?" Joe asked, before exclaiming, "My God! Do you mean *you and Tim*?"

"What?" Sue asked in a small husky voice. She looked blankly from the flush of Joe's face back to the smooth oval of Sara Porter's. She felt completely bewildered.

"Haven't you ever told her?" Sara asked.

"I forgot!" Joe said. "It's always seemed so natural to me and it's been going on so long—I've *forgotten* all about it, I swear!"

"That's an awfully nice thing to tell me, Joe," Sara said as she lightly touched his arm, then turned. "The thing is, Susan, Tim Garton and I have never married," she said. "It's one reason we live here, though it is one of the less important ones. And so poor Lucy Pendleton is over here this summer to guard Nan from our evil influence and she's rather a nervous type and not well, and I knew you'd understand if I decided not to add fuel to her fire by bringing two more *sinners* in under our roof. So, I've arranged a room for you up in the village."

Sara then began to laugh with relief at having finished what was a difficult speech. Now Sue felt herself to be smiling, too, for the first time since she'd seen Sara sitting so easily beside Joe in the dappled morning sunshine.

"All right?" she asked Sue.

"Of course!" Sue said, feeling happy suddenly. "But we'll be at your house a lot, won't we? Joe says it's not just heavenly, but *heavenly*!"

"It is. And you'll be there as much as we can keep you," she said, adding, "except for sleeping." And now Sara listened expertly to the sound of a half-dozen bells striking twelve thirty all over the little town. "We'll all be there if we can just manage to *get there*. Come on! We'll come down after lunch and get your bags."

Sue laughed and ran after Sara Porter with one hand clutching at the corner of Joe's coat.

"I do think she's swell!" Sue whispered as they hurried toward the little black Fiat parked at the curb.

"Sure," he said. "She's fine. But what about all those other people?" Joe hated to think of anyone in the world enjoying La Prairie with the familiarity that he had more than once enjoyed it. It had honestly never occurred to him that Sara ever had other guests. A whole summer's dreams of showing the place to his sweet Sue, of being there with her and with Sara and Tim tumbled into the hard sunlight before his squinting eyes, and he sighed.

"Sue," Sara directed, "you'll sit on Joe's lap in front, as the whole backseat is full of food, as you see?" An unnecessary observation, Sue thought as the three eased themselves into the tiny car.

iii

The streets of Veytaux were almost empty. An occasional worker on a bicycle pedalled home to his late lunch, not even the close heat of lake level slowing his hungry speed.

The little car went fast. Susan, sitting high on Joe's knees, felt the moving air curve around her head, behind her brown and naked ears, even under her beribboned bun of hair.

They were out of town suddenly. To their left the glitter of Lac Léman lay smooth and uninterrupted. Along the shore lay some ugly villas with windows that looked as if their shutters had been closed since the last visit of Edward VII, these unsuccessfully veiled by trees. The road ran on beside the water in a gentle curve.

Joe smiled at Sue's cry of delight.

"Yes, but look up," he said. "The lake's nothing."

She turned her head obediently to the right and tipped it back, trying to see to the top of the steep hill that rose almost straight out of the water. For a moment she said nothing. It was all too strange.

The whole great slope that seemed to stretch on ahead as far as the lake itself was wrinkled and ridged by ten thousand crooked walls of stone, gray-brown and as beautiful as the skin of an ancient elephant. And in each uneven wrinkle—brimming and looping over every wall and filling, like caught emerald water, the little terraces—were grapevines. Their leaves gleamed mysteriously, like verdigris on a copper roof.

Not so fast! Sue almost cried out. She had never seen a countryside like this, rising so strangely from the road walls to the right and sinking on the left straight downward toward the flat blue lake. She asked, stupidly, "Where are all the trees?"

"Trees make shade and take food from the soil," Sara said as she shifted, sending the little car speeding along even faster. "Trees aren't good for the vines."

"It's as bare as the moon," Sue said with sudden seriousness, feeling Joe moving under her and knowing he was laughing. "Well, no trees and all these queer walls and funny color on the leaves . . ."

Sara laughed too. "But you're right! It is very queer, all of it. It's almost frightening to look at these million walls and know that every stone in them was carried on some man's back. They've never stopped working, ever since . . . ? Well, for hundreds and hundreds of years."

"The color's copper sulfate spray," Joe added. He felt as full of knowledge as a vineyeard keeper.

They passed a yellow building, tall and gaily shuttered, with painted red roofs. Sara tooted the horn and waved to some men who sat eating on a wall. Their bare necks, as brown and polished as wood, their faces looking strangely pale as they lifted their chins to gesture in a jovial way toward the car.

"They look nice," Sue murmurred. The men's paleness, she thought, probably came from how they were bent over working all the time. She timidly waved at a solitary *vigneron* who wore a foolish-looking woman's floppy hat of faded cretonne. When he waved back at her she was suddenly filled with a creamy contentment, like a kitten's.

"Now, Sue, now!" Joe pressed his arms tightly around her tiny waist and she could feel his proud excitement. "Now! Around this curve . . . and *there*! You see those big old trees? And the roofs? That's . . ."

"La Prairie?"

"No, that's an old monastery, a farm now, that's just across the road. And now, to the left, Sue! That's it!"

Sue felt a shyness flood into her body again as she looked where Joe pointed clumsily with his one unhindered arm. She was almost overcome with dread at the thought of meeting more people. Sara Porter's little speech about "sin," which surprised Sue more than she realized, sounded again in memory. She felt a wave of shock to have learned that Sara and Tim Garton were not married—she'd always assumed his name was Porter. That she herself was not married to Joe Kelly seemed natural to her and didn't trouble her except when she remembered that she was deceiving her father. It was a shock to remember this was not acceptable for certain people. But to find that the people at La Prairie, that almost mythical couple, Tim-and-Sara, were like Joe and herself! This was such startling news as to seem improbable. Older people *should* be married, shouldn't they? Wasn't it unfair for them to be acting with the unconventionality of college lovers?

And all those strangers! Even Sara Porter had looked uncomfortable, in her remote way, as she had swiftly mentioned them. Sue wondered desperately if there would be *anybody* at La Prairie who was more or less her own age.

She drew in her stomach and tilted her head proudly. They'll all probably be horribly smart and clever—Joe was always quoting what had been said or done or eaten at La Prairie. The only thing she could think of was to try not to sniff and to pretend that her green tweed skirt had just been whisked out of an enormous wardrobe trunk, after much pondering by her of what to wear. If she held herself well she'd look taller and more unwrinkled and it was—as she remembered—always wiser not to talk.

"Look, Sue!" Joe tried to jiggle her on his cramped knees. "Do you see? There! You can see the roof now."

Sue nodded silently.

To their left, a little past the tree and hidden by the bulk of the old monestery, a driveway forked from the road and sank rapidly out of sight between two plain and heavy gateposts. Sara flicked the car expertly through them, cut off the engine, then coasted slowly down a short steep incline to the open garage.

On the right and above their heads was the road wall. The ground sloped downward so abruptly that on their left they looked into the tops of aged apple trees heavy with green fruit and the feathery empurpled bows of prune and plum. Under them wound a steep path past an old square basin-like watering trough. Sue could hear the steady trickle of its spout.

Susan sighed. Joe was right. It was lovely, *lovely*. She felt that this might really be the place where all her turmoil would be calmed, where she could find help for her every present need and trouble and worry.

"Hey! Where is everyone? Isn't anybody hungry?" Sue listened to Sara's calling out to the others, then lay back in Joe's strong arms looking at the house as avidly as if she might never see it again.

The garage was attached to the house, then it dropped with the slope of the land so that the front was almost two stories below, facing a terrace where there was a steadily flowing fountain. There were only two windows, one on either level, each filled with a luxuriant splash of tumbling, flickering petunias, white and deep purple. The walls were almost dust-colored, the shutters a muted green, above was the soft clay-red of the tiles of the roof. Sue felt a fastidious pleasure that the tones were right, as right as her own intuitive selections of greens and whites to blend with her gray eyes and her brown skin and her wild and sun-bleached hair.

Which room would I have, she wondered, if I were a good woman and could stay here? Joe says the house is long, stretched out facing the lake. Where is the lake? It must be very far below. What about this horrid woman who was making life difficult, making Sara Porter and me into whores? That's too funny. I wonder if she really means it?

Sara banged on the auto's horn, almost crossly, then sat back. Nothing happened. The fountain sounded clearly in the silent air and a little puffing breeze filled their nostrils with the scent of bees and rotting fruit.

"I don't know where everybody is. I thought they'd be out in the road looking starved . . ."

"How about my carrying all this in anyway, Sara?" Joe asked and flicked open the door with his elbow, shoving Sue off his lap and out gently, then unfolding himself rather stiffly from the small, low car. He looked with exaggerated amazement at the piles of paper bags and the heaped bundles in the back.

"My God! Well, at least we'll eat!"

"Don't rub it in," Sara told him mildly. "I can't help it if the house is full. Or if you and Sue are shameless. Or if one of my guests . . . ?"

"Hell, I'm sorry, Sara. I'm the rat."

"Yes, you are," she said.

Sue listened with astonishement as the two talked quietly, all the while Sara piling packages on Joe's enormous outstretched arms. He was blinking beatifically about him like a happy dog. She followed to look over the tiles of the sloping roof again and into the dark exciting squares of the flowered windows, on into the fruit-filled treetops.

She had never before heard him talk in such a relaxed way. With her he was almost always making love, fervent, demanding, and, with the people they had met this summer in the south of France and in the little taverns of Bavaria, he had always been passionately angry or excited or upset. His low voice—although it had never grown either loud or shrill—had always rushed and pressed upon her, whether with its own desires or with its angers against the extreme injustices others were witnessing on a daily basis. But now it was somnolent and amused.

She knew that if she were not so filled with shyness and the certainty of having to sniff or blow her nose within the next few minutes she might be jealous of Joe's happiness being found in something besides Sue herself, jealous too of Sara Porter and all these surroundings that made Joe so beamish.

She wondered why Sara called him Giuliano, as she did occasionally. Did it mean something secret between them? Sara *seemed* simple but was she, beneath her quiet manners, actually a grasping woman, a bitch?

Oh, please don't let Sara be a bitch, Sue prayed frantically. She's *got* to be nice! She's got to help me. The boat sails in seven days and I know Joe wants me to be on it, so why does he keep begging me not to go? And why do I *want* him to beg me not to leave him? It's too cruel, cruel. She's got to help me and soon.

"Here, Susan, give a hand," Sara was telling her.

Sue flushed. How could she have stood there so stupidly while they worked? What would they think of her? She sniffed and picked up a bag of tomatoes with awkward haste. As the bag split open, she stood staring in horror at a dozen round red devils rolling merrily down in to the dim garage.

But Sara laughed and said, "Don't you mind, Sue! They're that much nearer the kitchen. Here, take these instead." She piled three packages expertly in Sue's arms and said, "Come on, we'll let Daniel get the rest."

Instead of taking the steep path past the watering basin, Sara now led them into the cool garage and through a door in the far wall.

Sue and Joe followed her gingerly down some twisting steps, peering as best they could over their bundles into the cool darkness of the unfamiliar stairway. The house smelled fresh and airy and was quite without signs of life.

Sara stopped at the bottom of the stairs and they stood for a minute, listening. Susan stirred, hoping that they would not notice how her heart was thumping. Who would appear in this strange place? What would happen next? She felt like a lost child waiting for goblins from the depths.

Suddenly a door crashed open in the little hall in which they stood. Susan looked at the tiled floor, soft green and light gray, and then at the green wooden door and then let her eyes ride up the interminable length of legs of the one who stood there, legs hung with mussed thin cotton pajamas. They did not move. The hips were small and properly tied about with crumpled cloth and the thin lank torso was brown and wide-shouldered and as naked as it was born, and now Susan felt herself to be staring into blinking and bloodshot green eyes.

iv

In the half-second before he'd shut the door with a mumble that sounded rather like *jzza en sczzmhm*, Susan had decided that this was the darlingest, but the *darlingest*, boy she had ever seen.

She stood, ecstatically blank, seeing clearly against the soft green wood the rangy figure who'd been standing there, and she could easily imagine his half-shut eyes, as the sleepy garble of astonishment rang again in her ears with all the clarity of a French train whistle, all the magic sonority of an organ in a dim cathedral.

She flattened her flat little belly and reached with her one free hand, without even knowing it, for Joe's handkerchief. She needed a good blow. Her heart thumped delightedly.

"We'll put these things in the kitchen," Sara muttered. "Damn that lazy boy anyway! Oh, hello, Nor." She nodded at the tall girl who was arising slowly from the blue velvet chaise longue upon which she had been stretched. "We'll drop these things and be back in a minute to be polite."

She led them across a long light room toward the open wall along one side of the fireplace.

Sue picked her way down the three broad steps into the room and followed Sara, flicking one terrified look at this new person. Her mouth had turned dry and she was appalled to realized that in spite of her emotional nose-blow in the hall she would once more need to sniff, and *mightily*. Where else in the world were there as many enormous people as she had seen today?

She was used to Joe, so he didn't count, but Sara Porter had always seemed as tall to Sue as the city hall, and now here Sue was, peering up at yet more people who seemed even taller! And they were all thin. Her neck ached and she slowed down in front of the strange girl with a painful feeling that very soon her head would snap off and roll back off her shoulders with a hollow thump on the floor.

Suddenly it all seemed funny. She grinned and looked up into the benign brown eyes of one of the prettiest faces she had ever seen. She had a new certainty that she was after all so small that no matter what she did nobody would notice her.

Hurray, she thought lazily, I'll do what I like! I'll be Mosca the Gadfly. I'll have a little fun, maybe, and stop worrying myself thin over silly old Joe and whether he wants me and how many miles it is to Munich or Babylon or Oxford.

"Hello," Sue heard herself saying with a kind of passive amazement at her own nonchalance. This girl was one of the handsomest things in the world, certainly, slim, brown, dressed in impeccable white with high-heeled white pumps on her small feet and her silky dark hair piled on top of her head in a way that almost belligerently accentuated her extreme height.

If I didn't feel a little crazy, Susan thought, I'd be paralyzed by her, but *paralyzed*! Poor girl, though, she's so tall I bet it's hard for her to get dates.

"I'm Honor Tennant," the girl said. She spoke slowly, as if she were thinking of something else.

"I think I saw your brother."

"Dan? Yes. I heard his door while you were in the hall. That's too bad. I've been meaning to get him up before Sara got home. But he won't be long, now he's seen you. If you'll give me some of your bundles . . . here, let me just put these things on the table and I'll take you upstairs."

"But what about Mrs. Porter? Hadn't I better . . . ?"

"No. Leave them here. Sara will find them. She likes to be let alone when she's cooking. Anyway, I think what's-his-name went into the kitchen with her."

"You mean Joe?" Sue felt faintly resentful at this tall beautiful girl's complete dismissal of her love. She frowned and went on: "That's Joe Kelly. Please excuse us for not introducing ourselves."

"Yes, I know," Honor said, as if bored. "Star football, Rhodes fellow, all that. He looks nice. But don't worry about introductions. Sara should have done it and she always gets into a twitch before meals and I don't know where Tim is. I know you're Susan Harper, though, we we're at least safe on that point. And I do know we're all awfully glad that you're here."

She started to walk off with the long strides of her long legs toward the wide door through which Sue had just come. Sue ran after as an amused exasperation struggled in her. Suddenly she laughed aloud and darted quickly past Honor and up the stairs to the dim cool hall.

"You know," she said, her voice sounding rather thick to her own interested ears, "I am really scared to death and so have decided to say just what I want to, for once, while I'm here. I'm catching a terrible, but *terrible*, cold." She paused, then added, unnecessarily, "In my head."

Honor stopped her deliberate progress toward the stairs and looked quietly at Sue.

"Gosh, that's too bad," she said seriously, as if this were somehow an important thing about which she suddenly—in spite of her apparent boredom with the world—felt pierced to the very quick of her being. She looked with real concern in her lovely brown eyes, into the strangely twinkling gray ones of Sue, which—because Sue was above her on the stairs—were on a level with her. Then Honor walked on.

They went on up the twisting stair on granite steps. The walls were rough white plaster. There were green tiles on the little landing and green woodwork. Sue, bewildered and excited though she was, was again overwhelmed by the same aesthetic safistfaction that had risen in her in first seeing La Prairie from the car.

Honor turned a final left, Sue following her into a small airy room. She noticed a beautiful desk, a couch bed, a fat squat chair covered with pale cretonne, and long white organdy curtains billowing softly between apple-green and white walls, before the two wide windows which seemed half-filled by boxes of opulent petunias, white and purple. This is the room I saw first, she thought, exultantly. I looked up at these flowers and wondered if I should be here! Sue could hear the fountain below.

Honor stood for a minute, her head bent, as if she, too, were listening or waiting for something. Then she said, "You know, I'm really awfully sorry about your cold. They're hell, so ignominious somehow. I'll give you some face tissues, for hankies.

"And I know what you mean about being scared to speak," she went on almost hurriedly. "I know what you mean. I was too scared when I first came here. It's different now, but my sister's really pretty overpowering. I don't know why . . . I don't think she means to be, but she is. She's nice, though. Wait 'til you see Tim. He'll take the curse off it. And anyhow, I know you won't be scared long." Then Honor suddenly turned away.

She's embarrassed at talking so much, Susan thought. She watched Honor, as the girl stood by the old wooden desk and stroked a curve of its low fluted backboard with one finger. She's embarrassed, and how queer that her hands are short and plump! Sue laughed again softly. She felt much less intimidated now that Honor Tennant had talked even so inconclusively to her.

"You have a strange name."

Honor looked up as if she had forgotten for a second that she was not alone. Her face lightened but she only answered briefly, "Yes." Then, as if ashamed of her curtness, she almost rattled on, "My mother wanted it to be Norah but Father drew the line at that, so it's Honor, which is, of course, even *more* Irish than Norah, though in America there aren't as many cooks named that. Not that I'd mind being one either, just so long as I was a *good* one, cook I mean. Here. This is the dressing room. You'll find everything you want, I think, and that door to the left is the toilet. And help yourself to those tissues, they make swell hankies."

She smiled vaguely at Sue, ran one hand slowly through the top curls of her pile of soft brown hair, and disappeared rather heavily but majestically down the stairs.

Sue listened to her steps and smiled again to herself. Honor was *nice* and she felt somehow that it was because she herself had adopted an important new policy, clearly and definitely, as she'd stood only a few moments before in the bewildering strangeness downstairs.

That's all I need, she told herself triumphantly. With nerve, anybody can carry off a difficult situation—not that things have been *terribly* difficult so far—but they laughed at me when I sat down at La Prairie. I'll just act silly and say what I think. That will fool them all, all these tall people.

As she washed her hands and dried them sensually on the softest towel she'd used that summer, she wondered—and not for the first time—what made her feel so awkward and timid at the thought of this place. Certainly Joe had never offered anything but glowing praise for La Prairie and the people in it and the food and flowers and drink and the good beds and the freedom—all of it had always sounded pefect to her. She had longed to be here and now she was, if shaking a little again inside at the thought of having to go down those stone steps alone and wishing Honor had stayed with her.

Nonsense, she told herself savagely. You're almost twenty, and even if you are shorter than anybody, you do have a great deal of dignity.

She pulled out her three rather bent gold hairpins, shook her topknot loose, and wrapped it into place again expertly. As she poked the ribbon into place in front of her topknot, she stopped in order to look searchingly at herself in the mirror.

She scowled and—with quick determination—pulled the pins out again and did her hair all over again allowing it to sit in place more softly. It was easy to pinch into place the waves always lurking in her wildly gleaming, white-blonde hair. Yes, Joe was used to her and he didn't matter but she felt sure that Dan Tennant would like her better if she looked a little bit less like she'd been skinned.

She pulled deftly at the curls around her face to loosen them, leaving her fine brow bare, her little eyes looking wide and knowing. Then she moistened one finger and flicked her long eyelashes to point them before she looked at herself in the mirror with satisfaction.

Suddenly another violent sneeze rocked her and—for the second time that day—Sue felt as if she'd been jarred by an exploding charge of dynamite. She was sick and she was also being made dizzy by the realization that she would soon be so far away from Joe Kelly. She had never felt so overwhelmed and for a ghastly second she wondered if she was going to vomit as she stretched out one hand reaching blindly toward the washbasin. Then she stood, waiting impotently for the heartache to ebb away and leave her.

Oh, my poor Joe, she thought wildly, my poor, poor Joe. Why do you love me? What is going to happen to us?

The months and years stretched out like a cold cruel wasteland before her now. She shuddered with nausea, feeling again the loneliness of last year at school without him and the hopeless comfort of his passionate letters from Oxford, whose passion felt to her perfunctory, and knowing that this year they would be fewer and that then soon enough they would cease.

Why was it that she knew Joe could live without her? She didn't mind really that he had slept with other girls and that he would again. But why was it that she knew she herself would nevermore feel interest in any living soul? She knew, irrevocably, that what she gave Joe, her love, she had given him all of it, all! All! *All*!

And now she was shivering.

How long had she been standing there, clutching the side of the wash bowl? Honor would think she'd have gone to sleep—that is, if Honor thought of anything so dull as Sue.

Oh, I wish I were a great big woman, Sue thought. Then all these things would not matter half so much or they'd be more spread out over my more massive existence.

She blew her nose thoroughly. Yes, but *definitely*, a damned cold was creeping up on her. Sue felt utterly miserable and quite drained of all the excitement that for a few minutes downstairs had made her forget both her aching head and her breaking heart.

With a nervous look through the door into the little bedroom she quickly opened the cupboard nearest the washstand, as embarrassing as it was to poke about in other people's closets. As she'd thought, though, boxes of powder and a few small bottles of perfume stood there neatly on the first shelf. Beside them were two leather boxes, one of which held a manicure set. Susan felt sure that in the other, once obviously used for tiny tubes and bottles, would be odds and ends.

She opened it ferverishly and grinned with triumph. There was a jumble of lipsticks, hairpins, odd mismatched earrings and—yes!—a little flat box of aspirin.

She opened it and emptied three into her trembling hand, then swallowed them with a little water. Then she went quickly through the bedroom and felt her way down the unexpected curves of the dim stairwell and into the living room.

As she went, she touched her hair here and there carefully with an abstract satisfaction in the way it looked; it felt nice to have it loose again. Would that boy notice that she'd changed her hair since his first sight of her?

But what had Joe been doing all this time? She felt ashamed, realizing that she had not thought of him—the actual bone-and-blood man, the Joe who was her inward secret love—since she'd sat on his strong round thighs in the little car. She hurried to cover her confusion and as she went past the closed door where Dan Tennant had stood in his lovely mussed pajama bottoms, she turned her head resolutely away.

"Has anyone seen Joe?" she asked, her voice cracking slightly as she stood on the top of the three steps leading down into the the big room, now entirely empty.

V

Well, this is the damnedest place I was ever in, Susan thought irritably. I mean, I'm a guest here, after all, and people just keep disappearing!

She grasped the heavy linen curtain that hung by the steps and peered disdainfully about her. Not a soul, not even anyone asleep.

Then her face softened as she looked with a growing pleasure at the long high room. Like the rest she'd seen, this room had been plastered in rough white but here the wood was a dark gleaming brown, like the furniture, which she knew instinctively to be as fine as it was certain to be comfortable. Almost the entire side to her left was tall wide windows that stood open now, hung in thick linen striped softly in green and buff and blue, moving gently now in the noon breeze off the lake.

At the far end was the fireplace with a faded, sloppy red Moroccan cushion before it on the large gray-green rug. To the left an open doorway was curtained in the same striped linen as the one she held and through it she could see into what looked to be a green-tiled pantry whose walls gleamed with the rounds and ovals of stacked china and the soft shock of silver and pewter vessels hung on dark shelves.

On her right an enormous mirror, curved at the top like a great window into another room and framed in dull old gold, separated two long bookcases that quite covered the wall.

There were two couches and some chairs and the blue chaise longue where Honor had lain when they'd first arrived and a big rectangular table with grapes carved along its sides.

Sue sniffed absently, then walked quietly into the middle of the silent room. It was the most pleasant room she'd ever seen. And that mirror!

Colors looked more intense in the mirror, truer than life. It was like a beautiful dream, in which everything was more vivid than it usually appeared. And the room she saw in it was much clearer, somehow, than the real one. She stared into it, not even thinking to look at her own reflection so struck was she by all the rest.

There were the windows, past the green expanse of rug; the curtains swayed softly and the sunlight falling through them made a rosy yet cool light in the room. Through them she could see a blue much clearer and much more beautiful than the blue of the real sky behind her in the real windows.

And now coming though the middle opening was a man; his large eyes were much bluer than those of a real person, his hair certainly the bluish-silver she'd only seen in dreams. He walked softly toward her, moving his small light body in its white gleaming linen clothes as if he were a dancer, not gliding but with the grace with which all real people ought to move.

She watched him come silently toward her in the too-clear glass. Just as he was about to touch her, she turned around, blinking, and willed herself back into reality. It was not a shock, not even a slight disappointment as he still stood right there, smiling at her with his large blue eyes.

"Hello," he said. "I'm Timothy Garton. Has everyone else deserted you?"

For the second time that hour, this time more strongly than ever before in her life, Sue felt she had never, but *never*, before seen such an attractive man. Oh, she gasped silently. He's wonderful! He's sophisticated, as if he'd really lived and suffered and . . . ? He *lived*. She looked at him seriously.

(What a sweet child, Tim thought, and what a tiny one! She almost makes me feel like a tall man. Is this the way Daniel feels as he looks down at Nan? When Nan peers up at Daniel does she feel the faint sumission

that's in this woman's eyes? I suppose she is a woman and not a girl and I suppose things as small as this have average-size emotions. Is it harder for them, perhaps, less ground taken up, less to racket about in? She's extraordinarily sweet and so tiny too!)

Susan knew that if she didn't speak now she never would. Help! she said to herself, trying to pull herself from the compelling sureness of his gaze as if she were coming up for a breath after being underwater. His gaze swirled around her like the cold comfortable waters of a deep pool. This won't do, she thought now, with new determination.

"Hello," she said. "I'm . . ."

"Yes, I know," he said. "You're Susan and I cannot tell you how we've been looking forward to having you here . . ."

That's a lie, she thought. He's never given me a thought except to perhaps wish Joe wouldn't come barging in here dragging some girl like me, but I do rather like him for lying.

"And I'm really terribly sorry things are a little screwy for a few minutes and that we can't put you up here for the night. My sister will be right down. Sara's in the kitchen," he added, as if this was an important postscript. "We'll go through there but there's no real use bothering her. Just follow me."

He walked silently, with his great grace and ease, toward the wide door into the pantry. "That is," he added, turning around and smiling at her in a secret way, "you'll follow me if you know what's good for you."

Sue's heart now pounded alarmingly as she followed him across the room.

Nearing the steps that led into the pantry, she began to hear small noises and once in the light she saw a little office lined with shelves and cupboards. Beyond it the kitchen lay as part of the living room behind the fireplace wall.

Sue followed in Tim Garton's wary steps, noticing the great hood over the electric stove and a blue map of *La Gastronomie Italienne* on a cupboard door and the wide window beyond with one great white daisy in the Mexican jar upon the sill.

Sara was bent over the chopping board that was piled high with lettuces and did not look up as they came into the little room. "I hear you," she said to Tim. "You sound like rats. Lunch is in seven minutes. Have one for me, will you, and get up here in time to help carry it all out."

"Right," Tim said. "I will. Take it easy, darling."

Sue's heart thudded as if it, for that instant, believed he'd spoken to her. His voice was almost impersonal, neither fervent nor glib, not like the way an assistant director at a Hollywood party might say, *Dawww-ling!* He'd certainly been talking to Sara, hadn't he? Sue followed him down the cellar steps feeling lonely suddenly.

Would no one ever talk to her in that fond way? Would it always be the quick hot voice of passion or else nothing? I'm one of those women, she thought, who is made for lust, which is just my luck, and no one will ever say *darling* to me the way he just said it to Sara Porter, so easily, as if loving her were as simple as breathing or eating.

The thought made her gloomy.

As she sighed, she heard the wheeze in her breathing. She looked away, directing her gaze toward the walls on the sides of the cellar steps painted in the same plaster that had been painted a frolicking canary yellow with a thin green stripe at shoulder height to separate the yellow below from that white of the plaster above. A small light glowed in its feeble way at the bottom of the stairwell.

"Watch your step here, Susan," Tim said. "Follow closely by me. I'd hate to have you get lost under a strawberry box or something before Nan even got to meet you."

She followed him as he moved to the right through two different cellar rooms as cool as tombs and rich with the scent of ripening fruit and cucumbers and summer cabbages. She saw shelves filled with preserves put up in jars and in the next room the round gleaming bottoms of a thousand wine bottles. There, standing in the cold dim light of a single electrical bulb, stood Joe and Honor with Daniel Tennant.

Sue's heart stopped, it seemed, and she felt her head swim slightly to see all three men who now seemed to mean so much to her there underground together. Of course there was Honor, too, who was with them, and as Sue stood watching her, Honor shivered and put down the little glass she was holding onto a wooden table, then wrapped her long arms around what looked to Sue like such an incredibly small waist. There was gooseflesh on her arms and her eyes were melancholy.

Then there was Joe, his face—with the bang of dark curls above it—looking young and thick and tired. He, too, held a small glass so tiny it was almost hidden by the size of his right hand. With the other he leaned carefully against the damp wall.

Tim Garton stood between Sue and Honor and Sue began to feel she could hardly look at him for the love she felt for his small lithe body and his beautiful blue-white hair and dark eyes and for the half-smile on his wide mouth. His mouth made her shiver for the thought of all the secrets it might tell.

I am, she thought, going a little crazy.

And there was also Daniel Tennant, taller than anyone, his thin body hung as loosely as if his joints were tied together with old string instead of living gristle and tendon. His head was small and finely proportioned and seemed to sit on his neck lightly with a proud, arched poise. He wore a soft blue shirt; gray flannel slacks clothed his long legs. His bony arms ended in big if slender-knuckled hands.

Oh, she thought, this is terrible, then looked at the familiar bulk of her Joe almost desparately before she turned her enormous eyes on Tim, who smiled at her reassuringly. She felt her lips moving stiffly as she tried to answer with a grin, but then she was drawn back as if helplessly by the presence of this terrifying boy.

Sue stared up at him in the hard poor light of the one bulb in the dank ceiling and Dan looked down at her, politely. He had the biggest nose she'd ever seen and the rest of his face seemed to express amazement.

"Hello, again," she told him, hoping she didn't sound quite that weak.

"You've met," Honor observed, just as Joe and Tim began a jumble of now unnecessary introductions at which everybody laughed and then Dan bowed almost formally. He looked amazed or maybe cross, with his lips pulled tightly. Someone who will never love me, Sue thought sadly.

"You'd better hurry," Tim said. "Sara's whizzing around and I have no idea where Nan and Lucy are but lunch will be ready in make that six minutes."

As he spoke he was shaking bitters into two of the tiny glasses, then filled them with gin. He put one in Sue's hand and raised his own in a toast. "To happy days," he said, "or something. Joe reports that at Oxford you now say *chahs*!"

They all raised their glasses solemnly.

Sue was not sure she wouldn't choke as she'd never swallowed so much of anything quite so hot in one imitative gulp. She prayed she wouldn't, then blinked happily as she now felt perfectly safe. She sighed and as she did a most delightful warmth flooded through her and swirled downward into the seat of all her fervent sadness and suddenly she was glad.

"I liked that," Sue observed, now smiling at Honor, then looking shyly from lowered eyes at the silent Dan.

"Another?" Tim asked this eagerly.

"Oh, gosh, no! Tim," Honor said, "we've got to go help Sara. Come on!"

Dan swept his eyes movingly over the various expressions of resignation and disappointment that followed Honor's nearly violent statement. He sighed. For a moment Sue thought she would finally hear him say something aside from the untranslatable buzz of his exclamation in the bedroom door and he did now open his mouth. But then he shrugged, raised one shaggy eyebrow toward his carefully combed hair, put down his glass and—bowing slightly—passed in front of Susan and went out the door.

As she followed him out, Honor told him, "You're too young to have two drinks of gin before lunch anyway."

The boy finally spoke, "So're you."

To Susan his voice sounded like the mellowest notes from Benny Goodman's clarinet, only more *manly* somehow. She sighed and listened with a kind of muted awe to the two Tennants speaking to one another as she and Timothy Garton and her now silent Joe, whose arm lay almost protectively on the smaller, more frail man's thin shoulders, followed them through the cellars and up the narrow stairs.

"Who said I wasn't?" she asked

"What?"

"Too young," she persisted.

"Nobody."

"Well?"

"Well, it's simply different for a man. A man can drink more. He can drink younger."

"Oh no," she said. "Not gin."

"Yes," he said. "Anything."

"No," she said. "Gin's for women. It's very good for the misery, for one thing."

"Have you got the misery, then?" her brother asked.

"Not right now," she said. "But I *might* get it and . . ."

Their voices, intertwining, went on quietly, each with its own undercurrent of mirth. It was as if they were saying something quite different but putting it into ordinary if somewhat oddly-sorted-out words, so as not to startle those around them.

I wish I had a brother who'd speak to me that way, Sue thought. A brother might be so comforting.

Sue blinked as she stepped out at the top of the stairs into the white airy brightness of the little kitchen. They were all apparently seized by the same violent briskness as soon as they came within range of Sara, who stood putting glasses on a pewter tray that was already piled with silver and plates. Without stopping her work Sara began to speak to them and her tone sounded almost cross.

"About time! Dan, bring up some beer, will you? And Nor, you take that tray out and fix a table on the terrace, please. Susan will help you. And Tim, will you please go up and tell Nan, for God's sake, to stop writing and come down here. Lucy, too, of course."

Sara scowled at the tray, then muttered, "Napkins," then looked up quickly and cried sharply, "Oh wait, Tim, here's Nan!"

There was a light soft sound of someone running across the living room and taking the pantry steps in one stride. Sue held her breath, thinking, What next? Who might *this* be? She was almost dizzy now with excitement and aspirin and gin and the beer she had at the casino.

She gave one look at the small figure that seemed to fly into the pantry and pose there, then felt everyone look at her as she gasped. "Oh! You're Anne Garton Temple!"

Her cheeks were enflamed. She felt herself gaping, looking—she knew—like a moonstruck monkey, but she simply wasn't able to stop it. Finally, after what felt like an eternity of staring at the newcomer, Sue turned to Joe and asked reproachfully, "You didn't tell me?"

Then everybody laughed and Joe said, "Hell, Sue, I thought everybody knew Anne Garton Temple was Tim's sister. And I hadn't realized," he said, now grinning at Nan, "that we'd finally be meeting you."

Nan blushed and nodded and Tim walked quickly over and put an arm about her fragile shoulders.

"People usually say it the other way around," Tim said. "That I'm Nan's brother rather than she's my sister." He looked—quite without malice—into her upturned face.

They were the two loveliest people in the world, Sue decided, but the *loveliest*. She stood numbly as the introductions were made, then followed Honor out onto the long sunny terrace, Sue's mind still thrilled with the vision of the tiny fair-haired woman with Tim's arm lovingly around her.

How can anyone *that* famous be so little? Sue thought. Why she's hardly bigger than I am. And she looks so young, as young as the pictures on her books. But she can't be, Sue argued. I got my first book of her poems just as I'd finished Shelley, that was at least six years ago and I know she's in all the anthologies of modernist poets at school. She had to be forty, more. But she can't be, she looks no older than Sara. Oh dear, I wonder if I'll have done anything to be so famous by the time I've lived that long?

She sighed, rubbed her forehead. She now felt suddenly very tired and so sleepy she could hardly move. Her eyes hurt when she looked toward the wide and glittering lake that lay almost at their feet, yet also far, far below. Beyond the lake the hard black bulk of the mountains on the other shore felt almost like a physical blow.

How could she act in a way that made her seem so light and silly with all this sound around her and such a bad cold in her head?

"I *really* had no idea," she protested. Her own voice was now so husky it startled her.

"You mean about Nan?"

"Yes, that she was—that she is—what she is. I never thought I'd meet her. I have all her books. And plays! When I was in Chicago a year ago I saw *Hunter, No More!* four times. I thought it was *wonderful!*"

"Yes," Honor allowed. "She's swell. Maybe not quite Shakespeare but . . . ?"

"Oh, some of those early sonnets, and anyway, no one's Shakespeare except Shakespeare. And what other woman has *ever* written a play in verse that has run for weeks and months all over the world?"

"Okay, sure," Honor laughed. "I'm just as enthusiastic as you are and wait until you get to know her. But . . . ?" She looked hard at Sue, who stood leaning heavily against the table.

Sue was frowning under her thick dark brows, remembering those sonnets, those fine ringing lines.

"But, Sue," Honor continued. "You look like you have a fever. How do you feel? Did you find those hankies?"

Sue nodded. She was still overwhelmed with bewildered awe that she was in the same house as was Anne Garton Temple. She shook her head, trying then to answer Honor's question.

"No, really, I feel quite all right, thanks," Sue said, but then she sniffed.

"Yes?" Honor asked, still examining her quizzically.

"Yes, really. It's just that I forgot to eat any breakfast and now I'm in sort of a blur, with it's all being so queer and exciting and . . ."

"Oh, HELL-OH-oh!"

The girls looked up. On the balcony that stretched across half the length of the long house, a woman leaned over who was now waving at them. She had a nice smile and Sue smiled back at the woman, who had thick light-brown hair that was piled messily into a tousle at the back of her head. This was a big woman, from what Sue could see, with heavy breasts and broad shoulders.

This can't be the one who thinks I'm bad, Sue thought. She seems so friendly, so kind.

"Oh, hello, Lucy," Honor called up to her, with more easy geniality than Sue expected of her. "Lucy, this is our friend Susan Harper. Sue, Mrs. Pendleton."

"You poor child! Don't stand there breaking your neck looking up at me, but then I *would* stand in the most uncomfortable place for everyone!"

Lucy Pendleton spoke so warmly, her mouth was wide, her eyes bright blue, and she seemed to smile with her entire face. "Isn't it time for lunch?" she asked. "I've had *such* an absorbing morning but I'll be right down and try to do something useful," she said, then disappeared.

Sue looked at Honor, lifting her dark brows inquiringly. Honor was busy pushing deck chairs and arranging them around the table.

"She's a painter," Honor explained. "Watercolors. Friend of Nan's. Pick a comfortable chair, Sue, and sit right down. Everything will be out in a moment. You really look like you could do with a little nourishment."

Sue, after a moment of internal protest, did then sink gratefully into a chair. It felt so good to be sitting down. This was the first time she could remember being seated since, what? Was it two weeks ago on the train they'd taken to Munich? The thought of eating, though, made her feel a little queasy. She let her head lie back against the striped canvas back of the chair, pulling her feet up under her to sit on them, as she had as a child.

Honor now strode across to the gratings in front of the living room windows and called down, "Hey!"

"Yes, Mr. Kelly," she said. "I called. And you can tell that to Mr. Timothy Garton, also that rat Daniel Tennant, and tell them Sara says lunch is almost over and she thinks this is a very strange way for a newly arrived guest to behave to say nothing of . . ."

"Yes, Miss Tennant!" someone called.

Then there was a bang, then the subdued scuffling of feet through the cellar and Honor laughed. "Having a quicky, I suppose," she said aloud to no one in particular, then she walked over and sat down, then closed her eyes as if she were too bored to leave them open a moment longer.

Why does everyone here talk to Joe as if they know him better than I do? Sue wondered. She was without resentment, simply startled by the new ways she was seeing him in their having arrived at this place. There were tones in his voice she'd never heard before. She wondered why he was so different. She wondered also that she didn't seem to care very much.

She opened her eyes at the sound of footsteps and was horrified to see the tiny Nan Garton almost tottering under the weighty bulk of an enormous salad bowl.

"Oh, Miss *Garton*!" she exclaimed as she scrambled awkwardly out of the deck chair and dashed across the terrace to help. "You *musn't* carry all that! *Please* let me carry it!"

"Why, thank you, Susan," she said.

Susan, she thought. She called me *Susan.* As she took the bowl from Nan's hands, Sue felt almost overcome by the strangeness of this. Anxiety gripped her; had she taken the bowl too roughly from this woman? Never in her life had she seen anything so lovely, so fragile, as the woman who stood quietly and was now smiling at her. Her voice seemed to vanish. Had she really called her *Susan*?

"Oh, Lucy!" Nan Garton smiled affectionately at her friend who now approached. "How did it go today? Did you do good work?"

"A wonderful morning, Nan dear. And you?"

"I wrote hundreds of postcards," Nan said, even gaily. "For the first time in my life I've had the courage to write, 'Having a wonderful time! Wish you were here!'"

Susan smiled at the malicious way Nan Garton had rolled out the phrases that had never before sounded as silly as they did now, though they also sounded real.

"Ah, there's Sara," Lucy said, hurrying toward her as Sara walked carefully across the terrace with a tray of cheese on one arm and a great bowl of fruit held in the fingers of the other.

"Can I do something to help, Sara dear?" Lucy asked. "Or am I too late, as usual?"

"Never too late," Sara said, dryly. "Yes, please take this tray, if you will. And do forgive me, everybody, for having lunch so late."

She looked around and smiled impersonally just as Tim, followed by the two boys, all came to the table bearing rows of beer bottles.

"It's our fault, I'm afraid," Joe Kelly smiled, offering this in his softest voice.

"Oh, I'm terribly sorry. Joe Kelly, Mrs. Pendleton. Lucy, you remember my speaking of our friend who's at Oxford this year?"

Lucy smiled at Joe. "I wonder," she asked and as she was speaking she began helping herself to salad, then cutting a piece of the yellow-white cheese with great holes in it. "I wonder if you know any of the men who were at Balliol or Merton ten years ago or so? My nephew, you see . . . ?"

Susan listened as this mild chatter went on all around her and to the steady splash of water from the old fountain. She tried to eat. She was surprised that she was hungry and that she would have enjoyed the food but that her throat felt not sore but stiff. She thought she might be feeling better or maybe it was only the excitement that was getting her to forget her cold.

She looked again at Nan Garton's small and very vivid face in such contrast to the slow queenly Honor. Sue smiled to see them sitting side by side, the one's feet barely reaching the ground, the other's seemingly so long as to stretch halfway across the stone terrace.

Then she looked at the smooth face of Sara Porter, whose expression was remote. Her heart thumped suddenly at the thought that Sara might be able to help her, that she might tell Susan what to do. Of course, so far it had been rather hard to see anything of her but perhaps sometime during the afternoon there would be a few minutes. She would simply say, "Mrs. Porter, what do you think I ought to do? Joe and I really love each other, but Joe . . . ?"

"More beer, Susan?" Tim was looking at her half-empty glass and was leaning forward with the bottle toward her, struggling slightly as he rose from his chair.

"Here!" Dan said, pushing Tim back, and without even moving his body he stretched one long arm across Susan with the bottle poised above her glass.

"Cuff or plain?" he asked.

Sue, who really doubted she could swallow another sip, was simply thrilled to her very marrow at the sound of his deep voice and said, if breathlessly, "Oh, cuff, but *definitely*!"

He poured. She raised her glass and smiled at Joe over its white foam.

vi

It was now after lunch and Lucy Pendleton and Honor and Nan Garton stood together almost silently to wash the dishes in the kitchen. Sara had disappeared. Moments later Tim, too, was gone.

Joe Kelly stood dreamily in the hot sun on the outer edge of the flower-bordered terrace that ran the length of the house. He felt pleasantly full of fresh sweet nourishment that held no reproach, and he thought not of the ugly food he'd been eating while all the hidden people in that hideous place were starving. He thought of going into the shaded room, of lying down without speech or much thought to await digestion and the setting sun.

Sue was already inside, he knew, curled like an attractive foetus around a small striped cushion in the blue chaise, eyes shut, her mouth closed softly. Joe had stood looking at her before he'd come out onto the terrace, seeing with a new tenderness the smudges under her lashes and the way her delicate bones showed under the tight little yellow sweater, poor kid! Perhaps Sara was right; she was just too little to go bumming around the countryside with him.

He'd then looked up, almost shamefaced, at Dan Tennant, walking through the room from the kitchen. Right then Joe had begun to softly whistle.

"Shhhush!" Dan hissed, and Joe had, for a moment, felt angry, as if Joe didn't know his own girl was sleeping.

Joe scowled, then relaxed, as the green door closed and Dan disappeared. The young chap was right, after all. He, Joseph Kelly, was a thoughtless bastard. Then he grinned in complacency. He stretched and then ambled like a great heavy cat, a tom, out into the sun.

Below him the lake lay, mile after hard, shimmering mile, under the steep vine-covered terraces of the hill. He felt that he could easily throw a football in a curve wide enough to fly over the vineyards at his feet and have it land well out into the Léman. He could imagine the ripple, circling out and out, lapping tinily at the walls of the Château de Glérolles, growing weaker as they widened, coming at last in a faint diminishing curve to the far shores and the gloomy beach of Saint-Gingolph in France.

Joe spat richly and was astounded to see how foolish were his dreams of ever hitting the lake with a football or any other projectile. He peered nervously over the ledge of the terrace and saw, about twenty feet below, a square water basin set into the slope and on its edge, sat Dan, who was holding one long hand in a ruminative way, under the steady spout of water. He was wearing a pair of dirty white trunks and dark glasses.

Joe debated calling down to him, but felt sleepy and, besides, he wasn't sure he liked this cub-brother of Sara's. Dan might be all right when he got smoothed out a bit or else maybe learned not to be so *damned* smooth, Joe couldn't decide.

Like most of those who'd gone to Western colleges, Joe had an instinctive and almost self-righteous distrust of the clothes, the manners, the general self-assurance of the men who'd gone to Eastern schools. He knew that this, too, was partly by tacit agreement that he, as a Westerner, would remain as he was, less polished, but he liked those mannerisms none the more for that. The hair, for instance. Why the hell didn't Dan Tennant cut his hair and wear it short, like a man? Instead it was long and swept back in obviously nurtured waves from his high forehead and temples.

He looked pansy, Joe thought, and spat again, this time scowling.

Dan looked up, waved and smiled and suddenly seemed so like Sara that Joe found himself grinning down at him, caught up by a wave of affection.

"You got a cigarette?" Dan called.

Joe put his fingers to his lips, tipping his head backward toward the silent house then nodded. He then straddled the thick bed of zinnias and great gleaming daisies and slid down the steep slopes to the basin where Dan waited. The grass felt coarse beneath him and he remembered to vaguely worry about stains on these, his only pair of slacks.

Dan watched Joe inscrutibly from behind his dark glasses, all the while flapping one hand somnolently in the murmurring water.

Why the hell doesn't he say something? Joe wondered, feeling annoyed at the silence of this young pup, lording it over everyone because he'd gone to a big school in the East.

"Oh, I say, I'm sorry!" Joe said, and was rather startled to hear his own Oxonian accent, as intense as it was new. He fumbled in his pockets for cigarettes and matches.

Dan took the one Joe offered, lit it, then lit Joe's, too, with his dripping hand. "Thanks," he said.

"If you've got shorts," he said, pausing to smoke, "why not strip? Sara doesn't care."

"She can't see us, can she?"

"No, but she and Tim have to be careful about the peasants. We're foreigners here. There's no use our abusing the priviledge, so forth."

Dan's off-hand tone said he knew all about it, which exasperated Joe Kelly, who was deciding he'd sweat himself sick before he'd strip and be like this fellow. He dragged deeply on his cigarette, then asked, as if casually, "Been here often?"

"First time, but not, by God, the last. I came over from Grenoble about ten days ago. I should be there at school still but Sara said there was an empty room and . . ." Dan flopped limply off the edge of the basin and stretched his long thin limbs over the hot grass, sighing audibly with contentment.

Joe smiled to himself in triumph. "I've been here several times, damn near five, six. Lucky enough to have a long vacation here last year."

"Yes," Dan said. "Sara mentioned that she got a lot of work out of you. And she would. Nothing like my dear little older sister for slave driving. Well, I do envy you. My God, what a view."

Well, Joe thought, this Tennant chap isn't that bad. He began unbuttoning his shirt, then his slacks. He got out of his clothes, then rolled them into a shape that would cushion his head.

They lay, simmering quietly, sweat beading then cooling on each one's clean skin. Each man breathed slowly. Their eyes would open then close like those of a silent bird. Joe spoke once to say, "There's a lake steamer." Dan asked once in a soft grunt for another cigarette.

In the cool dim living room there was no noise except that of an occasional stuffy sigh from Sue, who was deeply asleep. She stirred only once or twice. Occasionally a frown would cross her face at some dream or a twinging muscle, then it fell still again.

Timothy slipped expertly over the second step, which was the one that creaked, and tiptoed past her, walking out through the sun-luminous curtains and onto the blazing terrace. He stood blinking for a moment, walked to the edge, and looked down.

There past the sturdy ridged stems of daisies swaying faintly in a small afternoon breeze on the slope past the thick grass lay Dan and Joe Kelly, sleeping.

(They are beautiful, he thought, lying like young dogs or carved amber bulls. God, am I already so old that I grow lyrical over the bodies of youth? I wish I could paint them, or do I? Is it better to say what I see, what I mean by seeing them, with opening buds, with the quick cruel upthrust of a crocus, the all-absorbing yellow of a tulip? One petal? The sensual sprawling orchid and its raw sex. Yes, they are all beauty. And I pity them to be so young and to not know what I now know, never to know what I know with my Sara, with the only woman.

Shall I go and tell them there is no need for them to look further, no use in trying other bodies or searching other minds? Shall I let them know that only I, in all the world, have found what all men look for, for the first time since the world began? They'd be right to think I'm crazy, I am crazy, but I'm sane, too, for the first time since my world began.)

A drink, Tim thought, might be more to the point. I'll wake them and we'll see. He then squatted down among the flowers, selecting a large-headed, thick, and heavy zinnia that he tossed. It fell lumpishly on Daniel's relaxed belly.

The boy awoke slowly and peered upward toward Tim's round and silver head. He squinted, then told him, "Hi," sleepily.

Joe, only half awake behind his eyelids, pulled himself unwillingly from a dream of a talk with Sara. In the dream there was Tim, the finest man he knew, leaning in from behind her like Cardinal Richelieu behind the queen. Joe was standing before them stalwartly, explaining in round Oxonian phrases, like a self-assured poetical don, the reasons he needed to send Sue packing.

He was only half awake and could see the dream so clearly. "And for another thing," he was saying in a loud clear voice, "I am only twenty-one or -two, there's no real proof of my birthdate on the orphan registers and Judge So-and-So and Doctor Such-and-Such have staked a lot to get me to Oxford on this Rhodes and . . ."

"Yes," Sara said, her voice cutting across his, "and you are hot for life," as Tim's eyes, blue and wide and as hard as an archangel's, stared at him.

"No!" Joe said. "Sara! I haven't got another girl! No, I love her, she's the only woman I've ever stayed with but I want to finish school with a First and if I'm alone I can get a First in Greats and if I'm with her I will be all absorbed by loving. God, this is my only chance. Can't you see, you damned woman, that you've got to help me? You have a brain behind that smooth face, a heart behind those small round breasts. You can tell her what I've never had the guts to, help me! Help me and later you'll be glad." He then turned to the short lithe man who looked at him cooly and nodded, almost impercetibly. Joe felt a great hot flash of relief. Men! Men stood together. As the dream ended he was smiling broadly.

"What the hell are you grinning about?"

Joe blinked, helpless against the slanting glare of the sun off the lake. Tim Garton stood beside him now, standing on the hot and sloping grass. Joe sat up, blinked again.

"It's almost four, you two," Tim said, as he squatted down and took a pack of cigarettes from his pocket, then held the packet out. Each boy drowsily took one. They lit their cigarettes, the smoke drifting into the blueing air.

"Your Susan's still asleep, Joe," Tim said. "She's tired out from the walking, of course." Tim's smooth goat-like face was blank. "I was wondering if you'd like me to go down to Veytaux and pick up your suitcases? You could tell me the name of your hotel and I . . ."

"Oh, hell no, Tim. Sue and I can . . ."

"No," he said. "She's really out on her feet, Joe."

Joe wondered why he didn't resent this, the way people responded to his woman with an almost feminine partisanship. He'd known Tim Garton for several years now, known him in that vague, half-suspicious, half-idolatrous way that marks the difference between youthful admiration and more aged estimation, and he swore to himself whenever he thought of the quick body and the full sensual mouth of the older man that never would he trust him with his own woman. And yet here, for the first time, he was listening to Tim's quiet appraisal of his own love's tiredness, with no qualm. He lay on the cooling grass, wondering.

Suddenly Joe opened his eyes, shrewdly.

"You want to be down alone with Sara, don't you?" He asked the question bluntly and then lay in a torment of embarrassment, conscious that Tim and young Tennant were looking at him as if he had broken wind before their mothers.

Dan glanced over with his flat face looking toward the flatter lake as Tim considered Joe gravely, then spoke.

"Yes, of course I do," he said at last. "You two understand quite well that Sara is a quiet one. But now, what with one thing and another, she's damn near frazzled and I'd like to take her out for a while before supper and so on. She's looking forward to supper tonight. You know she is quite conceited about the meals here at La Prairie and her own cooking. So of course she's got everything more or less ready already. And François is coming down later to serve. But I think I'll take her out for a little ride and get her away from the house and counting laundry and thinking about the marketing and all the general, well, *bitchiness*." With that he gazed upward toward the house.

There was a silence then before Joe cleared his throat to say, "God, Tim," and looked with true misery at the older man, Joe's whole being flooded with affection for him, also a nameless dolor. "I wish you'd tell me if Sue and I . . . ?"

Tim's face contracted. "Christ *no!*" he said, speaking almost violently and laid his hand for a second on Joe's warm and silky thigh. "You. You and Dan and Honor and Nan. Christ, don't ever think that. You know how it is, though, with a house so full of all ages and sizes. Please forget this, you two. Sara and I'll go down to town and get your bags and then we'll have a swell supper on the terrace if the wind holds off and . . ."

Dan, who'd been lying stone-faced with his gaze turned toward the black bulk of the French mountains, swung now back toward them, saying, "Go, my good man, my pseudo-so-called brother." He was commanding them loftily. "Kelly, tell the man your hotel."

"The Gare et Suisse."

"And Timothy, my boy," Dan went on, "keep Sara out until she's in a bonny mood again, for hunger creeps upon me and I would eat well tonight." Dan then waved his hand airily and heaved himself, in all his lanky bulk, up and onto his haunches so his small head was now perched like a bird's on his long and even scrawny neck.

(He's a good boy, Timothy Garton thought, and too perceptive for his years. How much does he know all the female hullabaloo that's going on, what with Lucy being such a cat and with Susan sleeping on the couch. Well, if he doesn't kill himself first he'll make as fine a man as his sister is a woman. Honor, too, for all I know. Yet we're both right to stay this way, decent and distant, with no hold of confidence one on the other.)

"Are you sure you don't want me to go down with you?" Joe asked the question wistfully, feeling the desparate certainty that this was his chance, perhaps the only one, to talk to Tim and Sara—or to someone, anyone—about the terrible decision that lay ahead of him. And he knew now that it was tonight he must make this decision. He could wait no longer. He *must* talk to them.

He stood up and announced, almost belligerantly, "I'll go with you. You're too goddamned little a guy, Tim, to haul our suitcases around," then beamed down affectionately at the man's impassive face. He put one hand on the man's shoulder, which seemed bony and birdlike under Joe's huge paw.

I've *got* to go with you, Tim, old chap, Joe thought. I know now you're the only person in the world who can tell me what to do with this lovely goddamned little woman I've got in my blood and around my neck and before me until I die. Help me! Ask me to come with you!

He then shook Tim back and forth slowly, beaming down at him with a smile on his big infantile face.

"Okay, then, Joe, you'll come along," Tim said, looking up at Joe pleasantly, his large blue eyes appearing clear and candid. "Let's get going, though, Sara wants to get back by six and I'd thought we might drive around the lake, then home on the corniche. The sun will be at our backs."

Tim turned toward the path up to the terrace, after one quick glance at Dan, catching sight of his squinting gaze. Tim's shoulders drooped now slightly, as if he were tired.

(Damn, damn, damn, he swore. My one chance! Why am I always so thoughtful and kind and generous—when you get right down to it, generally weak? Why don't I say to this tactless child, No, you cannot come. But Sara and I must get away, it's been weeks, months, God knows how long, since we've been alone. By Christ I'll get her far away, and soon! There are only a few days until they all leave and then we'll go to the south of France, to Cassis maybe, or Thorenc, or someplace nobody's ever heard of. And I'll have her all to myself. No hurt feelings, no female fights, no thoughtfulness, no cursed over-sensitive souls all over the goddamned place. I'll tell her this afternoon. We'll start to make plans. It will be fine. She'll hate to miss the chrysanthemums here but . . .)

He then looked at Dan again and said, "Dan, you'd better go into the house and mix yourself a drink. We're having La Prairie wine tonight and then maybe champage, so I'd suggest you coast over from beer with a good stiff vermouth and soda and that you take one up to Honor." Then Tim added, "Come on, Joe."

Joe followed him rather stiffly up the twisting steps, pulling on his shirt and fumbling clumsily with the zipper of his pants as he went. He felt happy. By Jove, it had looked for a minute like he wouldn't get Sara and Tim alone and now . . . ?

Then something hit him like a sandbag behind the knees. He grunted and fell sprawling, his hands clawing at the turf under the side of his face, and then at the tense body that twisted him farther and farther down the slick and grassy slope.

Joe cursed and writhed expertly on top of Dan Tennant's wiry figure. It had been more than a year since Joe last lunged and sweated down a barred football field, but he felt again the same hot and vicious anger, the excitement and the cunning that had made him one of the finest fullbacks in the United States of America.

(I'm a bastard, he thought. I am indeed and I like it. And I'll go get Sara and I'll spirit her off and we will escape and I'll tell her my secret plan.)

Joe grunted and grinned down into Dan's panting and impudent face.

"Smart fellow, eh?" Joe asked as he dug his fingers into the boney body beneath him.

"Damn right!" Dan said. He was panting, and just then he heard the sound of the little Fiat backing recklessly up the driveway, then honk once at the gate, he relaxed and lay quietly under Joe's hard and heavy body.

"I was tackle at dear old Princeton Prep," he told Joe, languidly. "Now, how about that drink, Joe? Tim recommends vermouth and he ought to know."

Joe got up from the ground slowly. Something was over and done with and it would never happen again and he felt that now his life was running surely in channels that he could not see and would never love.

"Right-o," he said and was amazed at himself that he felt no real resentment, only a kind of quiet anguish that he knew would never leave him again.

vii

Susan stared through the vanishing curtains of a strange dream of twisting leaves and tendrils with Joe all entwined about an old vine-ridden tree and herself tearing and pecking at the monstrous plant with her little beak and her tiny brittle claws.

Joe laughed at her gratingly, a sound like dry wood as her wings beat the air.

The tendrils turned into tough cloths, striped cruelly with bands of torturing red and green and yellow. She pulled up and wrenched, feeling the lines wrap themselves around her wings then her throat and over her open and panting beak.

Susan, now strangling, sat up wildly, opening her eyes. "Joe!" Her heart was pounding and as she saw him standing against the soft afternoon light glowing through the swaying curtains, she gasped in relief.

"You," she said. "You aren't caught, I mean . . . ?" She then laughed at her own foolishness as she lay blinking at him, then stretched voluptuously against the soft velvet of the couch.

Joe looked both dark and strong and to Sue he seemed more natural than he'd been all day. It was as if something was no longer troubling him or, if he had been troubled, she didn't know. Perhaps it was only she herself who was troubled?

"Joe, darling," she said with sudden resolution. "Sit down here and talk to me." She moved in order to make a little empty half circle with her body on the chaise. "I want to ask you something."

Joe began to sit down, then frowned and straightened himself. "I'd like to, Sue, but . . . ? That is, Tennant and I . . . ?"

"Dan Tennant?" she asked. "What about him? He's a child. He can wait."

Joe smiled involuntarily at Sue's scoffing dismissal of a person of her own age, then began to explain, "You see, we thought we'd have a little drink and then walk up to the village to look at our room at the inn. Of course, I know it will be all right but we thought it might be a nice walk, that is, there's not much to do here and Tim and Sara are out and since you've been asleep I . . . ?"

Susan knew now Joe was trying to get away from her and she felt suddenly desparate. She knew he was irrevocably bored with her, that he would rather do anything than sit beside her in this cool room and talk. She closed her eyes.

"Joe," she said. "I've got to talk to you." Her tight voice sounded small and foolish to her buzzing ears. "Don't put me off. I've decided something and I have got to tell you. Now. So go tell Dan and bring your drink up here if you want but please come back."

She heard him sigh, heard him moving softly away.

She felt quite cool. It was without surprise that she recognized the complete blankness of her brain. She was not at all upset. It seemed clear to her that when the time came, and it was apparently almost upon her, she would do what she had to do, as a woman would in giving birth to a child. She didn't know what would come out but she was irresistibly moved to talk with her love, to say to him things yet unthought of, to finish something. She'd felt this way before and nothing had happened, but *this* time.

Sue lay quietly on the couch waiting.

A few moments later she heard Joe's soft and heavy steps. She opened her eyes and saw him standing beside her, a tall glass in either hand, his heavy brows now dark and somber above his clearly puzzled eyes. When he noticed that she was watching him he started, almost sleepily, then smiled down at her.

"Here, my sweet Sue," he murmurred. He handed her one of the glasses, then sat down on the couch beside her.

She took a sip of the liquid, pale and brown, which was pleasantly mild and so cold the glass was already covered with dew. She wiped her hand absently on her skirt, then set the glass on the floor beside her.

"Joe," she said, "we've got to settle this business."

Joe kept twirling his glass between his enormous heavy hands and did not look at her.

"Oh, *darling*!" Her voice broke suddenly, sounding almost like a cry and she had to clear her throat for camouflage. "Don't just sit there! I don't want to sound like an hysterical female and everything but we've simply got to make up our minds! My boat sails in only a few days."

Seven days, she cried out within herself. *Seven!* Time's passing, it's growing late, it's almost evening of one day and where is everybody? Sara? Tim? Won't someone help me?

Joe was still gazing downward and as Susan stared at him it seemed that he had never looked so handsome, so strong. She felt suddenly that he knew exactly what they were going to do. She was relieved and a little proud of his ruthlessness so that when he finally spoke his words were like a blow in the face, after the conviction she was certain she had seen in him.

"I don't know," he said. "I don't know." He sounded miserable.

For a moment she was too shocked and disappointed to speak. Then she said, in a weak voice, "But I thought . . . ?"

Joe put down his glass with a thump and finally looked at her squarely. His eyes looked hot and unhappy.

"I don't know what all this is about, Sue," he said in a rather complaining tone. "I thought everything was all set. God, you know I can't live without you. I thought you wanted to come to England with me. I thought it was all decided that you'd stay in London or someplace and then when I was through we could get married if you wanted to and . . ." His voice trailed off as he dropped his eyes.

She sighed. What was the use? She felt very tired and her head still ached and here they were back in the same old groove, saying the same old things. She'd felt for a moment that now was the time to finish all their arguments, that now, for some miraculous reason, they'd be able to decide, but she'd been wrong.

Joe peered at her. Perhaps he felt ashamed as he looked at her tiny body with its weary bones, looked into her darkly shadowed eyes. Perhaps he wanted to finish things. He straightened his shoulders, then gulped his drink.

"Susan!" he said, then grinned suddenly, infectiously. "You know, I feel as if I were going to have a tooth pulled or something and I wonder why?"

Sue smiled back at him. "I've been feeling rather that way, too, darling, on the brink somehow? It's the altitude maybe?" Now she frowned. "But you know, Joe, we really do have to decide what I'm to do. I thought I'd talk with Sara Porter. Yes, that's what I'll do. You know her and she seems like such a sensible person."

Joe looked over. "What makes you think so?"

"Well, she's quiet and she seems so resolute and . . ."

"It's a funny thing about Sara," he said. "Everyone speaks of her as if she were all that, so practical, so dependable, and she *is*! And yet nobody knows anything about her, really, except maybe Tim. She never lets you know a single intimate thing. And yet she's not the negative personality that that might indicate. She's a force at least as far as I'm concerned and yet I don't quite know her. God knows she never says a word about what she thinks or feels . . ."

Sue stirred. "I thought I'd talk to her. I like her. I have the feeling she could tell me what to do."

"*I* can tell you what to do. Stay with me. Oh, Sue, my sweet Susan, stay with me!"

As he slid to his knees on the floor before her, his face seemed to crumple. His hands, cold from the sweating glass, pressed on her flushed cheeks, then down her throat and onto her tender pointed breasts. She shuddered, her free arm going round his heavy head. For a moment she lay there, feeling his familiar thick-breathing weight against her. Her heart thudded. She stirred uneasily, then suddenly stiffened.

"Stop, Joe," she said. "Sit up. We can't." She twitched away with irritation swelling within her. How dare he take advantage, yes, take advantage! That's all it was to know so well her weakness and her hunger for him, to know how abject was her love. She pushed him away viciously.

Joe bent over to pick up his glass. His face was flushed, his lips were curled in a secret smile.

"So you want to leave me," he said softly, a statement. He didn't look at her. "So you want to talk it all over with Sara, just girls together. Christ, women. You cannot even believe what your own blood is telling you."

Sue was suddenly so furious that her hand shook. She looked down at the brown drops that spilled from her glass and lay for a second gleaming before they melted into the rubbed velvet of the couch. She waited until her hand was as steady as she hoped her voice would be, then spoke slowly and clearly, saying to him:

"I know what I'm going to do, Joe. I'm going back to America."

She tried then not to witness the look of sheer relief that flared across his face and brightened his hot brown eyes. She prayed she'd one day forget she'd seen it as she went on calmly, "I'll go back to school and then, if you finish at Oxford and I finish there and if you haven't found another girl and I haven't fallen in love with yet another local hero, we might see one another again."

There was a long silence. Upstairs a door banged. They listened with a particularly polite attention to the first rush of water as it filled a bathtub. Joe finally spoke.

"Look, Sue," he said. "I think you're crazy. I think you should think this over. You should talk to Sara, see what she says. Talk to anyone at all, I don't see what the rush is. We have plenty of time to decide. Why don't you talk to Tim? You know now what I think, of course . . . ?"

Yes, I do, Sue thought bitterly. But why can't you say what you think, she wondered, because I'm so little? Because you think I haven't brains enough to see what you *really* think, you poor stupid child?

"I might," she said, agreeing automatically. "Or maybe I won't. I think perhaps I won't talk to anyone, that maybe I know already."

He looked almost panic-stricken and gulped at his glass. "No," he protested. "You'd better see what they think. Tim's the swellest person in the world, *he'll* tell you."

"Why don't you ask him then?"

"Ask him what? *I* don't need to ask him anything. I know what we should do without getting anyone's advice. You ought to follow me to London."

"Oh, please, stop," she said. "You've said that so often it sounds like famous last words. Round and round. I'm tired of it." She looked away.

"All right," he said stiffly. "If that's the way you feel, maybe you're right after all. Maybe you had better go home."

Joe stood up, his face averted, then walked to the window.

It's to hide his relief, Sue thought and winced. She called to him softly, "Joe, Joe darling, please forgive me. Come here. I'm a little cranky from drinking all that beer and gin, then falling asleep so hard. Come here!"

He turned slowly and went to her side.

"Look, Sue," he said. "We're all mixed up about this thing. I think it would be best to wait. You're right. I'm a hypocrite and sometimes I do really think you ought to go home. Most of the time I don't. I want you near me, I want to sleep with you. I want you near me to eat with and drink with. I get so damned lonely at Oxford, pretending I don't mind being the crude Yankee, going to damned silly teas for Rhodes men, trying to ape the manner of the well-born Oxonians or else trying awfully hard to act the part of Wild West rodeo riders, using slang I haven't thought of since I used to read the Sunday funny papers when I was a kid at home. And I don't understand English girls. And I *need* you. Sue, we're made for each other, you know that, at least in bed."

Joe stopped, looked at her seriously, then moistened his full lips.

She lay before him without moving. At last she was getting some of what she'd asked for. She felt stunned and that she'd been within a spiritual hare's breath of turning tail and throwing herself in his big fumbling passionate arms.

She drew in her breath and stared up at him, her eyes very bright, mouth curved into a hypnotized half smile.

"So?" she said it provocatively. She was daring him.

Joe was silent for a moment. His eyes shifted. He then finished the last tepid swallow in his glass.

"So," he said. "I want you to wait until tomorrow morning to decide. You know what I think. In a way it would be cutting our own throats to stay together this year. It will hurt your father and it would make things damned hard for me at college. But I don't know if we can live without one another."

He then turned away abruptly and she was horrified to find herself wondering coldly if the little tremor in his voice was sincere. He had sounded so *very* frank, so very man-to-man. Had he suddenly come to some decision of his own? It would be almost funny if after all her feminine worrying and shilly-shallyings it was finally *Joe* who took matters in his own hands and decided everything for her.

She shivered at the thought that maybe he already knew, that he was simply waiting until she felt fresher and better in the morning to tell her she must go. Oh God, to have Joe tell her the bitter truth that she'd always seen herself telling him? That would be unbearable.

"You're right, darling," she was almost stuttering. "I think we ought to wait. I'll come down and talk to Sara tomorrow morning. Everything will seem clearer. Let's wait. Let's not decide now. Let's forget all this and have some fun."

She held out her hands to him, and Joe pulled her up. As she walked toward the terrace with his hand hot and pulsing on her shoulder she was thinking, Fools! I know what we must do and *he* knows, as well, and we go on pretending and putting it off and I go on praying that somebody will be strong enough or foolish enough to convince me to do what neither of us really wants. We both know what we're going to do. How can we keep on being so false with one another? Oh, why can't anyone help me? Why must I decide all alone?

"Let's go play the gramaphone," Joe said.

2

Near dawn the doctor looked at the woman and raised his arms, then let them slap sorrowfully against his fat sides. She felt the first screw turn in an iron collar that was being afixed around her throat, the tight cold band that never again was fully loosened, so that even when she was an old woman she sounded her words tightly and coldly, as if through heavy iron.

That morning her husband still lived, after a fashion. He had withered and his lips were drawn back snarlingly from his dry teeth. As men lifted him onto the stretcher his arms clawed the air with short despairing movements, like that of a newborn child. The woman looked at him and he at her, but did either see?

After the operation she lay on a narrow hospital cot listening to his sick wretching in the next room. Doctors came in and told her of incisions and embolisms and then lifted their hands and let them fall, like philosophers.

The next day, however, he still lived, still after a fashion. As the stretcher took him toward the operating room he smiled dreamily and she felt one more screw settling into place in the iron collar. She smiled at him and then lay down carefully on the bed to wait for the doctors to come in and raise their arms in their helpless way.

She waited several hours without moving and she'd planned that when they came she would not look at them. Just as she opened her eyes she saw their hands, still covered with the thin spotted gloves, fall slowly toward their sides and slap faintly agaisnt their aprons. She smiled. She kept smiling even when they said the man was still alive.

i

Lucy Pendleton woke a little later than usual on the morning of August 31. She lay still for a moment, running her tongue over her dry lips and blinking painfully at the light streaming through the one big window that led onto the balcony, then she turned to look at the little shagreen-covered clock by her bed.

It was only seven ten. Oh God, how could she fill in the time before eight o'clock and her breakfast? And what if her breakfast was late, as it often had been? But what could you expect in a house run as carelessly as this one? If it weren't for a little direction that she herself, ill as she often felt, had been forced to give now and then, she was sure she'd *never* get anything to eat.

She closed her eyes and a tear rolled slowly from each one, down her face and onto the skin of her neck. She lay quietly, feeling them with a certain amount of grim pleasure. Finally she reached one hand under the pile of soft pillows—she never slept with less than six piled cosily around her shoulders to ward off asthma—and pulled out a damp and wadded-up handkerchief. She shook it out with a gloomy kind of pride in its humidity, then dabbed her eyes. Her breath caught. She sounded like a tired child as she sighed.

She might as well get up and kill a little time fixing her hair. She was sure François had noticed it the day before, all soft from a shampoo. As he'd laid her tray reverently across her knees, she'd peered at him sharply but it was impossible to tell much from his dark, rather bristly face. Really, Sara should be more particular about his shaving! She most certainly would be were he *her* servant. She'd felt strongly that he was somehow conscious of all her soft brown beautiful hair.

She stuck her feet into her green leather Pullman slippers, straightened her pale pink satin nightgown, noting the insertions of ecru lace, then pulled on her green chintz wrapper. It always pleased her to button its long rows of white buttons. Arranging the frilled bosom and puffed sleeves made her feel charming and old-fashioned and completely womanly.

Lucy Pendleton then stood before the bureau and shook out her two thick braids. No wonder! What man could resist hair such as this, even the ignorant peasant they kept as a valet? Not a single gray hair and each strand as fine as silk! With every stroke of her good strong brush she thought of the almost worshipful care with which the little Swiss coiffeur in Veytaux had touched her—it was actually so funny!—the last time she'd had her hair done. He'd been almost trembling and had become quite pale as he'd wound his fingers through the thick heaviness of her braids.

She stopped then, suddenly remembering with disgust what Tim and Sara said when she'd told them—rather what they'd *not* said but had implied. There was no avoiding it, the two were filthy minded. Just because a man was gentle and dainty and had a lovely face and speaking voice there was no proof he was . . . ?

They were filthy and her blood felt hot to think of it every time she allowed herself to think, as happened again and again over this whole dreadful summer. Those two managed to imply something so low and foul about even the most innocent things and now things were worse, with Sara's younger brother and sister here, being taught to laugh in the same perverted way. They were all awful, all of them, even . . .

Lucy put her brush down and resolutely started toward the door. She would speak to Nan this very moment as this could go on no longer. Could Nan not *see* how she was allowing the atmosphere of this place to coursen her? To make her as loose and common as the rest of them? How *could* Nan have let her morale slip so during the course of their time here, the whole summer but especially since young Dan and Honor came?

No, before it was too late, Nan had to be spoken to.

But with her hand upon the doorknob Lucy stopped. It was only seven thirty and Nan had mentioned the night before that she wanted to sleep until eight. Why, God only knew, Lucy thought. She was suddenly furious. Always before, Nan had been *happy* to have little exchanges of ideas in the freshness of the morning. It's the atmosphere of La Prairie, Lucy thought, where it's all *slack*.

Nan never slept that late in Philadelphia, even after a concert. It was Tim and Sara who were changing her.

The last thing Lucy had heard the night before—as they'd stood saying good night at the foot of the stairs—was Sara's light, breathy voice commanding them, "Everybody sleep late tomorrow! You're all tired, even if you don't know it. You're tired from the change of altitude and from our batting around in Dijon."

They'd all still been in their hats and sweaters from their drive around the lake.

Lucy frowned and spoke up in disagreement. "*Everybody* may be but I'm not everybody, my dear." That should have shown Sara how grossly imperative she had been, but the woman had apparently been born without the appreciation for subtlety. Sara laughed, saying, "Lucy, I'm talking to you especially. I hate to have you driving yourself, up painting at dawn, wearing yourself out."

She found herself then softening as she remembered the tone of real concern and affection in Sara's voice. It was a pity that Lucy so thoroughly disapproved of the poor creature. This only showed that young people, even those as thoroughly repulsed as was Sara, were drawn toward Lucy's sympathy and understanding. Had things only been a little different . . .

Her face stiffened once again as she remembered what she thought of as *the situation*. No matter how nice they might seem, these people were spurning all the moral teachings of their families and breaking their parents' hearts in the bargain. They were nothing but common criminals and should be treated as such. She'd often said so to Nan, and not even Sara's clever and beguiling ways, nor all Tim's gallantries, would ever shake her poor opinion of them. Tim Garton—even if he was her beloved Nan's brother—was a weakling and Sara—in spite of the apparent decency of her family and Nan's pathetic defense of her—was a bad woman.

Last night! This was the reason she'd awakened feeling so excited and upset this morning. Even Nan would have to agree that it was deliberate, how Sara had shooed them—as if they were two old ladies, *old!*—off to bed, saying they were tired, then stayed up until early morning herself, drinking and talking.

The insolence. She'd lain awake tossing and turning for hours listening to the muffled laughter that came from downstairs. It was obvious that Tim and Sara had deliberately got the children drunk and that they were telling them their usual battery of filthy jokes. Anyone could tell this from the lewd way they all laughed.

But even such behavior, its thoughtlessness of the comfort of the decent people in the household—had not upset Lucy as much as did the deceitful way Sara had sent her and Nan packing. Lucy was not used to being considered de trop, particularly by young people who tended to admire her, and now she stood before the mirror suddenly trembling with anger, knowing she would never forget the impotent rage it had made her feel as she lay listening to the thoughtless voices downstairs, hardly getting any sleep at all.

She wondered if poor Nan had comprehended the severity of the insult. Certainly Nan's face, as they'd said good night, had betrayed no signs. She needed to talk to Nan. Lucy could now barely contain herself.

She was staring at herself in the small oval mirror above the bureau as she whacked almost viciously at her hair with the brush and felt her anger dissolve into a rush of homesickness. Oh, how she longed for her own comfortable dressing table upon which sat her own carefully polished silver set. The table had three mirrors and a low comfortable stool. How she hated the heavy color and the silly mirror of this wretched mannish bureau. It was no wonder she always felt messy as she could hardly see herself to dress.

Sara could not have put her in a more thoroughly hateful room, this was no doubt purposeful, as she'd probably learned from Nan that blue was Lucy's worst color, especially the hard cold blue that covered the chaise longue and the bed and the windows. She'd have easily heard from Nan or even Timothy that nothing upset her more than plastered walls.

Could it have been Nan who'd written secretly to ask Sara to give her just what would make her most unhappy? Nan, who knew her better than anyone? Who knew, too, how dreadfully sensitive Lucy was to her surroundings? But, no, not even Tim's malignant influence would have made her own dear Nan behave as horribly as this. It had to be Sara, who had in someway divined . . . ?

And now Lucy's eyes again burned with tears and she hurried over to wash her face at the washstand behind the ghastly blue screen. Her face felt swollen. She opened the medicine cupboard and searched through the masses of tubes and jars and bottles and sticks for the lotion for her eyes that she always carried with her, as one never knew! How good it felt, how lucky Lucy was, to have brought along all these supplies!

She used both the white and the pink toothpastes that morning. She'd read that the white would neutralize mouth acids and the pink was for the stains caused by nicotine. Then she used a little mouthwash, then a gentle patting of her face with astringent, then another drop of lotion and one for her hands and now she was beginning to feel awake.

She pulled the windows open to a sun already high. She smiled disdainfully at the thought of all the people sleeping all over this house, while she alone was wide awake to the beauty of the morning. Typical of them, aside from her own dear Nan, who might, she thought, be awake too.

She tiptoed along the balcony toward Nan's windows and looked into the dim room. Nan lay like a tiny child with her face lifted trustfully toward a bar of sunlight that slanted across it. Her hair was gold and spread out in a fan over her naked shoulders, and Lucy's heart contracted with love.

She looked in, sighed sharply, thinking how odd it was that Nan hadn't heard her. Of course, Lucy hadn't called out loudly enough to have actually awakened her but she'd felt so strongly that Nan would already be awake, waiting to share this beautiful morning with Lucy alone.

How young she looked lying there. Who'd believe that Nan—seeing her like this—was only two years younger than was Lucy herself? And yet people said, confidentially of course, that Nan did not stand up to the light half as well as did Lucy. Who was it, that man on the boat, who'd been *amazed* when Lucy told him she was the older. He had, in fact, refused to believe it.

But that was the way Lucy was, utterly frank, instead of letting people build illusions all too easily shattered. She was probably the most frank and forthright woman she knew, in her own estimation. It was hard to be so relentlessly truthful but it was better than the alternative, which was fooling other people, as even poor Nan did, with all her youthfulness and ingenuity.

Now she heard a sudden slapping step on the path and Lucy lept into the shadow of her window. François, late as usual, was hurrying down from the village. Lucy's heart thudded with exasperation as she saw it was almost eight. This meant her breakfast would not be up until at least a quarter past the hour. She felt suddenly weak with hunger as she threw herself down on the detestble blue chaise.

This was Sara's fault, of course. It was a ridiculous idea to have this lanky villager come clear from the village every morning to serve their breakfasts. And it wasn't that François was inefficient—indeed, he served very well and cleaned like a madman all morning and the few times he'd helped with dinners he'd done so beautifully.

It was simply to feel Sara's outrageous vanity about her cooking that she refused to keep a servant in the house and instead made this poor man climb up and down the hill from the village, sometimes twice a day. Of course Sara was a good cook but it made Lucy almost laugh to see how Sara used this to attract attention.

God knew, it was easy to build a reputation, she thought, with one or two excellent dishes. She herself enjoyed the tremendous successes of her own monthly Sunday-night suppers and knew well the delight of having people ask for her recipes, but all this had come from years of experience, of searching through ancient cookbooks and of traveling and above all from Lucy's deep understanding of people.

To see this girl pretending to know something about gastronomy was too funny to bear, was, in fact, enraging.

She heard her stomach rumbling and she began to stir uncomfortably. If François didn't hurry she might faint. She looked again at the clock, ten past. He likely wouldn't be up for another *five minutes*!

Lucy moved quietly to the bureau and slipped open the top drawer. There, beneath her folded slips, there, toward the back, yes, *there*! She crammed a handful of the little chocolate drops into her mouth, shut the drawer forcefully, then sat down again, now breathing faster in anticipation.

The chocolate melted and ran deliciously down her throat and she was calmer, her breath steadying her and becoming more quiet.

They were so good.

François's steps sounded cautiously on the stone stairs and Lucy hurried back to bed, fluffing her hair out as she passed the mirror. She pulled the sheet up to cover half of her large chintz-emblazened breasts just as he tapped on the closed door with early-morning discretion.

"Yes?" She sang it gaily on two notes as she wiped a little chocolate from the corner of her mouth.

ii

It was almost nine o'clock before Lucy thought to glance up from the last pages of *Hasty Wedding*. She'd known all along that that lovely girl was innocent, still her heart had beat with anxiety toward the last, but now everything was put to right.

Lucy placed the mystery on the bedside table with the other books she'd brought with her from America. She smiled as she read their titles: *Ways and Means*, *A Philosophy of Solitude*, *The Pasquier Chronicles*, *Science and Health*.

She gave herself credit that she'd at least opened the last book and had read a page, well, half a page, after François left. She was truly amazed at her own sudden interest in the kind of cheap thrillers she'd always scorned, and a little ashamed of herself. As soon as she left La Prairie, with its shelf of these books in every room, she'd get back to her taste for good literature.

Another minor thing—but indicative of the entire subversive atmosphere of the place—that if a woman with as strong a will as hers could find herself growing even slightly lax about her reading, what might a weaker person risk and about more important things?

Lucy absently licked her fingers, the better to lick up the last crumbs of her breakfast roll. There was a thin smear of honey on the side of the plate so she cleaned that too. She did wish François would learn to bring her only what she asked for, which was her accustomed cup of strong black coffee, but he refused and insisted on giving her the same pot of hot milk, the same pile of butter curls, the same crisp rolls that he brought to the others.

It was natural for the children to be hungry, as they were like young animals and it mattered not at all with a little thing like Nan that she lost her figure altogether. Still, a tall woman who cared *anything* about the dignity of her appearance had to be careful.

Lucy resolved—and this time really meant it—that tomorrow she would send the tray back downstairs untouched.

She now lifted it carefully to the end of the bed and crawled out from beneath the covers. Her decision made her feel much better, more strong and cheerful and now she hummed a little.

She was nearly dressed when she heard Nan on the balcony. She was buttoning the front of her shirtmaker dress with hurried, slightly trembling fingers before she realized that Nan's high sweet voice wasn't addressing her; rather, it was calling to someone on the terrace below.

She moved to the window and looked out to see Nan, her hair blowing like a golden cloud around the shoulders of her soft, corn-colored dressing gown, was leaning over the railing of the balcony with her arms dangling down, and Lucy's lips puckered into a hard knot as her mouth flooded with bitterness.

Abandoned! That was how Nan Garten looked, *abandoned,* lolling about like that at the edge of the balcony with her negligee half open and calling out.

But who was it below?

Lucy peered down to see Tim and Sara sitting at one end of the green terrace table drinking beer and eating something from a little pewter bowl. Each was looking up at Nan and they were now all laughing. Lucy wondered if Sara had seen her, but—if so—there was no sign of this on her smooth, if silly, face.

"Come on, darling," Nan was saying. "Do please throw me one more!"

"You don't want pretzels for breakfast," Tim was saying, still laughing. "They're not for the likes of you."

"Oh, go ahead," Sara said. "Let Nan have them. She's got to learn the facts of life sometime."

Nan cried out as her frail little body tottered half over the railing as she reached to catch what Sara had thrown as Lucy watched, feeling agonized.

"Here," Tim said, "try this one," his pretzel landing almost at Lucy's feet as she ducked back into the shadow of the detestible blue curtains. She reeled, she almost fell, as she heard Nan say, "Tim, you did that on purpose, you old bastard."

Lucy picked up a handkerchief, looked at it dully, let it drop. She then felt under the pillows for the wet wad she'd used earlier and—closing her own door quietly behind her—let herself into Nan's room without knocking, there to burst into a flood of heart-rending, noisy sobs.

iii

Through her sobs, Lucy Pendleton then heard the sound of feet hurrying across the linoleum floor, then the light throbbing of Nan's voice. She felt a hand touching the flesh of her own shaking shoulder.

"Lucy, dear, what's wrong? Are you ill?"

"Ill? Of course I'm not ill!" Lucy listened to the croaking of her own voice with astonishment as she shrugged away from Nan's light touch. She then leaned against the wall, as if her legs would no longer carry her, and sobbed wildly in true anguish.

"Oh, Nan," she said, groping for her friend's long, slender fingers, which were not there. Lucy opened her eyes to see Nan Garton sitting quietly in bed, the covers pulled up, her large eyes looking oddly blank, even as her small square face watched the spectacle ensuing before her. It looked as if she was thinking of elephants, muffins. Her wide mouth was held in a polite, if slightly pained, smile.

Lucy's own eyes cleared. She abruptly stopped sobbing.

"Nan!" she cried, throwing her head back, flattening both hands against the wall, all the tragedy of the ages in her anguished voice.

There was then a long silence in which Lucy felt her throat thickening, daring not to look at the small woman in the bed for fear she'd see more of that ghastly polite tolerance. Lucy began to sob again, now in a harsh and ugly way, no longer caring about how the line of her throat looked as she thrust her head back, nor about her harsh tone of voice.

"But, Lucy, my poor dear Lucy, please do tell me what's wrong, won't you?" Nan asked. "Don't cry like that. Come and sit here beside me."

Lucy weaved blindly toward the low bed and sank down upon its edge, mopping at her eyes with the wet hankie. She sighed in a noisy, wavering way. Never had she been this miserable.

"Oh, Nan," Lucy asked. "What has *happened* to you?"

Nan looked at her with obvious surprise, then glanced toward the open window, as she stared at the lake over the tops of the apple trees. "Tim and Sara are still down there, Lucy, and they can hear you." Nan didn't look at her.

"Of course," Lucy said, "how typical, Nan Garten, always thinking of what other will think of *you*! They can't hear us, they only listen to themselves. Do you ever really consider me? How can you act this way, how can you be so weak?" She mopped her streaming eyes, waved the sodden hankie. "It's soaked," she said. "I cried all night!"

Nan's face was guileless, as she asked, "Would you like one of mine?"

"No, this is all right. I'll try not to make such a fool of myself, an old fool, but if you knew what I've been going through as I've watched you change this summer. It's a terrible change, Nan. And it's not just being so uncomfortable and being forced to live in this questionable atmosphere, with its irregular hours and slipshod meals that's exhausted me so. It's that I've had to sit helplessly by as you've allowed yourself to be cheapened. You know how I've always revered you and . . ."

"Lucy!" Nan's voice was now full of gentle ridicule.

"Don't laugh at me! Yes, I've *revered* you as the finest, purest woman I've ever known. Your manners, the way you carry yourself, the manner in which you speak, and *now* listen to you!" Lucy groaned, now twisting her hand in desperation.

"Listen to what, Lucy?" Nan asked. "I really think you're exaggerating. You do know, don't you, that I love you just as I always have and . . ."

"Don't change the subject!" Lucy said harshly. "I heard you out there on the balcony talking to those two. I heard what you called Timothy and can tell you, Nan Garten, that the very fact that you'd let such a word cross your lips is as horrible to me as *poison*!"

Lucy, tired suddenly, stopped. What was the use of fighting for her love? She felt again what she'd often felt that summer, that Nan was now lost to her, that never again would she be with her darling as they'd been that wonderful winter after the death of Nan's husband, when it was only the two of them and they were so happy together in the little studio in the woods.

"I'm an old fool," Lucy mumbled. "Forget it. Forget all I've said."

Lucy stood at the door stiffly. In her heart, however, she was still crying, screaming in fact like a wounded animal, begging in her mind for Nan to love her, for her to take her back, for her to be the beautiful gracious fairy creature of those other blissful days. Nan, she whimpered in her heart, I'm old and ugly and I hate all the world but you, you're my darling. Take me back, feed me with your beauty, comfort me with your gifts. Feed me, I'm so hungry.

Nan opened her hands, as if she'd heard, and left them open, lying like two lilies on the soft green blanket.

"Please, Lucy," she said softly. "Tell me what's wrong. This is such a lovely place and you're so unhappy. Why is this?"

Lucy fought the need to throw herself on her knees beside the bed, then smiled waveringly, saying, "Do I seem unhappy? I'm surprised you've noticed, you're so busy being with your brother and all these relatives of Sara's. Please don't worry about *me,* Nan, as I can manage perfectly well."

Face puckered as if she'd eaten alum, Lucy's heart was breaking.

"Oh, Lucy," Nan said, "don't make things harder for me."

Lucy's heart thudded to life. She'd known this, she'd *felt* that Nan wasn't as lighthearted and happy as she'd been acting over all these horrible lonely weeks. She'd known that Nan was secretly needing her. She wanted to run to the bed, to sit eagerly on its edge.

Nan looked at her. "You've changed, too, Lucy darling, you know? You don't seem to enjoy anything anymore. I try to think of things to do, a picnic in the woods? You *used to* like that. And Sara does her best and never has food again that you say you can't eat and Tim . . ."

She was startled that Nan Garton should set about reprimanding her, after all Lucy had suffered this summer for Nan's sake. It was too incredible. She sighed, large tears welling in her swollen eyes.

"What *is* it?" Nan's voice now sounded sharp. She sighed. "Here, smoke, Lucy, it will help."

When Lucy spoke again she tried not to sob and to have her voice sound calmer. "You do know, Nan, that you're the person I love most in the world. We've alwys been close and since dear George passed beyond I have willingly devoted my entire life to helping you forget your grief. But now I find I cannot simply sit by and see the very things I've so admired in you and respected you for dragged down." She saw Nan's blank look and repeated it. "Yes! dragged in the dust. I've always thought," she then went on, "that I was the most fortunate person in the world to be so close to you, to listen to your beautiful—yes! *Beautiful*—way of speaking. And now . . ." Her voice quavered but she went on valiantly. "Now I hear you shouting down to them like some common *girl*, using words that you shouldn't ought to even know the meaning of."

An amused look flickered across Nan's attentive face and Lucy, seeing this, said, "You *shouldn't*!"

"Well, Lucy," she said. "You do remember that it's my business to know the English and American languages, don't you? I believe that word that you're delicately referring to is in each of them, but I do admit I've never before said it with so much real pleasure. That was fun."

"Oh, good, laugh! Laugh! You enjoy torturing me, anyone can see this from the way you make people laugh at me when I'm out of the room, but now I'm beyond caring."

"Lucy, dear, can you be fair? You are deliberately hurting yourself and over nothing. You make people leave you out. You do this on purpose. You seldom sit downstairs, you leave the moment there's any kind of merriment. If we ask you to come with us to Veytaux or even just to walk to the village you . . ."

"Yes, you *ask* me. First you all whisper behind my back then one says, 'Well, I suppose we'll *have* to ask Lucy.' And can you not honestly see that we are both being treated this way?"

Nan looked hurt, which made Lucy happy, so she hurried on. "That's right, it's not only me. If you're so dazzled by all the seeming attention you're getting from your own brother and from young Daniel Tennant, not to see it, then I need to simply tell you. That's right, Nan Garton. Can't you see how they laugh at us both, how they push us to one side, how they always pretend to defer to us as if we were a thousand years old, then go ahead and do what ever they want to do? Could you honestly feel, after all your experience with hero worship, how they flatter and kowtow to you simply because you're famous? Can't you see how they . . . ?"

"Who are *they*?" Nan asked, her face stony.

"Why . . . why, all of them! The two Tennants were all right when they came but they soon got their instructions." Lucy laughed in a mean way and went on. "And Sara Porter, or whatever it is she's calling herself, and I do admit, Nan, that you told me before we came what the situation was but I never thought I'd have to live on here all this time with a woman as smooth and as deceitful as *that* one is. And yes, I might as well say it. It's *Timothy*! Yes, your own dear little brother, whom you so adore! He's against you, too, thanks to his horrible mistress. He's as bad as the rest of them, trying to get rid of us all the time."

"What are you talking about?"

Lucy looked at the doll-like creature sitting back against her pillow who seemed to have only kindness in her voice. Nan now looked older than she had a few moments earlier, which made Lucy feel strangely lighter.

"Last night."

"Last night?" Nan asked. "We were all a little tired from the ride to Dijon and perhaps we'd eaten too much before we started but . . . ?"

"Oh, please do not be so damned charitable," Lucy exploded. "You *know* what I mean. Last night when that Sara sent us packing off to bed so she and Tim could stay up down there alone and talk to the children? What if Honor had just arrived? After all, she's been here for practically every weekend and, Nan, my blood simply *boiled*! For myself, for you too! How dare they? I asked myself, how dare they treat *Nan Garton* this way, after all she has done for them? How dare they send us upstairs as if we were two old ladies who . . . ?"

"Lucy, dear, don't you think you have that a little too much on your mind? After all Tim is only a few years younger than I am and I'm only two years younger than you."

"Nan, if I didn't know that you are the dearest, loveliest person in the world, I'd think . . . yes, I'd almost think . . ."

"What?" Nan asked.

"Oh, that's all right, let's forget it. I'll get used to it." Lucy's voice now sounded pathetically jaunty. She stared away, looking at the wall over her friend's shoulder with a resolute smile.

"What?" Nan asked. "Please tell me. We mustn't let these misunderstandings spoil all our good feelings for each other."

"Well, Nan, I will tell you frankly, then. It seems to me, and not for the first time either, that since we've come to this *awful* place you're letting yourself be influenced by the others to act just the way they do toward me. Of course I know I'm big and fat and I have no shape and do not tell me any differently! I know what you all think of me. I know I am not as young as the rest of you. But it does seem to me you forget you're nearly my age."

"I actually never think about it. We *are* a little older but what difference does this make?"

"What difference?" Lucy's tears were now past all control and they rolled from her enflamed eyes like hot drops of fire. She buried her head in her hands, her wet handkerchief falling to the floor. After a moment, feeling Nan's light fingers on her hair, she straightened.

"Oh, I know you must think I've lost my mind, Nan, and I really hate to be this way, but I truly don't feel well. I try not to show it, but I feel so weak, so tired, and I'm so disappointed sometimes, after all these years of wanting to go back to Europe and now the chance to be alone with you and you just *dawdle* here, when every day we could be drinking in the beauty in the famous galleries together, instead of staying in *this place*, letting Timothy and Sara wheedle you into wasting even more of our time. I thought we were going to . . ."

"But, Lucy, I told you before we came how quiet it would be."

"But, Nan! You said we'd only be here a little while, then we'd go to Fiesole and take a villa, just the two of us, and you'd write and I'd paint and . . . ?"

"I know. But you must remember that I wasn't yet sure that Tim and Sara really wanted us here or that we'd be happy. It's lovely here. I simply cannot leave for a little longer. I don't want to. I'm happier than I thought I could ever be and I feel sure you can paint beautiful things and . . ."

Lucy rose. Almost frantically she lit another cigarette and began to now pace. She saw herself in the little mirror above Nan's washstand: Her hair was touseled, her face swollen, her dress both mussed up and half unbuttoned. She looked as if she'd been attacked. She laughed fiercely. She didn't care.

She didn't care and Nan didn't care either, Lucy knew. She turned, one trembling hand pushed hard against the wooden mantle of the fireplace, the other flicking her cigarette.

"Work?" she asked, hearing her voice go high. "Work? Why you know I can't work in a place unless it's completely sympathetic to me, that it's utterly impossible, which you do happen to know, Nan Garton. And yet you force me to stay in a place—and do not suggest again that I go on alone to Italy as I refuse to leave you in such a place as this alone. You force me to stay here where the atmostphere is so hostile, so *foul*, with all the insults and petty suspicions and digs and sly remarks, that I could never hope to paint well. And nobody should know that better than you. Why, you've seen me do some of my best work, Nan. You do know what I'm capable of, you know the reviews I got from that last show. Nobody understands me as you do, as you used to, I should say."

Her voice caught on a hard, quick sob that softened into tears. She saw that Nan's large eyes were filling too. She waited, breath held. Had she at last made Nan see?

For a moment the silence deepened. The two women looked at one another as Lucy began to feel hopeful, then—and suddenly—happier. She watched as her friend's hands relaxed and lay limply against the covers of the bed and heard the sigh that escaped Nan's pale lips. She felt young again, young and beautiful and full of hope and desired by all men, and she raised her proud head.

"Lucy," Nan said, when she finally spoke. "I can't tell you how terribly sad I am that this summer has been painful for you. For me—even if you say I'm deluding myself, that I've been duped and flattered—it's felt perfect. I know we planned to go to Fiesole, Lucy, but I'm not going."

Neither spoke so Nan went on. "You paint beautiful pictures, Lucy. I know you can paint them here if you will let yourself. Some of the flowers you've done this summer are beyond lovely. Won't you try to paint, Lucy dear? Won't you forgive me and try to paint? You mustn't feel left out, Lucy dear. We all love your work, just as we all love you. But," and Nan went on more firmly now, having wiped a single tear from her cheek. "I am not going to leave Timothy. I'm not going to Fiesole. I'm not leaving here until our boat sails." She finished speaking and closed her eyes.

Lucy stared for a moment, seeing as clearly as she'd ever seen anything in her life the fine almost dusty eyebrows, the faint lines around the mouth of her beloved. She listened to Nan's slow and now exhausted breathing. Never would she forget that sound, nor those faint lines nor the fine arch of her brow. Never would she forgive this small woman, never, she thought, and sobbed once more.

"Oh," Lucy cried out, as if she'd been struck. "Nan Garton, you are cruel! You're selfish. You love no one but your own brother!" And she rushed from the room, the door slamming behind her.

Nan's face changed not at all.

3

For the next eleven days the two of them—the man and his wife—watched his left leg die.

At first he was dazed. Then he began to wonder about the cage that was over it and at last to lift his head a little and to peer down at the leg when the nurses shifted the covers.

It lay, white and beautiful, on many small sandbags. To the woman, who knew, it seemed to be no longer a part of the man, but to him it was still his own leg, even as it was a wolf that tore and foamed bloodily in every vein, and it was a long twisted red-hot cable and at the same time a drop of ice-cold color. He looked at his leg reproachfully.

When the doctors came in and tapped and pressed at, say, the knee, he would smile and tell them joyfully that they were pressing on his ankle or his toes. The woman would try to swallow, but it was difficult.

He grew more cunning as the days passed. He tried every wile of his wily, cunning nature to get her to help him die. Of course bribery could not touch her, but he sometimes felt sure that she might easily bribe his sister or her brother and sister, someone. He remembered where his every cent was banked and offered it all for poison. Then he threatened, then cajoled, then wept and even tried to kiss the woman with some passion to get her to give him a razor blade or a knife or to help him to the window ledge. This went on for many days and nights and at strange times the woman longed to help him but she could not.

She watched quietly while the dead leg rotted on its pillows. It was true, what she had read, that the toenails of corpses grew prodigiously as these before her sprouted like curving yellowish shells from the withered toes, as, with time, the flesh around them turned an ardent brown. There were one or two red blotches on the inside of the calf, which spread slowly over the cold white flesh. Above the knee, on the inside, a greater blotch widened hideously, looking as if it would turn to jelly at the touch of a finger.

On about the eighth day she told the nurse to put gauze soaked with cologne water on the leg. The man looked at her and though he never spoke of it, she felt his gratitude and his fearsome humiliation, for he was the most fastidious person she had ever known and the most sensitive to smells.

On the tenth day, while she stood by the bed remembering with a kind of muted anguish his light agile dancing figure and the way he knew that his legs were his best feature, and wondered how to tell him, he told her. Yes, she said, it must come off. Soon, soon, he said.

On the twelfth day—after an hour's delay while a growth was taken from someone's brain—it was amputated: it was the worst hour so far. But finally he could go once more into the operating room and he smiled again, dreamily, wearily, as the stretcher took him away from her and for one dreadful moment the iron band loosened and she almost cried out with agony. Only two tears were shed and it was soon over. There was a cold sweat on her forehead. She prayed fearfully that it would never happen again.

She laid herself carefully down, once more, and waited for the doctors, who, this time, hardly even raised their hands.

She hurried past them as the stretcher hissed familiarly along the corridor, then watched without expression while the man's wasted body was lifted onto the bed. The stump of his leg, swatched now like a Turk's head, bobbed and quivered heavily for a moment, then his enormous blue eyes opened once in his grayish face, and then he was sick. But both he and the woman were uplifted by the miraculous sense of feedom and of relief and even cleanliness.

i

When Nan Garton turned in her bed and woke up enough to feel their warmth, it was still so early in the morning of August 31 that the rays were almost horizontal. She kept her eyes shut, almost smiling at the brightness behind her lids.

A little girl again, her mind dreamed. I'm little and am lying in the sun in the sewing room and if I open my eyes I shall see Mother's basket with my new plaid gingham school dress spilling out of it and the gold thimble with "Stratford-on-Avon" written around it. It's exciting to awaken not in my own bed and in a moment Father will climb slowly up the stairs and stop outside the door, then he will come in quietly and look at me, with my pretty hair upon the pillow and my eyelids held softly shut. And he'll be surprised when I open my eyes, his sudden weight beside my couch making the floor creak.

"Nanny," he'll say. "My little Anne." He'll whisper it. "You have a brother, now, and I have a son," and his full and beautiful mouth will tremble, the drop of whiskey caught in the soft hair of his beard flashing with little rainbows.

Older now and today school starts, the Misses Huntington's Academy for Young Ladies and Gentlemen, and Timothy will go with me. What a lovely day. I shall hold his hand tightly and all the girls will say, "Oh, your darling little brother! Let me have him, no, me!" But Timothy will look only at me and we'll walk through the sunlight of this warm and sparkling day safe together, my new Ferris waist feeling stiff and curvy, almost like a grown-up woman's corset.

Mother will be watching for us and will cry a little and say, "If your dear father could only have seen you!" but inside I know Timothy will never really miss Father because I'm there to protect him and nurse him in a white dress like an angel's when he is ill and he will need only me.

Now I'm sad. Timothy, promise me you'll never hide from me again. I won't tell Mother this time but don't sneak cigarettes in the old piano box. Love me or I'll tell. Tea at the Parker House, and, oh, he's grown, he's older, will college make him leave me? He loves that girl, no this one. He's home again, sad and thin and he needs me. War and he's strange and when he's wounded he calls for me and I'm the one who nurses him more gently than a man was ever nursed. I am the one who understands him so the ugly woman in the cape can stay away.

Nan stirred and squinted her still half-shut eyes against the brightness of the sun and its growing warmth. She wanted to stay in bed yet awhile in dreams, though they seemed empty ones. She hated waking up yet something inside her felt she was right on the brink of a great surprise that would bring enormous joy.

She savored the excitement delicately, her mind growing more clear as the overlapping dreams receded.

Nan opened her eyes slowly, thinking, Yes, I'm here in my brother's house and I'm happy. I should be sad, I suppose, that he's so completely himself and satisfied without me. Maybe I am a little sad but I also feel like the most wonderful thing is about to happen and I am breathless.

A light morning wind blew suddenly into the room, lifting one long curtain silkily across her face. It was the color of Chablis, pungent, frail, and she looked through this color curiously as it brushed over her cheek and slurried over her fair loose hair. The room seemed far away.

The white wall seemed to shimmer and pulse like yellow water in a crystal vase and the dark green curtains were as straight as rose stems, the pale curtains between them as invisible as smoke seen through smoke.

Rich browns in the chairs, the books on the mantlepiece, browns and greens in the rug transmuted into dim blurred shadows both strange and beautiful to her. I am not me, she thought. I'm a fish.

Then the thin silky curtain drifted off her face and she closed her eyes against reality.

In the next room was the sound of Lucy getting up so vigorously, running water, making noise of swirling, gargling, that she was already sounding disapproving. Perhaps I have a guilty conscious but why should I, it's not yet eight and we all agreed to stay in bed later today.

Nan then reproved herself. What had come over her to lately find fault with everything her poor Lucy did? It hurt Lucy almost physically to have to loll about, as she put it. Why then should Nan be so impatient, comdemning her for what was only an act of self-denial?

Oh, please, dear God, she thought, help me be more patient and loving, to see clearly and with an open heart.

She lay for a moment, praying lazily but intensely, and then relaxed. The day, she decided, would be one of pure selflessness. She saw that she had grown too demanding lately. She must try to understand why other people acted as they did. She would think with their brains, act with their bodies.

She smiled at the picture of herself sitting and acting as Honor Tennant would. What would it be like to be a great smooth cool statue, slow moving, silent, impersonal? Did Honor really feel and suffer? Could anything so big and goddess-like know ordinary emotions, enjoy mortal pleasures such as washing and brushing her hair?

No, I'd rather be me. I'd rather be me than Daniel, too; he's so young, so awkward, so trusting still. He makes me feel at least three hundred years old. And yet I like to feel old, because I know that you and Daniel think I am beautiful. Yes, beautiful! His eyes gleam with delight when I come into the room, and he sees every change in my hair, my dress. I like that. It makes me feel attractive. It can't matter to him: it won't hurt him to fall a little bit in love with me and I need it.

That's it: I need to be noticed, flattered. Perhaps Lucy is right. Perhaps I've grown a little silly and flighty this summer, hoping that a boy will notice the flower in my hair, hoping that he will leap to his feet when I come near him, hoping I will hear his breath grow shorter. But Timothy, Timothy—and here Nan felt her mouth droop—it's you I really wait for. You notice, you flatter, you smile as before but all you really live for is your Sara. And I'm glad and it's right and I like her. Even if I wanted not to I do like her but . . .

There was the sound of light steps on the balcony. Nan's mind flashed into blankness and on her face was a moment of gentle innocence.

If Lucy calls me I simply won't answer, I will not. I told her I wanted to sleep in this morning. I cannot stand another scene, another of her early-morning orgies of blame, tears, repentance, the weeping, every morning, the weeping. Oh, Timothy, why don't you hide me from all this? If Lucy calls *Nah-han* in that insufferable bleating voice of hers, I will scream.

"*Nah-han*!" Lucy's shadow fell darkly across Nan's face.

Nan saw red circles against her eyelids. Her throat stiffened with the effort she had to make not to swallow. She breathed softly, thinking dispassionately, How pretty I must look, in here with my hair spread out on the pillow, like a princess in a fairytale. I'll think of flowers. That will keep me from opening my eyes. Yes, petunias, dark purple velvet ones with silver in their folds. Petunias just opened, and under their sticky leaves I'll have one zinnia, brick-red, heavy, cruel. I will find one poppy in the meadow and put it in the dim leaf shadow. Shall I use wheat, to lift it high above? Would harebells be too blue?

The big woman sighed sharply, then the shadow slid off Nan and moved away, heading toward Lucy's room again.

Suddenly Nan now felt much ashamed of herself. How can I? she moaned. What makes me so selfish? I have so much. And my poor friend is so alone! What makes me act this way?

Nan started from the bed, pulling her light silk robe about her with a vague desire to rush to Lucy, to embrace her and beg her forgiveness.

But François's steps could now be heard as they slapped flatly on the terrace. It was later than she thought. She was silly. Breakfast would soon be up and Lucy would still love her.

She walked to the mirror above her washstand and looked at herself coldly before she threw back her shoulders, lifted her outstretched arms and began to count: one and two and three, as she began to touch her toes with a series of birdlike swoopings.

ii

Nan felt tears trickling like ants behind her eyes; she tried desperately not to yawn. She wanted to cry out, "Oh, Lucy, my poor stupid Lucy, can't you even see how boring all this grows? Don't you even care how ugly weeping makes you?"

Instead she heard herself murmuring consolingly, trying to help her friend pour out the long stream of bitterness that was in her. However did Lucy think of all these things? Nan wondered. What part of her brain invented such a fantastic parade of cruelty and insult? Has she always been this way? And am I so especially dull, Nan asked herself, that I, too, do not see these slights and deliberate taunts that Lucy says are all about us, here at La Prairie?

Nan tried to remember about Lucy. Everything before the summer seemed remote. There was this summer and then there was being a child again, helping dress Timothy on a cold morning, wrapping his cut knee. Oh, my brother, do you remember . . . ?

Lucy was weeping. Poor Lucy. What was it really about Nan's saying the word *bastard*? It was funny, it remained funny until she saw Lucy's haggard eyes and listened to the real shock in her voice. There's no use to feel happy with that face in front of her.

There was a ray of sunlight on the edge of the pillow that lay like hollow ice, and its edge gleamed with blue and scarlet. If she closed her eyes Nan could see the colors merging, dancing, shattering themselves and coming together again, dancing in and out too fast to follow with anything but the mind's eye.

"Your dear brother . . . Sara . . . Those two . . . ? Oh, that Sara . . ."

Nan sighed and heard her own voice sounding gentler than usual, while inside she saw again the dazzling happiness that had looked up at her such a short time ago, when she'd called from her balcony down to Timothy and Sara. She'd stood there longing to speak, hearing his deep voice and wishing that she dared call, dared force him to stop talking with his love. I must not, she'd told herself fiercely.

But I *want* him to look up at me, standing here in my soft silk with my hair blowing. Sara is so young, so happy, no wonder he looks only at her. I'm old with the beginnings of wrinkles around my eyes. Sara's hands are thin while mine are like little claws.

Nan had gone to the mirror and stood there saying, Don't be a ninny, Nan, don't be a ninny. Be strong. Go out on the balcony, Nan Garton.

And so she had indeed gone out and at the memory of their loving thoughtless faces that lifted up to her so trustingly she felt warmed again. They love me, Nan thought. They want me to call down to them. Perhaps Timothy was willing me to call out to them to say hello to him.

What was Lucy saying now? Nan must try to be more attentive. Now it was something about their age and she heard herself replying, her voice gentle and sincere, "Why, Lucy darling, I . . . I . . . I never think about it at all. We *are* a little older, but what difference does it make?"

What difference does it make? Oh God, Nan cried fiercely, why do I say such stupid nothings and so politely? Deference? I weep to know that my own breasts will go flat and loose, my arms bony. I weep to see that soon my neck may be dry and stringy, my hair too dull for brushing to revive it. Deference? I still see myself firm and round and fresh, and the years are bitter to me, remembering that lonely time when I was young and full. Wasted. Wasted and now what do I have? My youth is gone untasted. Timothy gone, I'm left a screwy widow woman, with only Lucy for my comfort, and am desolate.

Nan wiped one tear from her cheek. Lucy thinks I'm crying with her. Perhaps that will make her feel happier. I'm a hypocrite.

It seemed weird to her that she could go on talking so reasonably, so thoughtfully, while inside another woman spoke. Another? There were several. One wept for loneliness, another turned her eyes away from the swelling frantic ugliness of Lucy's tears, yet another spoke coldly and surely, saying what all of them knew, that she cannot leave Timothy, not now.

She'd never spoken so straightly to her friend and she listened to her own voice with a kind of timid amazement as she said she would not leave La Prairie. I am betraying my promise. I am breaking Lucy's heart. What has come over me? But I cannot, must not leave. I feel there is something for me to wait for. Something is going to happen to make me see clearly at last.

The crash of Lucy's slamming door was as tiny to her as a spider's footstep. Nan felt cool and exhausted as if filled with floating pebbles.

iii

To the meadow, to the meadow, and her feet made a little dance of hurrying down the cool twisted stairs. I am escaping. I have already escaped. No more tears, no more of my poor Lucy's moanings. Stay with me, flagons, comfort me with apples, for I am sick of love. That's not right. Where are my wits? Hasten to the meadows, Nan Garton. Get thee to thy vases.

Nan laughed softly.

The two baskets she'd put in the lower hall the night before stood on the tile floor, empty except for shears and the enormous pair of blue and yellow work gloves she'd bought at the Bazar Francais in Veytaux. Everything was ready for her, then, to go out the door and down the path and into the knee-deep flowers where she longed to be.

But she hesitated. Through half-pulled curtains she looked up almost unwillingly into the living room. It was bright with fresh wax cream in the sun. She stepped quickly down into it and hurried toward the mirror, frowning faintly. I'll just look, she reasoned, that won't hurt. It's just such a beautiful mirror and the colors in it. But she knew that the real reason she ran toward it was that she might see Timothy there. He might be watching on the terrace, going or coming, and she could see him in the mirror and not even speak. Looking could not matter. The mirror made things so clear.

The mirror was empty. Still the room looked better in it, she saw, less polished and polite in the bright sun. But Tim was not there and Nan turned away.

"Madam!" François said. "You will excuse me but Monsieur has disappeared!"

Nan raised her eyebrows coolly, hoping that she did not show anything but polite interest. Damn, François! How did he know she was looking for Timothy when she hardly knew this herself?

"Yes," the valet's voice continued deeply while his dark eyes burned far back in his skull. "Completely vanished." He looked somberly at her as his cigarette fumed behind him.

Nan summoned her best French. "Temporarily, I hope."

"Madame is correct, temporarily." And with a high cackling laugh François disappeared around the corner, leaving one tiny pile of ash in the middle of one green tile.

He's as crazy as a moth, Nan thought, and now she ran lightly back into the hall, swept up the two baskets and swept without a sound through the wide door, and passed along the white blowing curtains of Daniel's room, out to the middle path.

Crazy as a moon-drunk moth, crazy as a dragonfly, mad with mead from jasmine honey. Oh, Miss Garton, you *reee-eaally* should write! You *reee-eaally* do say the prettiest things, so poetical like!

I'll start with the tall flowers, she thought, as a kind of placid excitement, feeling them brush against her as she walked slowly through them. Sage, and mourning bride, surely, and maybe some Queen Anne's lace, a very little, and green oats, and will there be wheat? It must be gold, a deep gold for tonight. I'll wear my dress with gold threads in it. No one has ever seen it. Timothy will love it, with the gold weight on the table and me and a cloud of gold.

She moved slowly over the steep slopes, under the flickering leaves of ancient fruit trees. The birds were almost silent. Bees sang, though, around the ripening plums and pears, and she sank upon her knees and watched solemnly while a snail with a fine gleaming black-striped shell swept over a gnarled root. Buddha's curls were snails, she thought. Snail shells have the curve of infinity.

She snipped with complete absorption at the flower stems, leaving them now short, now tall. Sometimes she stood for several minutes looking down at the colors in her basket, before she started off across the meadow for one stock of wild snapdragon that she remembered near the vineyard wall, or a late ranunculus that flashed down by the brook.

She felt as light as a new lamb. She was conscious of the bones moving delicately within their warm firm envelope and she licked her upper lip and tasted salt in the beads of sweat that lay there with true sensual delight. She felt again the excitement that had been building up inside her all this summer, as she grew gradually more at peace and at ease with the greater peace of this place.

I should be worried, sad, ashamed of myself, Nan thought dreamily, but I'm not. There is my friend, morbid and lonely in her room, painting her ugly backgrounds in a kind of masochistic fury. There are Honor and Daniel. Young people are always so sad, so tender and bewildered. There is Timothy, my brother, gone from me. I should be, and am sad. But down here under these trees, on these flowery slopes . . .

One wild strawberry, dark and tiny, grew secretly under the thick leaves by the wall. She put a harebell beside it and then stood looking through quick tears at the blue lake far below her.

Help me to be kind, she prayed. Dear God, make me a patient and loving person. Make others love me as I love them. Make Timothy . . .

iv

She heard the car horn, short and insistent above the sound of bees and a little brook and turned unwillingly back toward the house. Suddenly she felt hot and tired and the full baskets dragged her faintly freckled arms. The slopes of the meadow seemed deeper than they should. When she reached the top of the path she was breathless and the flowers she picked so lovingly looked limp and bedraggled and she was touched by a little wave of self-pity. Lucy was right, she thought, why should I waste my time fixing beautiful vases for blind eyes? Who cares if I work all day?

In her room, though, where François had left the green shutters bowed against the sun and all the colors were cool, she put water on her face and brushed back her hot hair and felt gay again.

I'm hungry, she suddenly decided. I, Nan Garton, the bird woman, the frail spirit who lives on one almond and a sliver of ripe peach, am *starved*! What will there be for lunch? Hurry. Run down fast, get past Lucy's room and run to the kitchen to help Sara carve great pink hams, open jars of pâté from Strasbourg, bottles of black cured Greek olives, tins of herring, Polish chickens. To cut thick wedges of brown bread, slice through the smooth flesh of a mild cheese from the mountains, put butter in its tub upon the table! Pile up grapes and plums and the last four-season strawberries on a silver tray. Hurry!

But at the living room step Nan paused. People were talking in the kitchen, strangers. She all but growled. Would she ever be old enough to stop minding when she had to meet new people? A woman your age, she told herself severely, should be ashamed to be hovering out here like a timid school girl! What had Sara said about the visitors? Nan could not exactly remember. She took a deep breath and ran across the room and up the steps to the kitchen, thinking, Now! Quick! Let's get this over with!

In the flash of time between her sight of them all standing there and her first words, she knew she would certainly never forget them. They were like a picture, stiff and strange, of some scene from a once-familiar play. The green and white squares they all stood upon, and the white walls with one vivid blue-green poster, and the wide window with its white curtains blowing and the single daisy in the jar: it was naïve and beautiful, like the setting for a village melodrama.

Sara stood at the left, quick and tall, with one brown hand laid lightly on a pile of lettuce leaves. Honor, in the background by the cellar stairs, leaned against Daniel, with her eyes dark and brooding above her small red mouth, and Daniel leaned against the wall. In front of him Timothy sagged like a clown against the younger man's crooked knee, Nan's brother's face frozen into a wild leer, pretending to be Harpo Marx or, perhaps, a monkey. Half turned away from Timothy and grinning affectionately was a tall happy boy with dark hair and warm small brown eyes. And between them stood the tiny girl. Her hair gleamed almost white above her dark gold skin. She had gray eyes, the biggest eyes Nan had ever seen and seemingly the most startled.

All their eyes looked straight at Nan: Sara's pale green and sardonic, Daniel's their echo, Honor's black and sad above the bright blue merriment of Timothy's, and the new boy's like a wise ape's, but it was the enormous unblinking gaze of that wee woman that held Nan's own.

Oh, she thought, instinctively dismayed, she's littler than I! She is lovely and so young. Will Dan even look at me now? Will Timothy? Oh, I hate her! No, Nan, she told herself: Discipline, discipline! I must learn to see clearly.

"Oh!" the little girl gasped. She cried out huskily as if she had seen an archangel, "It's *Anne Garton Temple*!"

The picture they all had made standing there with their eyes turned toward Nan was now broken to pieces as everybody laughed and Nan felt herself grow warm and pleased at Susan Harper's excitement, and Joe Kelly's flattery. She knew this was foolish but how strangely nice it was to be recognized so far from America, away from publicity pictures and her fan mail.

She was embarrassed to feel herself blush, then blush harder still. Timothy came across the kitchen and put his arm around her shoulder. Darling Timothy, knowing exactly how silly and how pleased she felt.

They scattered suddenly before Sara's command directing the three men into the cellars, with Susan following after Honor like a bemused kitten. As the girl gave a last glance back at Nan, she almost tripped over the step into the terrace.

"Who are they, Sara darling?" Nan felt so amused and happy that she could hardly whisper. She leaned close to Sara as if to hear her secrets, and, as she hugged her elbows tightly against her waist, Nan's eyes were dancing.

Sara was counting spoonfuls of olive oil into the big wooden bowl in front of her, her lips moving. "They just got in, friends of ours, I told you last night after Joe called from town, remember? I used to know them in the West. They're staying up at the village."

"I like them."

Sara stuck one finger in the salad dressing and licked it and then ground more pepper into the bowl and abruptly she looked at Nan.

"Why?" she asked.

"Oh, I don't know. They're so funny, so sweet, like a . . . ? Oh, they seem so young and innocent!" And Nan began to laugh again softly.

"Yes, I like them too," Sara said warmly. Nan looked seriously at her from far behind her own gaiety and wondered if Sara meant it, or were those strange impersonal green eyes ever to be really warmed by any casual ordinary love? Would Sara really care if she never saw Susan or Joe again? Would she actually notice if Daniel, Honor, and Nan herself were to walk off the terrace into the blue air toward France? Even with Timothy, Sara's eyes never seemed to be unveiled, and Nan wondered how it was when the two were alone.

Nan caught her breath for in that instant she suddenly knew that Sara loved her brother with all of herself, brain, bone, and ghost. How had she ever doubted?

"Oh, Sara!" She cried softly and laid her cheek for a second on the other woman's thin brown arm. Then, laughing, Nan pushed all the piled green salad leaves roughly into a bowl and ran out into the sunshine with it.

She'll think I've gone crazy, but I don't care. I love her. Nan smiled, blinking at the glare from the hot lake and walked down the terrace toward the table.

When Susan rushed over—voice breaking, eyes wide with adoration—to help Nan carry the salad, the older woman beamed placidly, and when Lucy came swimming through the curtains onto the terrace Nan heard herself cry out affectionately, "How did it go today? Good work?" As if she had not seen the poor struggling woman and her foolish pictures only a while before.

Was it this morning, truly, that she had listened to Lucy's harsh sobs? Was it this morning or a life ago that Lucy had snarled at her, "Go on! Get out! Go!"

"You don't love anybody but your own brother," Lucy had said. But it was not true. Nan smiled. She loved everyone and everyone loved her. She looked gaily around, at Lucy, at little Susan's adoration, at Honor. And there coming across the terrace now were Dan, so thin and fine, and young Joe Kelly. They loved her. And Timothy! As he came into the sunlight, he looked straight at Nan with his eyes wide and winked faintly, first one eye and then the other, as he used to at dancing school. So she was happy. Dancing school! Do you remember, little brother?

V

The little tool room at the back of the house was cool and dim. And Nan loved to work there. It was almost like hiding. When she looked out of the windows and into the roots of lilies and well grass, she felt like a small silent animal peering from its burrow and she wondered why all rooms were not built halfway into earth like this one.

Nobody ever came here aside from François, of course, and Timothy and Sara, for hoes and twine when they gardened, and often the quiet man who tended to the vines. But there was never anyone when Nan Garton fixed the flowers. Perhaps she'd become invisible. Perhaps she had fern seeds in her shoes.

She hummed almost silently as she stood back to look at the last flower in the last vase, a spray of wine-colored nicotiana rising from the tassel of petunia, pink as store-bought strawberry ice cream, but something was wrong. She regarded the colors dreamily for several minutes, her face intent and as blank as a child's. She was thinking: I am almost completely absorbed, she thought, as much as I can ever be, because I'm almost not thinking about anything in the world aside from color and the shapes of flowers and their petals. I'm not thinking about what they will say and feel when they see my beautiful flowers and I'm hardly thinking about myself or what they think of me, so I am really as selfless at this moment as I am capable of being, although people say at certain times, like the peak of copulation or the moment of a sneeze, you almost stop thinking about yourself, the way I am now, not thinking about anything hardly, except this flower and its color and what to do.

She pulled a thick gold zinnia from the intricate pattern of another vase and with slow care wove it down among the stems of the poisonous pink flowers and hid it almost at the base of the tall upward-sweeping nicotiana.

There, she thought contentedly, there is an arrangement that I am sincerely and absolutely irrevocably sure would never win first prize even for originality at the annual show of the Garden Club. Thank you, dear ladies, for ignoring me. Thank you, you sweet-faced old hags, for forgetting just this once that I am Anne Garton Temple, the author of zubzubzub, the widow of zub, member of zubzub and zub. Thank you, daughters of the finest families with black ribbons holding up your waddles, for not knowing as much about flowers and how they grow and what they say as I do happen to know in the smallest of my tiny, clever, well-born fingers.

She stood for several more minutes looking at the vases that covered the tabletop and sat riotously on the cold floor. They were more beautiful than any others she had ever done. She thought so every time but now she was sure. The flowers were wild and passionate, staid, demure, in a language that spoke only for Nan herself, with epigrams, with small practical jokes, with now-and-then malicious undertones. She knew where every one of them would go and whether other people understood as she looked at them upon their mantles and their desks and dressing tables, and Nan cared not at all. She, in her own room, would be saying many things in every room in the house, unsuspected, silently, with amusement, with cold intelligence, with love.

She closed the door of the tool room behind her and shivered suddenly in the warmth that rose from the path. Inside the cold walls and floors had made the petunias send out their first sweet smell of twilight. Outside it was still midafternoon.

She leaned in as she passed the kitchen window and saw by the clock on the stove that there was a half hour before she had to start for tea. She ran up the path again and hurried across the tiny meadow that lay between the house and the vineyard to the shadow of a gnarled cherry tree.

There, Nan threw herself down onto the thick grass that lay beneath her silkily and rose high on every side of her like a mighty forest. I am hidden, she thought. I am safe. Nothing can see me here.

Above her the twisted branches of this old tree curved protectively. She could see sky through their leaves and, if she raised her head a little from the steep slope on which she lay, the blue waters of the lake.

> Bow down, thou sweet cherry tree,
> And give my mother some . . .
> Then the top bow of the cherry tree
> Bent down to her knee,
> And so you see, Joseph,
> There are cherries for me,
> And so you see, Joseph,
> There are cherries for three.

It should seem strange, Nan thought while the stiff music of the song ran in her head, that I've been so rude to my poor friend. It should seem strange that I am not ashamed. How does it happen that after so many years of being sweet and gentle and thoughtful and caring terribly what people thought of me, I have suddenly grown resolute? Will she cease to love me? I think not. She says I love only my brother. Is that wrong? She says so, but she loves only me. Perhaps that is because I am the only thing she has. But is Timothy the only thing I have? Yes, yes, he is! He's all I want.

A bee blundered low. Nan looked up at it with wide and staring eyes and saw its soft brown belly in the silver blur of wings at its sides.

Oh, Timothy, she cried, you are all I want, your love and compassion. Why do I feel so, why am I a slave to my little brother, my child brother walking beside me on the long streets, standing close beside me in dancing school, lying wasted and sad at my house after the war? Where are you now? Why do I break my good friend's heart staying here, when I see that you no longer need me? Lucy needs me and I hate her for it. You do not as you have Sara. But I stay on here. I *must* stay.

All this summer I have never felt stronger inside. Why? Is something happening to me to make me see you more clearly? Soon, now, soon I shall know. But know what? What do I want to know? Will all my sadness end? How do I know this? Inside me. Yes, I simply feel this is so.

She thought with a strange dispassionate bitterness of years behind her. Work had filled them, but they were empty. Would work make her happy now? Would love? Would religion?

Since she was twenty-two or twenty-three—it seemed too long ago to count one year either way—she had worked numbly, resolutely. She had studied the writing of other than her own people and had learned new tongues. She twisted the words in her mind into a trillion meanings and had put some of this on paper. And her people, the other humans around her, had heard in her verses some sound of truth. They had lapped up the crumbs of comfort from the dishes brewed for her own hunger.

Yes, for too many years now she had injected into others that fine needle of her own spiritual narcosis. It made them feel less of their secret agonies. And she knew herself not their benefactor, but their evildoer.

I doped, she said sternly to herself beneath the cherry tree, because I was doped myself. Work is no cure-all. Work can absorb one, like a blotting pad or Pantopon, or like a creeping cancer behind the Pantopon. But what is the cancer? Why have I had to work so hard for so long? Am I afraid to stop? Have all these years of research, of best sellers, of ships' reporters and press photographs, been dragged on because I was afraid to stop?

Is it my love, my little brother, that has pushed me? Is it because I have nothing else that I try to hide behind this ghastly curtain of literary importance? Oh, Timothy, why did we have to grow up?

Why could we not stay small and loving, meeting only each other without question, without cavil?

But I have stopped. I *have* stopped work. And Timothy is still here. I see him all day long. I see him in the mirror even when he is not here. And yet I seem to be able to go on without him. If I should stop work today, or if I should write a book today, I could do it without asking him, without begging for his thoughts, his opinions, his most secret reactions. I could burn it in the fire without thinking, What will Timothy say? What would he have said? I am no longer afraid. I do not know why but I know now that if I write again it will be because I can see clearly, not because I am blind. Not yet, but soon.

And love? Oh, dear God—and Nan looked up through the immovable branches of the trees with amusement in her eyes—how much I have thought of love all these years! How much I have read of it! How much I have written! But I know nothing.

When Lucy Pendleton, so ostentatious as she safely spares me, leaping into my conversation with gallantry and thoughtfulness at the mere breathing of my husband's name when I let my voice falter then, lowering my eyes with the required hint of heartbreak, what do I remember really? Where is George Temple? Was he ever my bedfellow, that quiet little Wall Street magnate with his potbelly and his exhausted grateful eyes? Did we ever love each other? Did he ever see my aching womanhood?

And others? All the young men at literary teas and that boy who seized my hand in the harbor at Rio and pressed it against the hot satiny skin under his shirt and before that all the shy eligible dolts at teas and coming-out parties . . . Oh, you poor youths, how could you find what I really was behind all my walls of fright and mother-taught propriety? How could you dare look further than my stiff face and my archly fluttering fingers? How could you know that I was sweet and true and aching to be loved?

How could George Temple ever have known? Or had he? Did he know the dreadful fear and the hatred I felt for him, the scorn? Did he ever know, years later, the sad pity and all the yearning tender love I felt when I saw him old before he should have been and suddenly weak and shy before me? Did he ever know how much I *liked* him, years too late?

Oh, Timothy, why did you never tell me all these things about love? When I was young and burdened with manners taught me by my elders? Why did you not tell me of their silliness? Why are you always there, so still and sympathetic? Was that your way of helping me? At Saturday-night circles you would dance with me so solemn and young in your white kid gloves and I would look at other girls whirling decorously on the arms of older men and love you passionately for making me look popular. I would long for the compliments of some perennial bachelor upon my proper girlish clothing, and when you told me I was beautiful I loved you for it. Why, why did you never tell me to just be calm and easy and not to care?

Why did I have to learn for myself when I'm sure you knew all the time? You could've told me about poor George Temple and those young men everywhere and not being stiff and frightened of them. You knew. And all these years I have been waiting to learn. Now it may be too late. You are gone. I am past those clumsy fumblings of the boy in Rio but I feel no disgust for them, no impatience now, that kind of love, and the love I have waited for from you, are past me now. I'm ready for something. I am waiting. I am no longer sad.

Is it religion then? When I was eleven and again when I was seventeen, I knelt upon a prie-dieu, waiting for a vision. I felt wings about me and I yearned to be holy. Now, sometimes, going into a dim church, hearing the music that beats out about the clerestory and underneath the arches of the chancel, smelling the dark overtones of incense and feeling the brush of the priest's robes past my closed hands and my down-bent head, I still think I have a vocation, that *this* is my life. But later I know that that is the beauty, the sensual ecstasy that sweeps me toward faith. I am not a true believer, unquestioning. The crucifix above my bed I leave there because it is a pure example of the fifteenth-century German carving, not because it is for me a symbol of the body of Jesus Christ, my Lord. I am not religious, though at times I long to be. I long to kneel with Timothy in the little chapel in San Marco and see tears creep down between his fingers, past his ring of amethyst.

All this is wrong. I do not need a Lucy to tell me. I need no one. No one.

Nan sat up. She was almost gasping and felt herself to be on the verge of some great and terrible discovery. She looked wildly about her at the swing, grasses that bent over her, and at the close curving branches of the cherry tree and at the far lake. What instinct had she brushed? Where had she wandered in her thoughts?

She felt excited. But she knew, surely, that there was nothing more. She must wait.

She stood up, rather stiffly, and slid down the little bank to the terrace. It must be time for tea.

As she walked toward a rendezvous with Lucy and Honor, she felt as small and secret as an amoeba. They cannot even see me, she thought scornfully. They do not know me. They think I'm there, loving them and needing them, and I am really here, within myself, waiting.

vi

Tea was good. Nan ate avidly. She heard the hard crust of bread beneath her teeth with pure delight and felt the tea flow hotly down her throat. She'd been *hungry*.

Lucy sat opposite her talking quickly, obviously happy that Honor was not there too.

All I have to do, Nan thought with a certain amount of complacent cunning, is to be wide-eyed and funny. All I have to do is say, Oh yes! and open my eyes wide and pretend to need people. That makes them feel important. I've always known this. I knew it when I was six and Father with his silky beard would tell me how he wanted to protect me. I know it now when Daniel dances with me as if I were made of porcelain. I know it when poor Lucy scolds me.

She is not scolding me now except in her own way. I have made her happy by talking of concerts we have heard together, pictures we have seen, people we have laughed at. She knows nothing about me.

Timothy is the only one who knows anything about me. He's the only one I love. It's because he stands alone, I think. He is not like Father or young Dan or Lucy and all the others, taken in by my cringing will to be loved, my need to be needed.

Oh, hurry, hurry, she prayed, her face smiling vaguely. Something is getting ready. Something is forming, slowly, surely, through all this strange summer. I am learning. But what is it?

She stood up. Lucy had begun to sob and Nan stood looking down at her, seeing the straggly brown hair, the fat hands clenched over the face, and beyond them—and more importantly—the blue waters of the ageless lake.

What is she crying about? Tea was good. I was good. What does it matter that Joe and his Sue are not married, if my own Timothy is not married to his love, if Daniel and his quiet sister Honor are not married, even? All that is immaterial. I am not shocked by Susan. I am not jealous of Sara. I am but faintly interested in the gawky Tennants. Lucy, this poor harried weeping wreck, is not much more than an interruption. I do not care anymore, ever, if I wound her sensitive feelings.

"I'm sorry, Lucy," she heard herself saying. She listened to her own warm sympathetic voice with a terrible glee. "I must stay with him," she heard herself say. "He may need me."

Poor stupid blind woman, she thought. You hear me talking of my brother. You think I love him, perhaps incestuously. Do you not know that I'm waiting for something else? You must think I stay here in this place you hate with such a venomous jealousy because I am held by an unnatural love for Timothy. You can never see that it is my love for him that is freeing me.

They walked on without speaking. Behind them the little terrace of the café settled into silence and a striped cat leapt up on their table and licked at the plates where a butter pat had been.

vii

When they rounded the last curve of the road, Nan saw Dan Tennant leaning on the iron gate. She glanced quickly at Lucy.

Oh, I hope he goes before we get there, she wished fervently. Will he notice that Lucy has been crying? Will Lucy lilt over him, the way she usually does? Will he stop me and make me talk? No, no! I want to go to my room and lie on the bed. I am thinking of something.

But Daniel stood resolutely there and—as they approached him—Nan felt her face smiling. She looked up into serious deep eyes, which were so ridiculously like Sara's green ones, yet different because of his maleness.

"Hello, Dan."

"Hello," he said. "Hello, Lucy."

There was an awkward pause. Finally Lucy sniffed and smiled gaily and said, "Well! Well, I don't know about you young people but I must go and get ready for Sara's little entertainment. Don't stay out here too long in the cool of the evening, Nan darling."

She hurried away, her head held high. Nan looked at Dan half in apology, half in amusement. He raised an eyebrow.

"The sun still rides the heavens, ma'am," he said in his deepest voice. "The cool of the evening is yet far from us. Mrs. Pendleton exaggerates somewhat."

Nan looked up at him again as he stood leaning his bare elbows easily upon the wall. She then came through the gate and stood beside him. She was impatient, also bored by his queer unformed pomposity, but he excited her. She was almost startled to admit that she liked to be near him. He was clean and he smelled good, like all the Tennants. She leaned nearer, sniffing imperceptibly, enjoying herself in a minor way and at the same time hating herself for hoping her nearness would upset him.

For a moment or two they said nothing. Then Dan swung around abruptly and cleared his throat.

"Lake's nice now, isn't it?" He sounded grumpy.

Nan turned with him and stood leaning against the warm stone wall without touching him.

"Yes," she said in a small voice. Inside she said, I really am a bitch.

The idea was surprising to her—it made her feel almost complacent. Then she was ashamed of herself and although she thought she wanted to be quite alone in her room for a time before she dressed, she said warmly, "Do you want to help me find the one blossom of Queen Anne's lace, Daniel? It must be tall and about three inches across."

He looked down at her and raised one eyebrow slightly and answered in a stiff way, "Yes, I'd rather like to, thank you."

Suddenly Daniel smiled.

For a dreadful moment she wondered if he thought she was a silly old woman, but now Nan felt all right again and she took his hand.

"Hurry then," she said. "It's growing late. Lucy will scold me if I keep dinner waiting. Party tonight, too, and I have a new dress for it."

They slid down the steep bank instead of walking properly out along the path, Nan feeling excited and happy. The shadows lay long and blue on the meadow. Birds called softly and flew shudderingly from one heavy bow to another. There was the faint smell of rotting plums.

"This is the best part of the day," she murmurred. She started to pull her hand from his, but he held onto her. His fingers felt chilled now and sticky suddenly.

"Nan," he said harshly.

Nan looked up at him and felt terribly sorry for his pain. She knew he was not really in love with her but that the world here at this moment, so beautiful, must seem terrible to him.

"Nan," he said, looking down at her and scowling, holding her fingers in his own moist hand, "do you know anything about:

'Blue-veined and yellowish,
Ambiguous to clasp,
And secret as a fish,
And sudden as an asp . . .'

And so on and so forth, something like that?"

Nan slid her hand. Her mind raced as furiously as an important mouse among all the phrases and old stanzas that were stacked up in neat tremendous piles in her memory. She sometimes hated the way she went on saving them, more and more. They were good. They were apt. If she gave herself time, as now, she could always pull out the quotation for a given moment. She knew all this to be impressive and once or twice this summer she had felt that perhaps young Daniel was teasing her, trying to catch her out. And once or twice she'd been almost piqued to find that his brain, so much younger and less ordered, held line after line of some of her best reserve of more or less immortal doggerel. So now she looked sharply at him in the soft twilight, before she went on in a slow voice:

"It doubles to a fist,
Or droops composed and chill;
The socket of my wrist
Controls it at my will.
It leaps to my command,
Tautened or trembling lax;
It lies within your hand
Anatomy of wax."

Her voice sank to a whisper. She could not hear Daniel breathing although he stood very nearby, but the sound of the little brook came clearly to her, borne from the end of the meadow on a current of blueing air.

"There's more," Dan said finally.

"Oh, oh yes, something or other . . . I forget and then:

"Now, compact as stone,
My hand preserves a shape
Too utterly its own."

"And now come help me, Daniel," she said, "or it will be dark and I must find one more flower. Come on."

Nan ran across the grass without looking back at him. Why had he made her go on? What might he think of her for so obviously leaving out that stanza? Why had he thought of that poem at all?

If I had seen a thorn
Broken to grape vine bud;
If I'd ever borne
Child of our mingled blood;
Elixirs might escape . . .

The little brat! Nan felt too cross and disappointed. Why did he push his own youthful agonies impertinently into her life? She wanted things to be as they had been earlier in the summer, easy and silly. She remembered with nostalgia the giddy way Dan and Honor made her feel and how she'd laughed and how poor Lucy had disapproved to see her young again with them. And now things were growing solemn. She wished parts of time would stand still. It was tiresome to have Daniel this way.

It was an interruption. She was waiting for something. She knew this now with her whole being. Daniel and his quotations and his would-be sardonic face above his long delicate body were keeping her from waiting as she longed too. She felt a dreadful impatience and was frightened to find herself on the edge of screaming at him to go away. Be gone! she wanted to yell.

What would he think? She smiled involuntarily seeing his horror, knowing how his dream of her as the moon creature, the goddess in an eggshell, would be torn apart by her shrill shout.

"You win, Nan, that time anyway," he observed. Was he mocking her again? "Your fund of famous quotations, ma'am, is limitless. I'll catch you before the summer's over, though. What will you do for me if I win?"

This is better, she thought, looking up easily now at his brooding young face and his twinkling eyes. He's stopped being solemn, but I wish he'd go. Go, Dan, hurry, leave me!

"Dan, I was going to ask you . . ." She hesitated, appreciating the timid and ingenious note in her own voice, savoring half-ironically the subtle girlishness. "Dan, would you mind taking me out sometime this winter? I mean, to places like Harlem, and . . ."

"Oh God, Nan! That would be marvelous!" His voice cracked, he cleared it in a perfunctory way. "What about . . . well . . . ?"

And as he talked, Nan felt almost excited with the part of herself that was not willing him still to leave. It would be fun to see strange places with this boy and to hear music played in the smoky little rooms she'd read about.

"What would Lucy say?" she asked suddenly and they looked at each other and the darkening air and they laughed and laughed. Oh, he was charming, such an adorable boy! She had such fun laughing with him in the meadow there, and everywhere, about La Prairie!

She was brought up short, surprised when he stopped and said, "Nan, here's the flower."

He bent down and pulled up one stock of Queen Ann's lace, root and all, and thrust it into her hand. Then without looking at her, he said in a stiff voice, "Will you dance with me tonight?" then, "Do you mind if I run up to the house instead of walking back with you?" and he was gone.

She looked after Daniel loping away as if he'd been bee-stung under the tree toward the path. Here I was wishing he'd go, wondering how to tell him to, and now he's gone! And I am a little hurt; really, he's odd. And I do love him for going. Maybe he felt me telling him to go. Or maybe he suddenly needed to go to the toilet. Anyway, thank you, Daniel.

She smiled dreamily, instead holding the coarse stem of the flower in both her hands, looking down at the root of it all filled with the earth against the stiff yellow of her dangling hat.

I must stand very still, she thought.

viii

The little brook was louder now but the birds were silent. One bee whizzing through the cool sweet air made a strong sound that lasted in Nan's ears long after it had vanished. She stood, as if naked, feeling the currents of the evening flow around her as tangibly as silk. And her eyes saw as they had never seen before.

They saw the lake that she'd often looked down into and the far blackness of the French shoreline and the old trees bending close above her. They saw grass about her knees and the spires of wild sage disappearing with their blue blossoms into blue air. The frosty web of lace in her hand, dry and alive; the bell of her yellow skirt; the soft curves of her own breasts—she looked down at all this as she had done and as she would do again and knew that never before had she seen and never again would she see. She knew, too, that all her life from this moment would be different.

At last she was *seeing clearly* as she had so long prayed to see, her whole being transfigured, lifted up in revelation. She knew now with the knowledge that poured through her like mighty music, that to see clearly means to love without demand. It means to love selflessly.

She knew that all her life she loved possessively, hungrily, absorbingly, and that now such foul destructive hunger was gone from her. She knew her tormenting love for Timothy and her preoccupation with their past together had been a long escape. And escape would never more be necessary for now she was free, unhampered by a greedy soul. The love and gratitude of other people was no longer food for her. Demanding nothing, she would never more be lonely.

She felt light, bodiless almost. The trees, the air, the far mountains seemed to vibrate above and around her in a kind of ecstatic dance. She sank to her knees. She was as empty as a shell.

Finally she began to think again, but more easily than ever before in her life. She knew she must tell Timothy what had happened. He would be glad. He would give thanks with her, to see her at last free from him, as he'd always been free of her. Now she knew that until this moment in the meadow he loved her more truly than she'd been capable of loving him, and he would rejoice to know her liberated.

Yes, she must tell him. At last she knew what she had been waiting for all this beautiful, difficult summer in the strange peace she'd found here. Her feeling of gaiety and easiness and health, stronger than since she was a child, had been a preparation. She must hurry and tell her beloved brother that she'd cast out the devil of loving him the wrong way. She was free of him. At last she loved him, and all things, truly.

ix

On the darkening stairs Nan then heard music from the living room, but faintly. She hurried up them and it seemed natural that her feet should make no sound at all upon the stone. In her head and quite without sacrilege ran the first measures of "Es ist vollbracht." It is *consummated*, she told herself. I must tell Timothy as soon as I can. I must tell him that I've cast him out, that I am free now to live and love without asking for return.

She sped silently down the hall toward her door.

Honor Tennant stood beside it, her hand raised. To Nan, who in her present state had forgotten the actuality of people and how they looked and sounded, and how they took up space, Honor looked like a creature from some other world. She loomed in the dim light larger than possible, her face seemed white as eggshell, her eye sockets deep as symmetrical caverns out of which she peered. Honor's hand, still and shapely, had a momentous quality about it as it hovered, ready to knock for Nan.

"Oh, Nan," she murmured, "I wanted to ask you . . . but you're out of breath."

"Am I?"

They stood for a moment without bothering to speak or to wonder much, looking at each other. Nan knew that Honor would now keep her from seeing Timothy before dinner but that did not seem to matter. She could tell him what happened later—even tomorrow would do. Perhaps, perhaps he knew anyway. But no she must tell him. In the meantime she felt kindly and rather drunk.

Nan smiled meaninglessly.

"But come in and tell me," she begged earnestly. "What do you want? Tell me what I can do." She grasped Honor's warm smooth arm. "Please do."

It seem very important to Nan, suddenly, to do something to test out her new freedom.

Honor was looking at her the way all the Tennants could. Sometimes Nan thought it was because they were so tall that their faces often wore an expression of almost haughty amusement and sometimes she wondered crossly if they were mocking her. But now she knew that the quiet smile in Honor's sad dark eyes was full of compassion and instead of resenting it she felt pleased to realize at last they were friends, loving each other without qualification.

"Come in," she said again. When they were in the room she turned on one of the lights and held out a box of cigarettes with a trembling hand that was vibrating like the wings of a moth.

"No, I can't stay. It's late. But Nan . . . what can we do about Susan?"

"Susan?"

For several seconds now Nan could not remember who bore that name nor why Honor should ask her what to do. What did it matter what they did, and for whom? Then she saw again the strange tiny blonde woman with her hair in a knot on her proud head and the large gray eyes watching over the rim of the beer glass at lunch, and suddenly Nan heard with a rush of warm amusement the blissful squeak in Susan's voice when she had cried out, "Why, it's *Nan Garton Temple*!" It seemed so long ago but so pleasant.

"Oh, Susan," she cried. "Of course! Why, is she ill? She looked rather dauncy at lunch, I thought."

Honor laughed softly. "*Dauncy*! That's a nice word. I've never heard it before, but I know what it means. Like *loppy*. My mother says *loppy*. No, it's about supper."

Honor then sat down on the edge of the wide dark bed. She moved like many people who are large, with deliberation and in flowing sections. Her white robe fell open and now she was left with this passion to look at the long sweep of her legs, brown and slender, and the flat softness of her girl's belly.

"It seems sort of a party, kind of. Nice, I think. Sara figures it will keep Lucy amused, probably, and it's fun. And do you know . . . ?" And Honor looked soberly at Nan, her voice suddenly vehemant.

"Do you know that Susan Harper, that poor little kid, has walked clear from Munich and hasn't a dress to her name? Tim and Dan and that fine conceited young man of hers are all right in slacks and coats but after all, we all planned vaguely to wear long dresses and I don't know . . . I just don't know . . ."

As her voice trailed off into silence, she sighed. Nan looked curiously at her. Honor's face was composed, her eyes were watching something more interesting than life, something up near the corner of the ceiling but beyond it.

I feel passive, Nan thought. I don't care. I am through worrying about being good or thoughtful or generous or making people admire me. Let Honor tell me what she wants. I may listen or I may not as I am free now from caring about her caring what I think.

Again they did not speak for what seemed like several minutes, a silence in which they were strangely easy. Honor lay on her side once again and said as if they hadn't stopped talking at all, "So I wondered if you'd let her wear something of yours. I don't like to ask you, I'd hate to have someone ask me to lend a dress to a stranger . . . but she seems awfully clean and everything . . . Maybe that blue and green housecoat sort of business that you've been wearing . . . ?"

Nan knew that she must answer but for a moment she was too peaceful to speak. It did not matter if she was rude or if Honor thought she'd gone daffy. She was so filled with ease and contentment, now that at last she was free of all the years of hunger and vain longings, she could not bear to speak.

"Of course *I* could lend her something or I could ask Lucy." Honor was apparently not entirely conscious of Nan's silence. "But I think we're either a little long up and down or a *leeeeetle, leeeeetle* big around and Sara says you have simply the most beautiful nighties. Why not a nightie for Sue?"

Nan jumped up as if she'd been stung or started up from a dream and left with what sounded to her own ears like that of foolishness and said energetically, "But of course, Honor darling! She's a sweet child. I *want* her to wear a dress of mine. She's so young and lovely and . . ."

And now she hurried across the room to the great dark armoire and pulled its door open dramatically.

"Here," Nan cried and thrust into Honor's arms a cloud of fragile yellow, all shot through with golden threads. "Take it," she cried again. "I want Susan to wear it. She will be beautiful in it."

Honor looked at the pile of stuff she held, then smiled. "No," she said slowly, "you've never worn this, Nan. I know, because I know everything you've worn this summer. You have such beautiful clothes . . . I like to look at them. And you've been saving this. No, it's too lovely."

"But I want Susan to wear it. I think it . . . Well, it's too young for me. She should wear it. Take it to her, Honor. Please. This is a *wonderful* idea."

Nan laughed excitedly. She did not feel empty and exhausted anymore but strong with delight instead. Part of it made her want almost violently to see Susan in the dress that she had saved all summer for Timothy's surprise. It seemed essential to her somehow to look at that billowy gleaming dress on another woman. It was right that Susan, Joe Kelly's light-o'-love, should be the entrancing one.

Honor rose slowly and stood in her stately way. Above the glimmer of the beautiful dress her eyes glowed as she looked down at Nan, then she moved toward the door.

"Let me!" Nan cried. "I'll open it!" She brushed against the tall girl and was conscious of the sharp smoothness of her hip bone.

Honor turned suddenly toward her. The girl's face was honey colored in the soft light from Nan's room against the darkness of the hallway; her mouth looked infinitely sweet.

"*Permettez-moi, chere Madame, de vous embraser,*" she murmurred laughingly.

Honor leaned down and in the most intimate gesture that Nan had ever received from another woman, kissed her delicately on either cheek.

"Nan," she said. "You are beautiful." Then Honor hurried down the long hall.

Nan, still feeling the moth-like touch of the girl's lips and hearing again the tiny crackle of the pile of gold-shot cloth between their bodies, stood looking after her.

"Me?" Nan wondered. "I am beautiful?" She spoke aloud, incredulously. She had often been told so but now it seemed as if she had never really heard this being said until the present moment. She knew that Honor had not said it only in gratitude over Susan's present.

Am I? Nan thought.

She went into her room and closed the door softly. I must tell Timothy, she thought. Not ask him: *tell* him.

She pulled off her clothes swiftly and got out the blue and green housecoat and laid it on the bed. It was not until she was brushing her hair, still damp from her quick bath, that she saw that someone had put a vase of flowers on her mantelpiece. It was the vase she'd meant for Honor's room and she laughed to see it there before her. It was a tall square hollow crystal, an old battery glass with a partition down the middle and she'd put a little ring of late field daisies stuck in pebbles in the bottom of one side. In the other was a tiny naked pink china Kewpie doll with "Made in Japan" marked across its buttocks. Then she'd filled the vase with clear water from the fountain knowing it was silly and maybe a little bit malicious.

Someone is playing jokes on me, she thought contentedly. I must tell all this to Timothy. I have so much to tell him.

I am beautiful, she thought. She said this seriously to the woman she saw looking at her in the mirror. Aloud she said, "Yes."

4

As soon as the anesthetic wore off, the wolves and the wires and the frozen colors came back, more intense, more intolerable. Ah, my foot, my foot! And the toes . . . Christ! My big toe, and all the others! How many toes? Six? Of course.

He looked down, the third day. His head pulled up from the pillows as if it were a sick tooth lifting itself, root and all, from its bleeding jaw-bed. He saw that he had no foot, no knee, never more a loin to ache with passion, and his great eyes widened with the secret laugh: The foot was still there, and all his leg, and only he to know it? He lay back, listening with sly amusement to the cries that were torn out of him by the flaming wires and the cold nails that wrapped around and pounded into his lost foot.

The fourth day he waited until the doctors had finished and the nurse and his woman. Then he lifted off the cover and looked down at the white turban that lay beside his visible leg, and with a clean ferocity he cut the air, once, sharply just below it. For a second, a second as sweet as death and as long as God, his lost foot was without pain. Then it rushed back. He heard his cries again, and his eyes grew cynical.

He tried it once more, the next day, and once he got the woman with her own long cold hand to cross the air above his invisible knee, but it never worked again.

Soon the mice began. They nibbled hungrily, bloodily, at the little pads of flesh under six toes, and occasionally rats came and tore at the whole foot. The bed was always tidy afterword: theoretical flesh does not make messes.

There was the leather shoe, like a doll's shoe, that was put on wet, and as it dried it twisted, twisted, twisted, until the foot curled under like a Chinese lady's, and the whole leg was pulled into a corkscrew-shape. Then when he would feel a scream bubbling behind his teeth, and ready to burst, the dried doll's shoe and all the flesh under it would be torn off, and mice, hundreds of mice, would rush in from all the cracks and creases of the bed and suck and nibble at the raw meat and the twanging, string-like muscle.

About two weeks after the amputation, he awoke from a nightmare of running, to find the white turban bobbing and flapping against the mattress, and suddenly he found that his poor foot had only five toes now, and that it was up almost under his knee. He sighed with relief, for he believed that if all that calf had finally gone, there would be much less to hurt. He was wrong, though. His leg only folded like an accordion and in every pleat red ants now scurried and stung, at least ten thousand of them burrowing and laying eggs and feeding themselves in the succulent creases.

He grew used to not seeing his leg anymore except in his dreams, but the ants never left him, nor the boot, nor various other things like having his nails pulled out slowly, nor especially the mice, and although he grew able, finally, to lie without noises most of the time, the presence of his theoretical foot was more real now than food or sleep or his love, and he would never lose it.

i

That morning, August 31, Daniel Tennant heard all the knocks on the door. The first was so gentle it had a kind of coyness about it. He woke almost before the knock began and lay there without moving even his eyelids.

The next was somewhat louder, although it still sounded covert, as if a conspirator or even a thickly veiled adventuress was signalling to him. He chuckled to himself and lay waiting for the next, which he knew would follow after a short but tense pause, and now it came: three dramatic pounding blows, echoing with painful force everywhere in the quiet house. Daniel winced, opened his eyes just enough to see the bottom of the door and the floor between it and his bed.

There was now a sharp sigh out in the hall. Then the door swung open noisily. François's large grimy tennis shoes stood on the green tiles.

"What?" the man asked. "Still asleep, my God!"

Daniel closed his eyes imperceptibly and—as a slight change in the morning routine—snored once.

"Ah, youth," he heard François mutter just as Daniel's toes were being seized and shaken from side to side, his eyes becoming wild as he stared up now into François's face.

"Arsjanashbousyen," Daniel gabbled thickly as recognition seemed to flood back in. He sank upon his tousled bed, panting slightly. "It's you," he murmurred in his vile French. "Thank God!

For one terrible moment, one minute, I thought I was back in the dungeon in Istanbul."

François cackled, eyes shining, almost dropping the tray he had balanced rather expertly along one forearm.

"Oh, Monsieur Daniel," he said, "Yesterday morning you said Cairo." He cackled again and leered down, with a roguish look, his face creased darkly under his four-day bristle.

"Cairo? Istanbul? What does it matter? I'm safe now that I'm here." Daniel sighed brokenly, then asked, "What is there for breakfast?"

François's face fell for an instant at Daniel's abrupt shift from romance to reality, then brightened as he picked his way daintily over rumpled clothes and books and shoes to the bedside. He rested one end of the tray on the edge of the little table as he pushed the lamp, ashtray, more books, and a pile of sticky peachstones casually onto the floor.

The crashing gradually subsided.

"Flute! How careless I've become! Pardon! And here Monsieur Daniel has his little breakfast! This morning I have created a new dish, eggs as all Americans love them!"

He settled the tray onto the table and whisked the cover of a large silver vegetable dish off a plate. There indeed were four fried eggs, all curled about with at least a half pound of beautiful broiled bacon. Daniel, looking at this and the pots of hot milk and hot coffee, the plates of toast and dishes of butter and jam, the bowl of grapes, and even the pitcher of water, wondered weakly how there was enough china left in the pantry for the other trays.

The food spread so elegantly before him made his stomach quiver, faintly but unmistakably, and he wondered idly if he had a slight hangover. He remembered with an almost ghastly pleasure the last drink he'd drunk the night before, after Sara and Honor had gone off to bed, when he and Tim had gone tidily out to the kitchen with the glasses of their unexpected bout and had had one last snort. They had not meant, any of them, to sit drinking and talking all night. Each was tired and Nan and Lucy had long since disappeared. But it had been good to sit there talking of food and people and pacifism and . . .

"Thank you, thank you, old fellow," Daniel said. "Now if only I had a cigarette I could almost forget the horrors of my past. I could almost forget that night in Cairo, or was it Pago Pago?"

François stiffened, stood trembling slightly like a melancholy pointer.

". . . but no, enough of that."

"Would Monsieur Daniel accept one of my cigarettes? Of course they are not like American ones, mine being slightly perfumed. They are called The Pride of the Harem. Perhaps they would remind Monsieur Daniel of . . . ?"

"Other days? Thank you, François. I shall accept one. My memories will be most pleasant, I assure you." Daniel smiled as lasciviously as he could manage and lay the cigarette beside his coffee cup. Then as François stood looking down at him eagerly, he sank back and closed his eyes again.

A long silence, then Daniel snored almost too faintly to be heard, and François sighed.

Dan heard him tiptoe to the door, stopping as he went to pick up a pair of slacks and to fold them over the back of a chair with a disapproving cluck of his tongue. The door closed.

Just outside his room the little fountain poured out its thin constant stream, monotonous and musical. A breeze changed its notes, flattening the water for some moments against the stone before the water flowed straight again. Daniel listened without knowing, not only there at that moment in his tousled bed, but everywhere about the house. Sometimes he would forget to understand what Sara or the others or even Nan were saying while his ears pricked toward the ancient trickle of the fountain. In his dreams the rhythm of those waters beat like his own heart or the pulse of blood. Away from it, anywhere out of hearing, he felt uneasy now.

Daniel stretched, then rolled so that his feet could hang down comfortably over the end of the bed.

When he was old and filthy rich, he'd decided, he would command a bed three meters long. It would have sheets of striped pajama silk, these suspended above his toes with a delicate framework of wrought silver so that his feet could point straight upward without being dragged at by the weight of bedding. There would be blankets, of course, of the very softest materials and they'd be fixed in a way that when he was cold they'd automatically unroll from the foot of the bed and cover as much of him as needed warmth.

It might be a little difficult to work that one out—he'd have to have one of his brilliant young secretaries devote himself to the problem. Then by a series of subtle blackmailings he would get the poor devil in his power entirely and buy the idea for a pittance or perhaps a small monthly pension, an idea that would then add another cool million or two to his pocket.

People all over the world who were as tall and as bony as Daniel—for in spite of his advanced age at that far-distant time, he would still be lean and hard and in perfect physical condition—people who for countless generations had been forced to sleep folded into uncomfortable positions or with their feet dangling over the bed-end and people of all lengths who had spent wretched nights when they were too sleepy to pull up an extra blanket over their chilled bodies, when it would inevitably be too short, would bless his name.

He, of course, would have one improvement in his own bed that would not be for general sale. Each night, or for as many nights as his whim dictated, a beautiful woman would be tucked somewhere into the mighty expanse of those striped-pajama-silk sheets and electrically regulated blankets. She would be of whatever size he wanted and of any color from moonbeam to a deep purplish brown. One of his most trusted secretaries would make it his sole responsibility to see that she was sweet smelling and in all other ways delightful.

Daniel yawned, then opened his eyes, struggling to stay awake.

"""Hot dog!" cried Mr. Pennyfeather!'" he quoted, then rolled toward the little table, looking as if it might sag under the heavily laden tray. He lay looking at the clutter of food for a moment before pouring himself a cup of sloppily put-together coffee.

Why in hell had François brought him all this food? The man was madly in love with him, of course. That was obvious from the way he giggled, fluttered, blushed like a schoolgirl at Dan's faintest look in his direction. But was there also a maternal feeling hidden somewhere in that hollow chest, along with all those girlish throbbings? Do I bring out the mother in him? Dan wondered irritably. Does he long to plump me up, to make me big and strong enough to fight life's battles?

Daniel spread strawberry jam thickly on a piece of his now cold toast and—while he was deciding whether it would be a good idea or not to eat in bed, watched three large drops of jam drip from his toast onto the pillow.

Damn and blast! What would Sara say?

For a moment Daniel felt almost panicky, then remembered he was no longer a small boy and that Sara, even in those far-distant days, had never beaten him nor even given him what might be called a tongue lashing. You'd think she was a demon, he thought, the way I cringe at the thought of her seeing this spotted pillow case. Anyway, she'll probably never see it and besides she's too polite and decent to mention it. Do I think she'd wait until the parson came to supper and then point at me and laugh stridently and tell everyone what I'd done? That I was a naughty rascal? You'd think so from the way I act.

Sara has me buffaloed is all, and she always has. She's thoughtful and never shouts or scolds and she's never cruel, yet I am still scared to death of what she'll say, even after all these years of being away at school and not even seeing her. She was good to me when I was little. Honor and I worshipped her and that's the trouble: We still do, even if we don't want to. We resent her importance to us; we'd rather spend all that admiration and consciousness on other people and she's there taking it.

Does she even want it? Daniel wondered. Does she even know that we are both obsessed with her?

But I never really thought of any of this before, that she might not even want us to think she's so almightly goddamned wonderful—I took it for grtanted that she loved us that way but I don't know that she does. In fact, I know she doesn't, as she doesn't seem to ask anything from us. And yet we're always thinking about her, wondering what she'll do and say and wear and whether she'll be in good spiritrs or pale and closed-mouthed as she sometimes is. That isn't right. We should be thinking more about women. I'm a man and should be thinking more about my future wife. I do, of course, but Sara's always there making me wonder what she'll think of the way my girl stands or eats cold chicken or gets drunk.

Daniel finished his coffee, then poured warm milk into the cup and drank that. He then carefully scraped at the red blotches on the pillow with the butter knife, licking it off, while his mind circled lazily around the surprising idea that his older sister might not find him as important as he found her.

He'd ask Honor. She was a quiet girl but she had pretty good ideas about some things. It would be rather embarrassing talking that way about Sara, of course. But Daniel felt he must find out, that a man should not live as long as he had without clarifying some of his more youthful impressions.

He stuck a fork into one of the eggs, which was quite stiff by now, then sighed with exasperation. What would he do with the damned things? François always looked so completely crushed when Daniel sent food back that he'd tried to hide them, putting them down the toilet, but that was disgusting. He'd even tried hiding his unwanted eggs in the clothes, which became even more disgusting when they were forgotten. He decided he might make a couple sandwiches for later.

Except he knew he would never eat them and that they would be put away and grow progressively nastier. Food was something to be enjoyed in public in this house, not nibbled in secrecy. He had never had such good things to eat before in his life and by God he was not going to start acting as if he were a sneaky child again in prep school, even to protect the heart of his slave from misery.

He ate three of the cold eggs, which did not take long. He then laid a piece of toast over the fourth egg so François might not notice it. Daniel wondered what had come over him that he no longer enjoyed the breakfasts that would have delighted him only a few months before. He was the type who matured rapidly, Daniel knew, and now ham and eggs were almost as odious to him as the liverwurst sandwich with chocolate malted milk that he'd so hungered for only a couple of years before. Daniel wished, almost passionately, that he had gone down to the wine celler before François had brought in this ghastly tray. Tim might have been there. They would have cracked two bottles of beer, had maybe had a wee nip of gin first, and a bowl of pretzels for something light from the icebox.

At the thought of the cold stream of beer washing from his throat the cloying taste of the jam and milk and stiff cold fried eggs, Daniel almost moaned aloud. He stretched back jerkily under the sheets and his eyes closed.

Why do I feel so different today? he wondered. It's a little like Christmas morning when I was a little kid. Are we going somewhere today? To Chamonix or Châtel-Saint-Denis? No? But something else very nice, but then everything is nice here. Last night, lighting a little fire so late at night after the long ride from Dijon and sitting there getting just a wee bit tight and talking with Tim and Sara was so good. Is it that we're all going to get dressed up tonight, at least the women are, and are having a party? I doubt this is what my excitement is about, I'm too old to get excited over things like this, but maybe we'll dance. Oh God! I can ask Nan to dance with me!

He threw one long arm restlessly over his face and now his breath came faster.

I can say, Nan, will you dance with me? Or, Nan, may I have this dance? It's perfectly simple—I've often done this before. She'll say, Why of course, Daniel, and look up at me and her eyes will widen as she smiles so she looks almost like she is blind. Then I'll hold out my arms and she'll be in them, like smoke, like a flower, like the most beautiful body that I've ever dreamed of and there, in my owns arms, she'll be and it will not be a dream. The music will rise around us like water, like passionate wings, hiding us, covering us.

There was a knock at the door and Daniel lay without breathing. The seocnd knock was louder. There was a pause, then he heard three bangs. He decided not to snore nor even open his eyes. He lay breathing quietly.

François opened the door and apparently stood looking at Daniel for a moment before he spoke. "I do not wish to disturb Monsieur Daniel," he announced into the air, "*if* he is asleep; however . . . ?" He paused to pick something up from the floor and to fling it scornfully into a corner. "Yesterday Madame Porter was most annoyed with me to find the room still unmade at lunchtime and what am I to do, I say to her, if young Monsieur Daniel is still in his bed? Should I clean around him as if he is a chair or perhaps a small insignificant tuffet?"

There was a silence. Daniel hid his face as he couldn't quite keep himself from grinning.

"Well," François said, "I can only say that I have at least done my part to keep the peace. Now if Madame makes things difficult, I will at least be innocent."

The door closed with the small but firm sound of his outraged nobility.

The old boy's right, Daniel told himself. You *must* get up. It looks like hell in here and how can he clean the room with me in it? People on the terrace can see in. Sara will be mightily peeved. I'll get up right now and take a shower.

But then in minutes Daniel was heavily asleep again, dreaming troubled but exciting dreams that made him sigh and cry out as if he were in pain.

ii

It was early when Honor first awoke that morning. Sun slanted low through the thin white curtains and a tender breeze sent them billowing, swaying their fat ruffles against the floorboards. The little fountain pouted and dripped right below her open windows. Birds sang frantically in all the trees. She felt happy as a healthy baby and in the same unthinking way.

As soon as she came to life enough to realize it, though, she was engulfed by a sickening wave of discouragement. The very thought of being alive was almost more than she could endure. The idea of another day, a whole day, to crawl through seemed vile to her. What would she do with it and with herself? And why should she do anything?

Perhaps she would lose her voice. She knew, though, that Tim suspected her from the last time of doing this to escape. It was so convenient but three times in one month would be overworking a good thing. She thought longingly of the blissful feeling of peace it gave her to sit in a room full of people knowing she need not answer any of their goddamned silly questions, that she needn't even listen to them.

Sara, of course, knew, as it was Sara who'd taught her how to escape in that way. Honor still remembered her own shocked outrage on that day when she'd been full of pity for her sister whose throat was too sore to speak, only to then have come upon Sara singing quietly to herself in the bathroom. Sara, who never mentioned it, never lost her voice again and this summer had never once shown that she knew what Honor's silences meant.

Honor wished Sara would, sometimes, engage. It would be good to be scolded or frowned at in displeasure instead of having her sister treat her always with such impassive courtesy.

She pulled a thin blanket up over her shoulders. The memory of her terrible dream made her uncomfortable and she shivered. She had only dreamed it a few times in her life, but now twice this summer the dream had sent her shaking and cold with sweat from her bed to sit half sick by the open window for the rest of the night.

She heard again—without wanting to—the dreadfully shrill screams of rage and filth that poured from her own mouth in those dream scenes and she felt the sting of her face where Sara slapped and slapped her, the blood under her own fingernails where she clawed at her older sister. It was awful. What made her dream like that? Should she talk to a psychiatrist when she went back to the university? Perhaps it meant she secretly hated Sara or maybe it was a revolt against too much of the famous "Tennant Reserve," too many years of polite good manners. Yes, that was probably it—she should ask Timothy.

Perhaps if she got up now she'd find him drifting somewhere through the airy freshness of the rooms downstairs. She began to throw the covers off, knowing she would find him, understanding this so clearly it was as if she'd made a rendezvous with him. Go to the mirror, her mind said, and you'll find Timothy. Look into the mirror and he will come, just as he came the night she felt so lonely and had gone down for fruit and had found him standing in the window. I saw him in the mirror, she thought, and stood looking at his white hair glimmering, his eyes. Then he came to me without speaking and led me to the couch and put a shawl over me and soon we were drinking hot milk and brandy and talking about what we remembered from Sunday school. She'd meant to tell him then about the dream that had sent her down there but it had seemed unimportant.

Why bother him? she wondered now. Why go downstairs?

She lay in a sort of torpor, feeling the blanket becoming too hot but not being bothered to push it away. Soon Honor was asleep, her face becoming young and smooth again and her mouth growing soft and loving, no longer drooping brokenheartedly.

iii

It was much later when Honor woke the second time.

She got up blindly, went swiftly into the dressing room, and began her meticulous toilet. She knew from experience that if she started to think she would grow too miserable to face the day, falling back asleep again in order to put off for a little longer having to talk to anyone or to answer with a smile.

I should take the veil, she thought, wiping herself vigorously after her shower. There is surely a sisterhood that has vows of silence. But I would miss my perfumed bathoil and looking down there at the enamel on my toenails and putting a little brown on my eyelids and running this little white pencil under my too-brittle fingernails.

She looked in the long mirror, assessing herself expertly. All she needed, certainly, was an ostrich-feather boa to be like a naughty drawing of a *directoire coquette*, her feet in silly satin mules, her hair piled up silkily into a soft bun on the top of her head and nothing on in between. A *directoire coquette* through the wrong end of an opera glass, she said. God am I big. I am beautiful but I am so enormous, so *tall.* Maybe it's glandular, maybe this is why I'm so unhappy. Other people don't seem to feel so low and miserable and lost as I do. They seem to have more normal-sized emotions. All mine are oversized, exaggerated, like me.

She put on panties carefully, then a white tennis dress. She slipped her feet into high-heeled white shoes, admiring her long brown legs. She felt as clean, as sterile, as boring as a dairy lunch.

Standing at her window, looking into the treetops, watching smoke from her cigarette blowing about aimlessly, she wondered what she might do. She might write home . . . ?

Just as she turned to the desk and her eyes caught a quick flash of yellow in the meadow, Honor brightened. She leaned far out, her mouth open to call excitedly to Nan, Darling Nan! Honor would run right down and pick flowers with her, she would carry her baskets.

But she didn't call. Was it worth changing her shoes? And would Nan even want her to be tagging along clumsily? What was the point of going clear to the end of the meadow, being bitten by flies, to pick flowers that would only wilt? She wasn't certain Nan even liked her.

I don't see how anyone could like me, Honor thought, with true bitterness, as I am a dull and sour woman, though I'm too young for this. I know this. I know I'm well on my way to becoming one of those ghastly boring neurotics who just adore to analyze themselves, thinking of no one else. But I am consumed—*consumed*!—by my despondency and truly hate the world. I am determined that the world hates me, which is simply a pity.

She looked with true disgust at her untidy bed, then left the room.

The stairs were cool and silent. Her high heels tapped lightly and she didn't bother trying to walk softly as she passed Daniel's room. What if she did wake him? It was late and he ought to be up. What if he was not there but was sitting on a wall watching the men work in the vineyards or was off talking with Tim and Sara? Honor's heart quivered with a small twinge of jealousy, but she immediately thought, Why should I care? How stupid. I say I don't want to be bothered with talking and am then envious imagining my brother having a conversation without me?

The living room was spotless and empty.

In the kitchen François saluted her with reserve. He hated her, she knew, because she refused to eat breakfast. She had hurt him irrevocably by leaving her tray untouched every morning until he finally came to believe her in her initial announcement that she wanted nothing at all until lunch. She now smiled sweetly at him as she took a glass from the cupboard.

"Will Mademoiselle permit me to assist her?"

"No, thank you, François."

"Very well, Mademoiselle."

"Thank you, François."

Honor started down the cellar steps, with her heels clicking loudly, hearing François bounding suddenly across the kitchen to stand at the top of the stairs.

"Mademoiselle!"

She turned slowly to look up at him. Do not *shout* at me, she thought irritably. "Yes, François?"

"Mademoiselle will not find Monsieur in the cellars."

"Monsieur?" Her voice was icy.

"Monsieur Garton has disappeared. Everyone is searching for him. I simply wished to inform Mademoiselle. It is nothing serious, of course, but . . ."

"A minor disappearance, that is to say?"

"Mademoiselle is correct."

"Thank you, François."

"Not at all. At your service, Mademoiselle."

Honor proceeded with elaborate dignity, hoping devoutly she would not trip at the bottom of the stairs as the man had in *The Diary of a Nobody*. She filled her glass with milk from the icebox and drank most of it. She didn't feel like going up through the kitchen again, having to listen to François's senseless interruptions.

Interruptions of *what*? she asked herself. My too-important thoughts? Do I even have any thoughts? Is *thinking* what I'm doing?

She carried her glass upstairs cautiously, proceding through the kitchen with her head held so high and haughtily that she almost did not see that the room was deserted. François is like me, preferring my room to my company.

He is luckier than I am, though, in that he never went to school and had to learn about how *sensitive* he is, or how to be so egocentric and masochistic and so on and so on and more than anything *bored.*

Honor stood in the door of the living room. Sun blazing in the smooth gravel of the terrace sent a hard light through the windows, glaring on the white walls. She pulled the heavy linen curtains part of the way along their rods and there they stood in straight loose folds, unmoving in the stillness of late morning. The light fell softly through, bars of mild blue and green and rose. Colors in the rooms all appeared to be mellower now. She picked up the glass she'd put down on the great dark table that was wreathed about with vine leaves. It was a lovely room. Sara could make anything lovely.

"Hello!"

She looked, quick as a lizard, into the empty mirror, before she turned toward the sound of Timothy Garton's voice.

"Hello," she said. She felt confused and a little embarrassed, as if she'd just been caught out doing something idiotic.

"What are you doing?" Tim came into the room from the terrace and sat down on the shabby red tuffet. "Don't you know billard balls are made from milk?"

"What about it?"

"Well, if you don't eat something when you drink milk, it'll make a little billard ball in your belly. Cramps. Crisis. Hot water bottles. Doctor, who diagnoses appendicitis. Cold water bottles, so forth."

"What should I do?" Honor asked as she sat down on the floor, leaning her back against the couch. For the first time that morning she felt easy, also a little excited, as if something extremely funny or wonderful might happen at any moment. Tim also made her feel so. She looked up at him and smiled.

Timothy, she said in the serious voice that resided deeply within herself, I love you. I could love you passionately, probably, but I don't because it's so good to love you this way, the way I do. You, with your odd spirit, are beautiful. I wish I were Sara.

"Where is everybody, Nor?" he asked.

"I like it when you call me that," she told him impulsively. "It's only for a few people." Then before he could answer she hurried on. "But 'where are you?' is the better question. François informed me with his customary air of mystery that you have disappeared, but if he thought he could use that news to crack my glacial calm he was bloody well fooled."

"What would Lucy say to hear you using such words?"

"Bloody? Oh, she'd probably think that's all right as it's *English*! She's like most small-town Americans, a terrible anglophile. Anyway, I don't care what she thinks. She'd speak and I wouldn't hear her, really. Where *were* you, though? They're all out looking for you."

Tim lowered his voice, leaned closer, his eyes dancing, and Honor was overcome with the sense of his delightful silliness though she knew that what he would now tell her might not be really amusing or exciting and probably not even wholly true, but the way Tim drawled with one corner of his mouth pulled up and his tired pale eyelids drooping made her feel like giggling before he even began to speak.

"You see . . . but here, don't you want to smoke? It'll help kill the taste of that foul milk. I got up early and picked some tomatoes in the garden and tickled around the edges of some lettuces. Then, really a bit dry, I went down to the celler and drank a bottle of beer and ate three stalks of celery and a pickled peach from the top of a jar marked *Not to be opened for three years from last July*, but for God's sake do not tell your sister! Then I went all over the house peeking through keyholes."

"I don't believe that."

"No?" Tim first leered like a satyr, then hugged his knees.

"No."

"You had on a pale-blue satin shift, very décolleté, with a pretty silly little white lace heart stuck on your, um, bosom, am I right?"

Honor now looked coldly past him. "I think it's despicable that a man of your upbringing should stoop . . . ?"

"What? A man such as I am is made for such pursuits and it's fun."

"I disapprove but go on."

"You see?" he asked. "Keyhole peeking appeals to everyone. Well, then I looked at Nan. She was right in front of the keyhole, practically. Very pretty, my sister is blooming. Her hair was spread all around her and if I'm not mistaken she was sleeping raw."

"*Nan*?"

"Well, maybe she had on something fairly diaphanous, a cobweb or two?"

And here Tim grinned and added, "I just skirted the edge of an ancient joke of great filth. I hope you didn't recognize it?"

"No, I don't know any filthy jokes. I don't like them."

"Neither do I, though I happen to know hundreds, which probably proves we are different in some way. *I* don't know. I wonder and wonder about it. Human behavior is such a *mighty* peculiar thing, Miss Honor."

And now she laughed in spite of herself as he sat waggling his large head solemly, to have her early-morning doldrums about Oh me and Why and How and Ah-me-how-sensitive-and-introspective-I-am flung back at her so neatly.

"Phooey," she said.

Tim looked at her.

"No," she said. "Not you. I was thinking about something else."

"Well, we Continental generally say *pfui*!" Tim told her in his best kindly old-uncle tone. "But to continue—and kindly pay attention because it's here I disappear—I skipped downstairs after my far-from-brotherly peek and took a little squint at Daniel. Couldn't see much, the keyhole in that old door being in a most inconvenient place, but there was the general impression of vast disorder."

"Mmmm," Honor agreed. "Dan's room."

"Then spent several enjoyable minutes gazing at the little white lace heart on your little blue bosom."

"Tim, please tell me. How did you really know I wore that nightie?"

"I peeked, I'm telling you. I'm a peeping Tim. Then to calm myself after the sight of you, I gathered my fortitude and went to spy on Madame Pendleton."

"Oh no!" Honor said, genuinely horrified. It seemed wrong to her—even if this was all an elaborate make-believe—that poor Lucy's ugly body should be spied on secretly.

"I know what you're thinking as your face is as transparent as water, my dear girl. But it's all right. There was nothing but a great expanse of chintz, all this moved and billowed about and very chaste. Just then, to my exquisite shame, François came tripping up the stairs and I sprang to my feet and as he started to speak I put my fingers to my lips to silence him, so he froze. I hissed, *I am invisible!* and with the man's usual quick and sensitive appreciation, which makes him a rascal and very nice to be with, he hissed back . . . ?"

There was a silence and finally Honor asked: "What?" though she really did not care. Still it was so pleasant to have Tim here with her, to be sitting lazily on the floor beside him and to be listening to his quiet voice telling her these tales.

"Oh, I don't remember," he said vaguely.

"I'll bet you were an awful liar when you were little."

"Yes. They say it's an escape. Maybe. Lying's great fun if you're careful not to lie about anything that's real."

"Yes, that's what Sara said."

"Has she told you many things like that?" Tim looked at Honor curiously and she realized it was the first time he'd ever referred to their childhood and she laughed bitterly.

"She didn't actually tell us, I suppose. But she made it plenty clear when she either approved or disapproved of things. And in her own peculiar way she saw to it that we suffered."

Honor was sorry now that they'd begun to talk about Sara, as it hardly seemed fair to speak of her to her lover, of times before he'd known her. Honor felt that it might give him an advantage over her sister, but now it was too late. She heard words that she had not before put together into sentences rushing from her.

"Oh yes, Sara was never one to spare us if she thought we'd done sonething wrong or bad or sneaky. She never touched us but she made us wretched, simply *wretched*, with her silent disapproval and I don't know exactly how. And she was terribly stuffy and rather Girl Scouty at the time, all about our doing a good deed daily and brushing our teeth and playing the game and so on."

"Really?" Tim looked highly amused.

"Oh yes! And table manners! And being seen and not heard when out in public, things such as these. But mostly she was stern about sneaking around and being a tattletale, that sort of business, which she simply abhored. That's what's so surprising now."

Honor's voice now died away. Oh God, she thought, how can I have been so indiscreet? Oh, Tim, forgive me!

He looked at her for a moment then, with a calm and speculative eye, asked, as if conversationally, "You mean about our not being married?"

Honor nodded. She was filled with misery.

"For heaven's sake, you look like a kicked puppy! You might have said something long ago. You Tennants are too damned discreet for your own good, you know? It's too bad, too, for a few people that Sara and I are not legally married. We will be as soon as we're able. With people like us, those who've known one another for a long time and have liked each other for all this while, it really doesn't matter. But I think most people probably ought to get married. So I don't think I advocate promiscuous cohabitation or all that damned foolishness. In fact, I abhore it."

Honor still said nothing.

"So does Sara," Tim added.

She frowned, then said crossly: "I don't need you to tell me that. I know my sister."

"Well, please don't snap at me. Here, have a cigarette, though you do smoke rather too much for a girl your age."

They smoked. They sat without speaking for a time. Upstairs they could hear the somnolent padding of François's tennis shoes and the occasional bump or clatter as he cleaned Nan's room. Once they heard Lucy Pendleton's painting chair being scraped across the floor. Once a train shrilled and rumbled distantly along the lake. Finally Tim slid off the tuffet and sat close to Honor on the floor, carefully not touching her.

"Are you in love?" he asked.

Honor didn't mind his asking, she was startled to realize. The very thing she would not even let her own self ask was all right being asked by him.

"Yes, I am. I am in love."

How queer it was that her voice did not crack, that she did not cry out, that instead she sounded as calm as if she were saying, "Yes, I'll have some tea. I'd like lemon, please."

"But how do you know?" Tim looked at her curiously again. "How does anyone ever know? I was in love several times before Sara and still I don't know."

"Well . . . ?" And now Honor hesitated. She was thinking hard. She wanted to tell Timothy as clearly as possible so he would know. He would help her. "Things like dreams," she said, "and all that and then that awful feeling of uncertainty and doubt and sickness and worry over it. People who say love's wonderful are *saps*, actually."

"It sounds like the real thing. Don't think I'll be flip about this, dear sweet Honor. That's my trouble in talking about terrible things, that we're all so afraid we've reduced them to trivialities, at least as far as intonation goes, but this does sound real."

"Yes, it is. He's a Jew, which complicates it all the more."

"You mean in your having children?"

"Not so much that but that Jews are double haunted now. That they are so hypersensitive, if you get me?"

"He's being noble, you mean?"

"God no. He doesn't even know how I feel about him. He's just being noble about humanity in general, as if he were another Jesus."

"One's enough, I always say. And you don't want to be another Mary waiting around for the Holy Ghost. Tell the man. Talk to him. Pull him off his high horse."

"Dan knows, a little, not much. Dan says such things as, 'Oh, one of my best friends at university is Jewish, you know . . . ?' I sometimes think my brother has the soul of a big-time politician."

"He is probably too intelligent for his own good."

That's right, Honor thought. My brother's not like Jacob—Dan is cautious. He might seem adventurous but he's secretly afraid of pain and hunger and public shame. Dan's the good kind to marry, not the poor and tortured soul like Jacob, not the outcast.

"He went to Vienna with money for refugees," Honor said. "He went disguised as a British art dealer; he did look quite the part. But that was four weeks ago. Now I'm afraid for him."

Tim rubbed his eyes as if he were tired and asked: "Tell me, Honor. Does he love you?"

"Yes, he does," she said, "but he doesn't *want* to love me. He hates me because . . . ? Well, because I'm healthy and I'm clean and I haven't suffered. And because I wear nail polish. I asked him what difference that would make in the fate of all the poor people if I suffered, too, but there's no changing his mind. He hates me for who I am, hates himself, too, for loving me instead of one of them, his own, one of the refugees."

She sighed now remembering the painful silence that would fall on Jacob's friends in a café when—earlier in the summer in Dijon—he'd take her with him to a meeting. The men would be crudely, horribly courteous, while the women laughed at her behind their hating eyes.

"But I like to be clean," she said. "In a revolution or a war I'd get dirty, I'm sure, but for now I prefer to be clean."

(You great full-bosomed beauty, Tim thought. You firm-bodied girl, keeping yourself, waiting to bear children, where will you find them? Will some desirous little soapbox revolutionist deign to impregnate you? Will you accept the caresses of an unwashed soldier who stinks? Where is the quiet home for you? Where can you hide the children you don't yet have? The best to hope for you, dear Honor, is the artful contraceptive passion of a neurasthenic professor. He will certainly use mouthwash and perhaps a dash of aftershave in the armpits. No, there is no danger here of your bearing great strong farmer sons. I congratulate you, Madame, on your sterility, on your fine thighs, your strong round breast, useless, meaningless, except for causing you your own secret pain.)

"Perhaps you should bring him here?" Tim asked. "We could fatten him up and he could see that though we take showers on a daily basis we still have some faint comprehension of the vast extent of human misery?"

Honor stared at Tim. "Oh *no*!" she said. "I never could, he'd be too uncomfortable. I don't want you to think he's a boor; he's cultured, his father was a doctor in Vienna and he does know how to use a fish fork. But months now of this work, his hiding and brooding in ghastly places and his not knowing where his family is, which is probably in the concentration camps—all this has made him queer. I don't wonder now that he hates me, resents me for my safe life. And he's gone now anyway. He's probably in a camp now too."

Honor stopped. She stared at Tim but wasn't seeing him. "And what would my sister have to say about it?"

"How do you mean?"

"I don't know. Every damned thing I do or say—or even bloody *think*—I am always wondering, What will Sara say?"

Tim seemed troubled. "Hey!" he said. "Hey, that's not right—I want to hear all about this, but first . . . I'll be right back."

He rose as easily as a cat, then bent down again and kissed Honor on the cheek. "I'll be back," he said again.

Honor knew, though, that he would not be back. She watched him hurry out onto the terrace and listened to the footsteps as they hastened off toward the vineyard, and she didn't care that he'd run away. She imagined he'd be back later, that later he might help her.

How good to have talked to Tim about Jacob! And about Sara's influence on her, which seemed more important almost than the details of her own sad love.

Honor took that whitened milk glass off into the kitchen then came back and lay back upon the blue chaise in the corner of the living room, her eyes open but not seeing.

iv

As Daniel hurried across the living room, he ran one hand nervously over his hastily shaved and powdered face. He hoped Sara—if she was in the kitchen—would be standing with her back to him so she wouldn't notice that he'd cut himself shaving under his chin. She hated that sort of thing.

He smiled at the remembrance of why his razor had slipped only a few moments before, feeling again the same uproarious astonishment that he'd felt then to think that any woman as that kid in the hall could possibly exist. How did she manage, really, to breathe? Did she sweat and get tired and have measles and all the other human things? Had he really actually seen her or had it been a dream that he'd opened his door and she'd been standing there in the dim hall with her arms full of bundles and her eyes as big as apples?

"What are you grinning about?"

Sara was looking at her brother coldly, then she turned from the sink piled high with fresh salad greens. "Hand me the big wooden bowl from that shelf, will you?"

Daniel reached for the bowl and handed it to her with a flourish that kept his cut chin hidden from her.

"Good morning, Madame," he said. "Or should I say good afternoon?"

"You're a lazy dog, Dan. But I suppose children do need their rest."

"You cannot shame me, woman, by taunting me with the fact of my youth. I'm proud to be one of America's hopes."

Sara, unsmiling, bent her head. Why do I keep up this kind of silly babbling? Daniel wondered irritably. Her face is thin and she looks tired.

He leaned against the cupboard and raised one eyebrow wearily. "Is there anything I can do to help? Do you want me to set the table?"

Sara's face broke into a warm smile. She shook her head, glanced out of the open window, her hands idle, her expression vague and dreamy. Daniel ate the heart of a little head of chicory as he watched her, wondering why he never in his life had asked, A penny for your thoughts, as he'd often wanted to. He tried to chew the crisp green nugget noiselessly but Sara heard him and looked at him, then moved resolutely to the spice shelf, her face grown resolute and alive again.

"Oh, Dan, hurry! Don't stand there. Honor and Joe Kelly are in the wine cellar. Go rescue them, *please*! Nor gave me her dying look when she went down, and you know how damned lazy she is unless she likes a person. Poor Joe's probably standing there freezing. Tim will be down in a minute. But you be barman until he comes."

"*Very* well, Madame!" Dan plucked another lettuce heart deftly from the pile as he went toward the steps. Then he turned.

"Sara," he asked softly, his face bright with sudden amusement, "did I really see that wee lass, sleekit whatchamadoodle?"

She looked blankly at him and then grinned. "You mean Susan Harper? I didn't know you were awake enough, there in the hall, to see anything at all. Yes. Why? Have you fallen for her?"

"Naturally," Dan agreed blandly, but as he went down into the coldness of the cellars he frowned. Women were silly. Even Sara bored him, often. Why should they all talk so glibly of such things as the biological attraction between people? And anyway, how could he ever even dream of seeing anything really desirable in any female in the world, after this summer and Nan Temple?

He sighed and touched his cut chin gently. Damn Sara! He was positive that she had seen it and masked the disugst that he knew such things made in her. Why was she so fussy? What the hell difference did it make whether a man cut his chin a little? Why be so damned finicky all the time?

He felt depressed and went glumly through the first rooms of the cellar without noticing the rows of richly colored fruit jars and the shelves of cool vegetables that usually pleased him.

As he came slouching through the low doorway to the wine cellar, Honor looked him over critically. She felt annoyed at Daniel, hated it when his face was still puffy with sleep, hated being stuck down in the cold with such a wooden young man as Joe Kelly.

If I were a *normal* woman, she suddenly thought, I'd be thrilled to the teeth to be standing in the same room as this All-American and a Rhodes scholar, who may be a scholar, all right, but is he a gentleman? He's too thick and too heavy and he looks like a lug. He's supposed to be brilliant, at least Tim and Sara said so the night before, but I don't see any signs of it.

The man bores me, Honor thought.

She watched coldly as her brother, resembling a giraffe, stood blinking under the thin light from the globe in the ceiling. Joe Kelly was nearly as tall as Daniel but he looked almost elephantine beside the stringy body of Daniel.

Why are people afraid of silence, she wondered, but I suppose I should say something? I suppose they're all lonely, and talking reassures everyone about being in communication with their fellow human beings, or something. She noticed that each of the young men looked increasingly uncomfortable as she stood there but that as soon as she'd formalized the meeting, telling everyone everyone's already-known name, things felt easier.

Daniel's voice was very deep, which meant he was feeling shy. Poor boy, and he had a nasty knick on his chin, as well. Thank goodness *she* was finally over being so terribly young and self-conscious!

"Pour yourself a drink," she advised him gently.

Daniel looked at her half-empty glass disapprovingly, then at Kelly's.

"Did *she* do that?" Daniel asked him. "I hate women bartenders."

"It's cold down here," Honor said. "You have to drink to keep limber. You pour him one, Mr. Kelly, will you? I can see he's in a terrible state."

"I am, thank you," Daniel said. "Why, thank you, suh, but if you all will be that kind and obliging, a dash more bitters, suh. That's right. Perfect. To your very good health and to yours, Madame."

Daniel clinked glasses punctiliously, then gulped back his drink and visibly shuddered.

"It's very bad to drink on an empty stomach," Honor said. "Isn't that right, Mr. Kelly?"

"Would you mind not calling me that?"

She liked the soft murmur of the stranger's voice. It was too bad he was so thick, she thought. She smiled at him apathetically and watched his small warm brown eyes, which were both sad and as deep as a monkey's. It seemed queer to her suddenly that this great hulk was that little Susan's lover, and she astonished herself with this thought.

"What's wrong?" Joe Kelly asked. "Have I put my foot in it?" He looked at her confusedly, with his face flushing.

Honor started, then laughed. "About your name, you mean? All right, no more Mr. Kelly, but I don't know you well enough to call you anything else just yet."

"She gets that from Sara," Daniel explained. "Sara's funny about names and being familiar and all that."

Honor frowned. How stupid of Dan to believe this was their sister's instruction.

"But of course," she said enthusiastically. "You must call me Honor and I will call you Joe."

To herself she added, Maybe, wondering why she should call this dull young man anything at all. She sipped her gin, shivered, listening inattentively to the hit-or-miss of the conversation between the two men standing with her, feeling herself to be a sullen child.

But where was Tim, would he ever finish what he'd begun saying to her that morning? Or would the coming of these two new visitors cause him to forget? And where was Susan?

Honor smiled to herself. She liked to look at people with clear outlines. She liked Susan with her delicate bones and her large teeth and eyes and her beautiful skin. When she'd first seen the tiny woman standing there in the living room with her bundles, she'd instinctively disliked her, because she seemed like an interruption. Now she'd come to like her. Indeed, she felt warm and *maternal* toward Susan, as she now recognized with amazement.

The only trouble with me, Honor thought as she sipped her gin, is that I need babies.

Then she heard Susan's hard little heels come tapping down the stairs and the sound of Tim, who was both talking and laughing.

By God, it's true, Dan cried out exultantly to himself. I did actually see this funny little thing! And he then stood looking down with pure delight at Susan, thinking he'd maybe never seen anything so cute. She wasn't exciting to him as she didn't really seem like a woman at all, more a type of delicious joke. He watched her talk and drink and pretend to be a grown-up and could feel his throat shaking with choked-off laughter.

He looked at his sister leaning back against the cold wall with her arms now folded tightly across her waist. Now there, he thought, was a fine big girl who someday, when she'd matured a little and had experienced more of life, would make some man a fine wife. She was, however, completely cold, of course. This supposed affair of hers with the crackpot student in Dijon was merely some fanciful idea. She really knew nothing at all of passion, Daniel insisted to himself. Girls were very different from men. Honor might be older than he was but—in experience—she was still a child when compared to him.

Kelly, given time, might be the kind who could teach Honor what was good for her—it was merely laughable to think he'd been lying in bed with the tiny woman who stood beside him. They were like a Saint Bernard and a Pekingese. Daniel swallowed hastily with a little snort of innocent mirth, taking the rest of his drink, then led the way without speaking up the stairs and into the kitchen.

V

Sunlight flickered through the leaves of the twisted old fruit trees that bent over the tables at the end of the terrace as if benevolently. The sound of voices was soft as the people sitting there talked vaguely, easily, after their lunch. The little fountain murmured and chuckled. Below, upon the white lake a whiter paddleboat churned almost gaily toward Chillon.

Daniel tipped back his head sleepily and let the last warming swallow of beer in his glass pour down his throat. He opened his eyes wider than they had been for several minutes looking about. What was everyone doing? By God, he had almost fallen asleep!

Little Susan lay curled up on the deck chair, one hand reached out automatically toward the dark somnolent bulk of Joe Kelly, and she looked sleepy too. Daniel wished she would stop sniffling. She was cute, though, with the hayfever or whatever it was she had. Her eyes were as big as a puzzled kitten's. She was terribly polite, in a solemn drunken way.

He wished Lucy would stop talking. She was a boring old bag. What did Nan see in her to bring her over here as her apparently chosen friend. Was it charity? Women were queer. Honor said that Lucy was a good foil for Nan, that this was probably the long and short of it.

Daniel smirked slightly as he looked at the two mismatched women sitting side-by-side across from him. Nan lay easily in the deck chair that made her seem smaller and more exquisite than she was. Her yellow dress curved roundly over her girlish breasts; her hair was a golden cloud. One hand, as relaxed and delicate as a skeleton of some sea bird, lifted a cigarette dreamily to her mouth then fell away again, while beside her Lucy smoked nervously.

Daniel looked at Lucy with impatient dislike, noting with the impervious cruelty of a very young man her fat strong fingers with their bitten nails, the brownish spots across the backs of her hands and wrists. He saw with disgust her shapeless mouth awkwardly smeared with lipstick, the monstrous tangle of her dank wadded-up hair. He speculated coldly on the probable shape of her large body without all the braces of whalebone and cloth. She undoubtedly had a strong smell, he'd already decided.

She and Nan Garton were the Dr. Jekyll and Mr. Hyde of womanhood. He recognized an apt criticism when he saw it and felt pleased with himself.

Honor would appreciate this if he felt like telling her. Honor hated Lucy Pendleton, he knew, though she had never said anything cruel about the old woman. Instead, the few times they had just spoken of her, Honor had been kindly and had smiled in that remote way that women can, smiling *meaningfully*. Why the hell couldn't women just say what they thought? he wondered.

Honor looked at him suddenly, as intently as if she'd heard him thinking. She held a crust of bread in one hand and lay back looking . . . No, she was not looking at him at all but at something in the apple boughs above him. He stretched one foot out in order to gently nudge her chair. Her brown eyes dropped their gaze—how large and somber they were. She stared unsmilingly at him for a strange moment and bit into her bread, looking displeased as if she loathed the taste of it.

Honor was a queer one. What she needed was some fun, he decided. When they got back to America, he'd try to take her out dancing occasionally if he wasn't too booked up during Christmas vacation and show her a good time. Or did she have a good time without him, with men he had never met? He felt a little ashamed of himself—why should Daniel feel patronizing toward Honor when he knew so little about her?

But then what did he know about anyone? He sighed and picked up his empty glass aimlessly and was suddenly filled with depression. What was the use of thinking about them, when they were all of them so secret? Was he a secret to them as well? He hoped so, and yet at the same time he felt almost unbearably lonesome. Through his head floated a tune that had been lurking there ever since his morning dreams. Now it was clear and strong and he knew it was Sibelius's "Valse Triste." It was corny, all right, but it haunted him now as it had done ever since he first heard it weeks before in a little record shop in Paris.

The song crept through his dreams with its sad and haunting rhythm so that nothing could clear it away. Playing it on the gramophone only made it worse and made him long intolerably to say things he could and should never say. It pressed him toward madness and made him feel Nan in his arms very close to his heart.

Daniel looked at her, suddenly sure that she, too, would be looking at him, but she was smiling at Timothy. Daniel shrugged his shoulders and shook his head to free it of the dangling melody that tricked him.

He watched Timothy smile back at his sister and then when the older man turned and looked solemnly at him he felt quite jolly all of a sudden and young again. To hell with feeling sad, Daniel thought. Women complicate things. Men, real men like Tim, are the answer.

Daniel looked back at his friend nonchalantly with his heart full of gratitude and affection. Tim Garton was a *real man*, that was it. That was why Tim was probably the most important person in the world for Daniel, as important as love and duty and so on, much more important even than romantic love and so much more important than . . .

Daniel sat up, startled. What was it he almost said? Was Timothy more important than Sara? Sara? Why, he'd known her since being born! She taught him how to walk and talk and speak. He got away from her, had pushed himself away from her, freed himself from being her little brother by a thousand acts of deliberate maturity. Why should it startle him now to find himself thinking of someone more important than she was when he had proved to himself for years now that she was unimportant? He could get along without her. Then why did he compare everything to her? Even after all these years? Why should his mind drag her into relevant things like his liking for Tim Garton? Damn Sara! Why couldn't she leave him alone?

Daniel looked at her, his face blank over his seething resentment, and was furious to see Sara's blank face looking back at him, mirrorlike. Then he grew even more furious to recognize the stab of almost womanly concern that surged in him, to notice once again the new thin line of her cheek, and the strange set to her mouth. Was she too tired with all of them living there with her and Tim? Was she pushing herself to work too hard to make things smooth and comfortable for all of them and to keep them peaceful and well fed? Why did she drive herself so? Was she some kind of martyr?

He looked anxiously at her, now full of worry. This summer had grown tighter as time passed with only occasional hours of laziness and gaiety such as last night, after Nan and her strange friend had gone upstairs. Then Sara had been like the girl he remembered from childhood but even more fun, full of laughing foolish talk and sudden exciting flashes of dark wisdom. Daniel had felt happy sitting there beside the cold fire in the night, with his brandy, and Honor a little tight in the big chair and Tim sitting beside Sara on the floor with his white head shining. Daniel felt it was fine to grow up and find that your sister was a real person instead of a conscientious nursemaid. And now she was gone again, turned back into a remote efficient woman who could make him feel uncomfortable and ill at ease with one look, could flatter him with glib subtlety and make him a fool altogether. Why did she hide? Was it his fault? Was it just that she was tired? Why didn't she stop worrying him?

Daniel pulled himself slowly to his feet and took the empty glass from Tim's hand. Lucy was bustling toward the kitchen pretending to be gay, lilting like a Salvation Army lassie. Perhaps she was getting on Sara's nerves? Dan followed Lucy with beer bottles in his fingers and went down into the cellar.

It was cold and quiet down there. He stood for a few moments looking intently at the green glass wine bottles lying on their sides.

"Hold, men, hold," he hummed thoughtlessly:

"We are very cold.
Inside and outside
We are very cold . . ."

He stuck the fingers and thumb of one hand into five little glasses left from the drink before lunch with Tim and Honor and the new people and finished the old song more loudly:

"If you don't give a silver,
Then give us gold!
Hold men . . .
Hold!"

"Damn right," Daniel said. "Damn right! That's the way!"

He walked upstairs carefully holding the fragile glasses before him like five thimbles and put them gently on the sideboard.

Honor looked at him impersonally and raised one eyebrow at Lucy Pendleton's broad soft back and Daniel nodded slightly. The old bag *was* a bore with her lilting chitter chatter chatter. Tomorrow would be his turn with lunch dishes, oh, *fabulous* day!

He was permitting himself one full look at Lucy as he strode toward the steps into the living room. Her eyes—wide, pale, blue, the strangest size he'd ever seen—now looked straight into his but she did not see him. Was she thinking of a fine phrase or of her demon lover?

Daniel shivered—what was he, a ghost? That everyone looked through him today? Were all of them ghosts?

vi

When the dishes were wiped and put away, Honor went gratefully to her room. Lucy Pendleton, poor Lucy, trying so hard to be young and to have fun . . . Lucy? She always made Honor feel tired out with pity and with her having to pay attention to the woman's foolish gabble. Why did people have to talk?

The little bedroom was fresh and beautifully empty. François had managed, somewhere between Honor's late rising and his noontime leap up to the village to shop, to leave it tidy. She grinned thinking of his discreetly agonizing description to her, one morning, of trying to clean poor Lucy's room with her in it.

"At least I get out," Honor had said to him bluntly.

François reared back, flushing, then covered his embarrassment with several coughs and a murmur, "But naturally, Mademoiselle is always most thoughtful."

He then flipped his duster, moved a vase, and plumped three pillows in the silent living room, before coming close to her and hissing, "Mademoiselle understands, of course, that *I* understand artists. I know that they must not be disturbed. I wait for Madame Pendleton to emerge from her chamber. She does not. I knock politely. I behold her in the middle of her room on her small stool, which appears somewhat *too* small. Around her are all the *accouterments* of the true artist . . . several pads of different-sized paper, boxes of paints, an easel, of course, palette, water bottle in spite of the immediate neighborhood of the washbasin on its stand, and naturally many vases and pots and jugs holding the various models that we collect for Madame. She looks up. I bow, indicating without speech my brushes and dusters. She speaks to me in a flood of what I know to be either German or Italian, perhaps both . . ."

At this point François had stolen one glance at Honor's face, then permitted himself a single cackle as he lowered his eyes.

"And then?" Honor asked it unwillingly, hating to encourage this malicious old auntie, but not being able to keep herself from being swept along by his relish of the description.

He sighed and shrugged. "Then? Then? After much hesitation—I do not like to interrupt the creation of even a minor masterpiece—I enter. Then, Mademoiselle, François cleans the chamber of Madame Pendleton as if it were his own mother's, in a thousand small dabs and darts, lifting first this pot of wilted begonias, then that vase of dead bluebells, dusting off the feet of the artist herself. François hesitates. After all he asked himself, should he disturb these living objects? And if so should he attempt to do so in French? Or in any of the other tongues that Madame seems to prefer? Should he say . . . ?"

And here François had ducked his head and sidled bustling from the room before the abrupt entrance of Sara. Honor burst out laughing and Sara, surprised at first, smiled as she seemed to comprehend the noise of dishes and spoons swelling from the kitchen like a cloud.

"Poor fellow," she murmured, picking up a duster from under the chair. "It is really harrowing to be surrounded by such sensitive plants as he! My God, how he suffers! How he broods."

Honor felt full of love remembering the warm funny way Sara spoke. Sara was *good*. How could she ever wish to leave her?

At the thought of quitting La Prairie, putting behind her the summer days and the sweet irksome company of her sister, the girl's heart sank and her stomach heaved a little with alarm. How could she want to escape all this comfort and all this beauty? School would be the same, with the infuriating red tape of registration for classes, and the rushing and fatigue and the heartbreaks, and the classes and leaves falling everywhere, and she would never see Jacob again. And now she knew she needed to pretend to be sophisticated.

She often thought of getting a job, but the barrier of her parents' amused disapproval was too much for her. Besides, what was she trying to do?

Oh, Jake! she called desperately. Jake! Why did we fall in love? Why did I have to love a small, thin, tortured man such as you instead of some proper stockbroker, the smooth young elegant handsome nitwit, who would bore my family but let them not worry about my bread and my bridge debts? Damn, damn, *damn*!

She stood by the window where the long white curtains hung motionless lazily wondering what to do with herself until teatime.

I'll write to Jacob, Honor decided. I said I wouldn't but if I don't I may go nutty or some such thing. He'll never get the letter so what harm will this do? I'll write him a really nice pleasant friendly letter, so that if he ever did get it by chance he wouldn't be upset and think I was neurotic or being a nymphomaniac or anything. Dear Jacob . . . my dear Jake . . .

Or I might start a short story instead. I might write about a tall sensitive girl with brown eyes and a bitter mouth. That would be something new. I could tell all about her intimate life and dreams. That would be new.

Where is Timothy? He understands that I have to get rid of Sara. He knows without my telling him more than I know myself, I think. If I don't get rid of all my old fears and sessions with Sara I can never *be*. The way I am now is not being. I am in a static state, static or stillborn, but where is Timothy?

She went into a little dressing room and took off all her clothes and stood looking at the white heap of them on the dark green floor. Finally she picked them up one by one with her toes, enjoying as she did the scarlet flash of her painted toenails. Then she rubbed her body with the rough mitt damp with cologne water and put on some lipstick. Finally she drank a large glass of water, put on a white burnoose, and lay herself down slowly on the bed.

Several pages of *Les faux-monnayeurs* meant nothing to her.

She started to get dressed. She needed to get in her walk up the hill with Nan and Lucy Pendleton but realized now how passionately she could not do it, could not possibly bear to listen to Lucy chattering without feeling her face growing stiff, wondering again disgustedly why Nan had linked herself to such a bore. No, it was impossible. Nan would go in a little while to poor Lucy's room and tell her that she had a bone in her leg or some-such antique nonsense, some 1890 quaintness that would make Lucy feel they were girls together, females who spoke the same intimate tongue. Honor hated to be female like that and exchange hints about monthly periods and so on. She would maybe take a shower—a long one—then go to Lucy's room and tell her she wasn't going. I might go a little early and tell her some more lies about high times in the sorority house . . . I suppose I should be ashamed of myself but she does love these stories and I do feel so damn sorry for her. If I thought I'd be like that at her age, so lonely and dull, I'd kill myself right now. Nan isn't that way. My parents aren't. The trouble with Lucy is that she seems to be hungry always and is so stupid that she cannot satisfy herself. God, will I ever be like that? This noon she gobbled with her crooked little finger held out to look elegant and then she sneaked food when we were supposed not to see. And I knew that it's not only food that she starved for . . .

Is Sara like that, in her own complex way? Is she trying to feed her own spirit on my devotion to her? Or does she even know that I'm devoted? I am. I love her more than anyone in the world probably.

But where is Tim?

There was a tap on the door. She knew that it was he, and she whispered, "Yes?"

He stood smiling down at her.

"May I sit for a while, Honor? Sara and I've been counting laundry and I'm dizzy.

"It's queer," he went on. "Laundry always stinks even with the most clean of people."

And with that Tim slipped to the floor beside her bed and sighed gratefully. Honor reached out her hand for a cigarette as he lit one and smiled back at him. She loved to see him there, so compact and real looking. It made her feel good.

For a few minutes they smoked and said nothing. The little fountain splashed beneath the window. A hornet thrust itself three or four times furiously against the white curtains. Finally Honor said, "Tim, I've been thinking as much as I'm capable of and I feel all mixed up, you know?"

He looked at her impassively. His eyes became warm and turned brilliantly blue. She felt he was so terribly sorry for her but there was no such thing as patronage in his whole soul.

"Yes. You seem to be. Maybe it's because you're in a foreign country and have been in love and are generally a little uprooted."

Honor rolled about almost peevishly on the bed as if she were a child.

"But I feel so *pointless*," she said with despair in her soft voice and in her hot brown eyes. "Why is it, Timothy? I'm young and good-looking and pretty intelligent most of the time. And I am simply consumed with boredom, boredom with my own self, and the life I've lead, and the time I waste, and sometimes I think it's Sara's fault."

"Well, I don't say you nay, do I?"

She laughed. "No. It's simply such a crazy idea that I almost contradict myself."

"It seems fairly plain. When you were young and didn't dare think for yourself, you depended upon Sara and . . ."

"Yes, for so many years I believed that what Sara did was the best, and what she said was the wittiest and the wisest, and what she wore was the most handsome. And now, damn it, I still do! Even when I fight against it, I think, would Sara wear this dress? Would Sara have said such a dull thing? And so on. It is hell."

"You're wrong, though, Nor, to let yourself be boring because of her influence. Of course I'm prejudiced . . . But if anything you should be even more interesting."

"But she spoiled everyone *else* for me, Tim!" She laughed. "No fooling, though most people seem stupid and gauche because of her. God knows I try to get away from her influence and be myself, even to the point of deliberately wearing clothes and doing things that she would absolutely sneer at, like . . . well, wearing high-heel shoes as I did this morning with slacks."

Timothy chuckled. "Anticlimax department. But I do see what you mean. But, Honor," and he hitched himself closer to her bed and put his hand, small and strong, over one of her long honey-colored ones, "I think you're confusing what Sara was when you were a little girl, and what *you* were, with what you both are now. You're still trying to be a child, with her, and make her what she was years ago. You must never confuse your love. You must love straight. I know you love Sara, but you're confused. You must kill that bad love, do away with it, cut it out as if it were diseased. This will maybe hurt you and always you'll hurt a little, but you will be stronger, Honor. You're letting false love poison you and turn into hatred that's dangerous for your whole life. This Sara you used to love is long gone but you—now a mature and intelligent woman—have let the old mildewed ghost of her haunt all your actions and thoughts, in part so you can blame anything you dislike about yourself on her. And you can't really love the Sara of today or yourself or anyone else in the world until you get rid of that ghost. You must kill it. You must kill what you love best, if your love for it is crooked and unhealthy."

Honor heard him sigh. "It's simply necessary. And even then," he went on in a minute, "you are never free."

It did not seem at all strange, she thought wonderingly, to have Tim speaking to her in this way. She knew that if anyone else had done it, even Jacob, she would've turned the things he said into a joke, and changed the whole color deliberately, frightened and startled by truth. But today in the small airy bedroom, she lay quietly accepting what she knew she must hear.

She looked at Tim sitting on the floor beside the bed. His eyes were almost closed and his head was thrown back so he appeared more than ever like a fine delicately boned goat. I hope he doesn't try to make it all easy, she thought passionately, or say anything about preaching sermons or anything like that.

"It's like my kitten," he went on as softly as if he were talking to himself. "When Sara went away once I got a kitten named Bazaine. Before she left, Bazaine was just a kitten, warm and capricious and sweet. But I grew very lonely and gradually Bazaine became the only important thing in my life. I dreamed of that little cat and I was happy only when it was close to me or crouched by my chair. The more intently I loved it the more it began to be like Sara in my mind and heart, so that my longing to have her come back was changed into a strange unhealthy obsession with my kitten that was without passion but all absorbing. Though I could hardly remember what Sara looked like, I saw her in the flat pointed face of the kitten and heard her voice in its little calls and murmurs.

"Then the cat grew sick and coughed and made pitiful messes everywhere. I told François to buy some chloroform and he said the kitten would get better. The next day was Sunday and I told him not to come down from the village. I wanted to have Bazaine alone.

"All day Sunday he lay in my arms. When I put him down for a moment or two he would lift one paw and touch my face. He smelled. Sometimes he tried to clean himself but he was too weak. I gave him warm milk with brandy but that made him sicker.

"Finally early Monday morning I had to sleep. I woke up about an hour later and it was getting light and I knew that if Bazaine was still alive I'd have to kill him. I went downstairs. He was lying on top of the bookcase with his head hanging far over the edge and his fur all in little points and his eyes half open.

"I was glad because I thought he was dead. But then he felt me in the room and tried to lift his head and fell onto the floor and couldn't get up.

"So I got a hammer and held him so that he couldn't see me and I hit his head. You'd think after the war and so on that I'd be good at killing and in a quick fashion. But it took a long time or so it seemed to me and even then I wasn't certain he was dead. And I sometimes still feel I'm going up and down and I think, Christ, isn't he dead yet? You see he was almost dead when I began it so it was hard to tell any difference.

"Then I was sick and then I drank some brandy. I went to sleep for about fifteen hours. And when I woke this was all straight somehow and the only thing in the world that mattered to me was to have Sara come back because Bazaine was just a kitten again and now I missed him as a kitten. Except for wondering if he was really dead."

Tim wiped a tear from his cheek and then looked at Honor. She watched him seriously as he stood up.

"You know, when I started to tell you that it seemed terribly important," he said as he stood by the door stretching himself. "I've never told anyone except Sara, of course, and now here I am starting out with the firm conviction that if I could only tell you about Bazaine, my little cat, you would understand all about love and so on, but I must be tetched. I need a drink. Do you?"

Honor shook her head.

He closed the door without a sound. In a few moments she heard a slight step on the terrace.

What Tim told her teemed and roiled within her. She lay still as death waiting for phrases and words and thoughts to shape them into some kind of order. She felt more at peace than she had for a long time.

The thing to do, of course, was to tell Sara, she thought suddenly. Of course! Why have I never done that? I'll simply tell her that I'm no longer a little girl and can no longer be dominated by her. I'll be cold and independent. Oh, Sara! I'll be lonely. I'm not made to be impersonal. I want to be wrapped about with domination and love . . . Sara's love. I hate her for it. I've got to get rid of you really, Sara, with my first cigarette, my first infatuation, but you and your niceties and your lovely imperious nature still haunt me.

I'll go see Lucy. I will purge my own disgust and feed her hunger with a few choice best bits of sororal lewdness. If my university sisters knew what they've been up to they would be beside themselves with jealousy. Is it wrong to tell that poor old pathetic woman a few lascivious lies? Today I'll talk to her about the secret order of carrot fetishists, I think.

She stood up and drew her burnoose about herself. She felt clean and peaceful and walked as straight as a knife through the gradual darkening of the halls toward Lucy's blue chamber.

vii

Going up to the village with Joe Kelly might've been fun. Daniel wondered lazily what had made the fellow change his mind suddenly after their decision a few minutes earlier. He'd come down to the cellar looking glum, with his heavy dark face scowling, and said rather wistfully that he thought he'd play the phonograph with Susan instead of walking up to the inn.

"How about joining us?" Joe had added eagerly, as he started up the stairs with two glasses of vermouth and soda. Daniel had shaken his head. If he could not go up the hill alone with Kelly he preferred to be by himself as he wanted to get away from women for a while.

He felt for the first time in his life that he was conscious of ten thousand looks and sounds and meanings and all of them seemed to come from women. Had women always been so clear and so complex while he was blind to them or was he suddenly imagining a lot of nonsense?

Out on the terrace, a few minutes earlier, he had abruptly recognized a deep understanding of Sara. She had become a sensitive and intelligent *creature*, one who existed as completely as he, instead of something to which he was thoroughly accustomed. He had known that she was tired because Lucy Pendleton was a troublemaker. He wanted her to be alone for a time with Timothy, wanted it as strongly as if he were Sara herself, worn out and depressed and bored with always being polite.

Daniel sat down on the cold floor and leaned his back against the leg of the high bar table. His drink was icy. He shivered in the dank air and wondered with some complacency how he had dared tackle Joe Kelly and whether Kelly had realized how strong Daniel would be. I'm a pretty deceptive fellow, he thought, deceptively tough. I'll bet he was amazed.

Why did Joe seem so queer when he saw that Tim and Sara had fled? He'd looked sick for just a moment as if he'd lost something, as if he was hopeless. Maybe I'd hurt him? Hell no! It's bad enough that I have a lot of hypersensitive women around me without crediting one of the hardest guys in America with tender feelings . . .

I like Joe Kelly. He seems like an oaf at first. He's all right, though, or Tim and Sara wouldn't bother with him. Otherwise he's independent. It would be good to be an orphan in some ways, free and clear and self-sufficient as Joe Kelly is. There's no complication, no compulsion to love, no need to hate anyone, no one like Sara to have to think about.

But I'm *free*. I come and go and have my own life. Then every once in a while, like now, I suddenly feel that the only place I can really have fun is where Sara is and I don't think that's right. Then I get peeved at her and think she's trying to interfere with my life, when I'm just being a bastard.

Right now I'm living here because I'm here instead of working at French verbs in Grenoble. Did she order me to come here? Is it her fault that I got fed up with sitting in classrooms taking notes on Molière with a lot of dingy Armenians and wide-eyed Poles, then going back to the boarding house and being silly once a week on cheap *vin* sold to us at champagne prices by the pimpish husband of the cook? I tell myself that this is perhaps my last chance ever to be a student in France. I tell myself that this is the chance of a lifetime. But maybe *this* is the chance of my life. I love it here in this beautiful house with Sara and her good food and not having to think of laundry and with Tim. I love it here because I can be close to Nan Garton. When this summer ends . . .

Daniel closed his eyes as if they pained him. He swore not to think about the end of these weeks. He shut his brain, patiently and again and again, to the cruel knowledge that he would need to be an American undergraduate once more and that Nan, the beautiful tiny alluring girl, would become a famous literary figure who was nearing her fifties. It was as fantastic as it was hideous. He was a man and she was a woman, that was all he could think of, really. It was hopeless . . .

Tim had said to take a drink to Honor. Daniel half stood up, then slumped down again onto the cold hard floor. She shouldn't drink so much. She was too young. In actual years she might be a little older than he was, but girls were less able to absorb alcohol than were men. It coarsened their muscles or something, or was it that it gave them bad labor pains? How soon would Honor start having babies? Of course it would simplify things if she'd fall in love with somebody instead of yearning over the starving revolutionary. It was so ridiculous to think that she thought she knew anything about real love yet.

Did any women? Did Sara even? She seemed independent. But he knew that she loved passionately, deeply: life, Tim, Daniel himself . . .

He was sick of love. There was too much about it, in the world.

Nan, Daniel said this all but soundlessly, I love you. Will you be my wife? I have only three more years of school and I'm sure I could make you love me.

Upstairs, music had started and was playing on and on, sounding like notes heard underwater. He whistled softly through his teeth. He hoped Kelly would not find the record of the "Valse Triste." Now he was playing a Brahms concerto. The piano came thick and faint and the deep chords of orchestra vibrated thinly on the wooden table legs. Daniel could feel them inside his skull.

> ". . . behold in thy body
> The yearnings of all men measured and told,
> Insatiate endless agonies of desire . . .
> What beauty is there but thou makest it?"

He thought vaguely of other lines, which came and went to his memory like flatfishes flickering at the sides of a glass bowl. He heard himself, suddenly, whistling the "Valse Triste." Damn them for playing it now! He leapt to his feet and walked stiffly from the dark coolness of the lower rooms, his face scowling.

Upstairs on the terrace, the air was warm. He stretched out and felt as his irritation changed into a sweet melancholy. All about him were the small sounds of twilight, swift dartings of birds through the upper branches, an occasional late bee. The last notes of his waltz faltered and stopped. He strolled quietly along the path to the gate, past the thick climbing banks of iris leaves. Petunias in the window boxes in Honor's room sent down their first heavy perfume of the evening.

He leaned against the wall by the gate. It still felt warm with sunlight. He heard the scream of the hungry pig from the farm up the hill. It sounded as a man might. Daniel shuddered and wished he had a cigarette.

Down the road, through the air that seemed now blue in the shady places, Nan Garton came softly, her hat dragging by its ribbons on one arm and her hips pushed easily under her full golden skirt. She looked small and tender. He compressed his lips to keep them from trembling and when she and the lumbering shattering of Lucy Pendleton that followed her were by the gate, Daniel said in his deepest voice, "Hello. Hello, Lucy."

viii

Honor looked pleasantly in the long mirror at herself and her buckled silver sandals as light and supple as gloves over her small brown feet. She was ready for supper.

She went silently down the steps. The air throbbed with easy beautiful notes from a violin. It was Lalo's Spanish business, such lovely crap, she thought.

She walked swiftly across the terrace, praying that little Susan and that young man of hers with his pouting baby-puss would not call to her. What did Sara and Tim see in such a lout? What did anyone see in his own friends, though? How could Nan Garton stand poor Lucy, with her stupid selfish face? How could Daniel stand the awkward squeaky boys that he brought home from school? How could she herself bear to look at, even, the pretty little painted mouths and childish eyes of the girls she lived with at the university? How could she ever again listen to their chatter, knowing that they would marry and have children and raise them to chatter or to hate chatter?

Through the kitchen window that opened widely onto the path to the tool room, Honor saw that someone had put out silver, linen, and plates. Sara had been there, getting things in line. She was serious about this party tonight, but why? Was it some secret anniversary or had she simply had enough of routine suppers, where they drank sherry, then sat down and tried to be gay and happy and to ignore poor Lucy's ghastly good manners as she subtly criticized everything that anybody liked?

She thought with love of Sara and Tim and prayed that they had driven far and fast and had felt they'd got away from all their relatives. I want to escape from mine, Honor thought, and probably Sara wants to get away from me. That shows I'm a grown-up. That I can stand to know this. When Tim ran up the hill and jumped into the little car with her, I could see through the window that her hand was on his knee and that she looked *happy*. Sara needs peace. I would give it to her if I could. But she needs no protection. She is mature. I am going to be cold and to stop all this subjection, all this thinking of her and what she would like and what she would do and think and wear.

Except for a gray light that came through the high windows half masked by plants on the banked earth outside, the tool room was quite dark. Honor switched on the light and smiled triumphantly.

She'd known Nan would leave her vases here. Often she looked, when nobody knew it, at the flowers sitting there after Nan had fixed them and was waiting for François or for Timothy to help her carry them into the house. Always she guessed, with excitement and even glee, where Nan would place the various strange and beautiful bunches of flowers, and almost always she was right, Honor's knowing instinctively what Nan was trying to say. She shook with inward amusement at some of the arrangements of blooms that appeared on certain desks and mantles.

Where was Nan? It was late. Would it be wrong of her to put the vases where she thought Nan might want them? François would be busy with supper as soon as he came and Nan was probably still at tea.

Honor carried a heavy pewter bowl of asters and nicotiana to the curve of the hall and put it down solidly there against the green tiles. In the dimness the lavenders and blues seemed to almost disappear like rounds of smoke.

She put a graceful, almost gaudily proper bouquet on Lucy's cluttered bookcase. But at least it's paintable, Honor thought, not without a touch of malice. Just look: It's utterly shattering in the intensity of its tonal values. With a background of old Chinese mud and dead junipers!

She carried the vases all over the house. Some of them were tiny, like the stiff little posy of marigolds for Tim's bathroom. Some were enormous and heavy like the jug of Saint John's wort Honor propped up against Daniel's closet door, placed in a manner that would force him to look at it before he dressed.

As she passed the kitchen window on her last trip to the tool room, Honor saw François. He stood with one long bony finger pressed against his temple and, as she looked at him, he sighed and said, "Ah, music."

"The 'Valse Triste,'" she said. "Monsieur Kelly has played it several times this afternoon."

"Mademoiselle does not love music, then?" François asked, sighing as dramatically as an old clown.

Honor smiled in a perfunctory way at him—the man was boring and he always managed to make her feel a little queer, as if he were the real part of the shadows of other people. She shivered with this thought and went again into the hard blaze of the tool room light.

The two vases that were left were for her own room and Nan's, she knew. There was a soft meaningless blob of pale lavender Scabiosas from the meadow with a few late yellow heads of clover. Then there was a glass battery jar filled with water over a drowned china doll holding a little ring of field daisies. It was for her, Honor was sure.

Nan might be cross to see that Honor suspected her long game of flowers but the temptation was too strong. She carried the heavy glass jar carefully along the terrace and up the stairs to Nan's room, where she set it down.

Honor laughed: it did look crazy there as it sat looming in deep shadow on the mantelpiece. What would Nan say when she saw it? There were silver bubbles on the petals of the daisies, more on the pink curvesome body of the little Kewpie.

She got the last vase of flowers and turned off the light in the cold tool room. As she left François darted toward her. "Mademoiselle Honor!" he cried. "Has Mademoiselle the time to stop one moment? One wishes to show her something."

Honor grinned and followed him into the living room. In the corner Joe Kelly lay alone with his eyes closed. Something quiet and reassuring was playing on the gramophone: Bach. There was no light in the long room except what came softly through the wide French windows.

François had pulled the carved table into the center of the floor and put out a rough lace that looked like fishnet to cover it. The bowls of dwarfed nasturtiums and wheat and bluebells that Honor had left in the kitchen for this table were placed carefully now down its middle. Polished wine glasses shone in the dim light, as did the precise lines of silver.

"It's lovely, François," she said.

He sucked in his breath and whispered sharply. "Oh no! The mirror!"

She looked past the table to the wide mirror that made a window from the floor to its curving top into a clearer room that held more light. At the mirror's base, just at the entrance to this other world, he had placed a row of fine begonias. Even in the trickery of twilight Honor could see that they were the most beautiful flowers she'd ever seen. The leaves curved and sprung with virility from their juicy stems and the shell-like petals of scarlet and gold and the delicately shaded blossoms glowed twice, once against the darkness of the floor and the low mirror and once again in the glass itself where the colors were stronger and more intense.

"Oh, François," she said. "It is *lovely*! Monsieur Garton will love them." And the man stirred happily.

"Is it not providence," he said, "that François raised them himself especially for this fete? It is fatality!" Then he sighed at the drama of his own words before slipping into the kitchen again.

Honor knew how pleased he was. It was as if she could lay her hand against his side and feel him purring.

She looked at Joe Kelly's dark bulk in the corner. His eyes were still closed. It was almost the end of the record. She hurried silently from the room and up the stairs.

Honor was startled to see Susan sitting on her bed looking somewhat woebegone. Honor had all but forgotten about the little widgeon. She placed the bowl of meadow flowers on her desk then looked at the girl.

"What's wrong?" she asked. "How's your cold? Would you like to take a shower?" Honor heard that her own voice sounded abrupt and almost cross. She was ashamed to see Susan's small head holding itself haughtily, like that of a wronged child.

Honor sat down with her on the bed. "Cigarette?" she asked, and when Susan nodded, she stretched to reach the table, gave one to each of them, and lit them.

Susan puffed then blew a great cloud of smoke expertly through her nostrils, saying, "Are you going to dress for dinner?" The casual tone of Susan's voice made Honor suspicious.

Then, before Honor could answer, Sue went on, "I know you'll think I'm crazy, but definitely *crazy*! But I don't have anything to wear. Isn't that silly? As a matter of fact I haven't worn anything but sweaters and skirts since I got off the boat three months ago. It will be funny, but *definitely*, to start dressing like a human being again when I get home." She then laughed nervously as she stubbed out the cigarette she'd just lit.

"And, yes!" she added. "I *would* like to take a shower. You don't think Mrs. Porter will mind, do you, if I just wear what I have on?"

Her mouth was tense as Susan tried to smile at Honor. Her eyes, however, under the ridiculously tight gold cap of hair, were warm and audacious like a spunky little cat's.

"I have an idea," Honor told her as she stood up. "Go run and take a shower and I'll be right back." She then hurried from the room.

And now as Honor stood at Nan's door she wondered how she even dare ask such an intimate thing of her as the loan of a dress from a woman for whom she'd never felt anything but timid admiration. Honor wanted to talk like, to be like her, ever since she'd met her but felt somehow that the difference in their size—with Nan at least—would pose an irrevocable barrier. Often this summer she'd seen in Nan's warm and friendly face the most speculative look she'd ever seen in a human's eyes, and this surprised her. It made her feel queer and as if it would be impossible to be quite free from constraint when they were together. The secret of the flowers was the only real bond that Honor felt between herself and Tim's intense and well-bred sister. How dare she be so impudent as to ask a thing like this? Honor wondered.

Hearing Lucy stirring about in her own room, Honor knocked on Nan's door as softly as she could, praying the other woman would not hear.

Just then Nan came running down the hall making hardly a sound as she moved along the hard floor. She looked strangely excited and more beautiful now than Honor had ever seen her.

It was easy, somehow, to ask her to loan Sue a dress as Nan was in a kind of dream, as if she had just been embraced.

She's an odd one, Honor thought, as she now stood by the door, her arms filled high with the fine golden tissue of the dress that Nan had never worn—as she knew—and had been thrown at her helter-skelter. She looked at the small square face that seemed to float in the light of the bedroom, only then remembering the flowers on the mantle, that silly teasing vase that had been meant for her. She smiled almost involuntarily and in a rush of sudden understanding and amusement, she bent down and kissed Nan's cheek, which was hot and oddly furry.

"Oh, Nan," she said, "you are so beautiful." Then she hurried away feeling very shy.

Back in her own room she threw the dress on the bed and called impatiently, "Susan." She saw the tiny white panties lying beside the neatly folded skirt on the chair and laughed. "Susan!" she called again.

Honor slipped off her burnoose and pulled her long tight green dress with the silver leaves around its skirt carefully over her piled-up hair, then looked at herself quickly, seeing if everything was all right.

Susan came in from the shower with a towel wrapped properly about her body. "Oh, Honor," she said. "You are so beautiful." And Honor smiled to hear the words she'd said only a few moments before.

"Look at this," she said. "Here, be quick, put it on!" But Susan just stared at her without comprehension.

"Drop the towel," Honor commanded. "And here, slip this over your head, you can pull your panties on later on when we do your hair."

She was almost frantic as she hurried Sue into the exquisitely full and floating gown that fell to the floor all about her, curving softly over her small breasts and showing off her sharp little shoulders. The gold threads woven through the cloth shone in a thousand twisted lines as Sue's tanned skin glowed in contrast.

Honor felt her heart twist as she looked at the other girl and longed for one sad moment to be as small and as sweet as this, knowing, if she were a man, she'd want to love just such a tiny, perfectly made person.

"I am dreaming," Susan told her. "Dreaming, but definitely! Shall I wear it, Honor? Will this be all right? And what about my feet?" She lifted the skirt to show her brown toes and was now looking down at them ruefully.

Honor laughed, feeling silly and happy. "Don't wear shoes, why should you? Your feet look nice just like that. You can pull on your white ones to dance," she said as she left the room. She was pushing at her own hair carelessly, saying, "Come down when you're ready. There's no hurry."

Suddenly she turned around and asked, "Are you scared of Sara now?"

"No! No!" Susan cried excitedly. "I'm suddenly afraid of nobody!" Then she picked up the volume of the great yellow skirt and whirled around on her slender feet.

Honor now hurried down the first curve of the stairs. The house felt tight and strangely expectant as a house always will when people are in their own rooms shaving, dressing, deciding on colors and scents to wear as they come together again at the supper table. Honor liked this time as the shadows were not quite frozen into their night shapes and there was a quiet feeling of delight and hurry everywhere throughout the house.

She went cautiously on down the stairs, which were almost dark now, and out onto the terrace. She stood by the fountain, head bent, listening to its unwavering trickle in the still air. Its basin would be just long enough for her, were she to lie down in it, she saw, its shape exactly like a coffin's. She could so easily imagine herself lying there, looking beautiful and fresh under the cool mountain water.

Just then Daniel came running up the path from the meadow. "Oh, there you are," he said. "I want to talk to you," he added, and Honor heard that his tone was harsh.

ix

Honor looked at her brother for several seconds before asking, with exaggerated calm, "What's the matter with you? You look like you've seen a ghoulie."

He laughed and stopped trying to hide his shortness of breath, now gulping noisily at the air like a fish. "I ran," he was trying to say.

"Obviously," she said. "But from what?"

"From nothing, my dear girl. There are no spirits in a high Swiss meadow that could faze this courageous young American, but I had an idea and I wanted to talk to you."

Honor turned and began to walk slowly toward the edge of the terrace. "Come," she said. "Let's walk a little."

"I've been walking. In fact I just ran down to the lake and back in about six minutes flat. Honor, wait for me!"

As he caught up she stepped close to him and murmured, "Remember, it's summer. Windows open. People upstairs quietly dressing, if you're about to make your true confessions."

He frowned impatiently. "True confessions?" he asked. "Stop being weighty, Nor. This is it, I've decided. You and I are leaving here tomorrow morning."

They walked on slowly to the terrace's edge, their long legs falling easily into step.

"What makes you think so?" Honor asked.

"Because I think it's a good idea, that's all. And it would be fun for you and me to take a little jaunt together. We haven't seen much of one another this summer."

Honor laughed. "But why this sudden need to be with me? I haven't noticed that it's kept you home for the last five or six years. What's this really about? Do you have a rendezvous with some little chippie on the Riviera and need me along for protection?'

"The *hell* with all that," Daniel told her fiercely. "Stop trying to be so tough, Nor, as you're a pathetic flop at it. No, I have *not* got a rendezvous, as you so archaically put it. I simply think it would be fun to have a little jaunt together, maybe go to Milano or someplace. Anyway, Sara's fed up with all these people being here and our leaving would help her."

"It's only the bitchiness that floats around in certain quarters that she doesn't like, if that's what you mean. In fact, you and I are a relief to her from having to worry about that sort of thing."

"Well . . ."

"Our going away wouldn't make it any easier for her to take the digs and hints of that old . . . poor Lucy. But you cannot blame Lucy. This entire business is difficult for a woman who believes in adultery as passionately as Sara does."

"Why don't you stand up for her? Go ahead, Nor! Lucy needn't have come here, quite aside from her being the most unpleasant old bag. She knew how things were and she came anyway."

"Yes," Honor said. "No doubt to protect Nan from everyone's wanton ways. And I knew she never dreamed that Nan would be happy, or anything aside from miserable. Lucy imagined herself as comforter—everyone loves that role. And poor Lucy was tricked by the fact that Sara isn't the common streetwalker she'd come to expect and that Timothy and Nan so obviously love one another. In fact, I feel terribly sorry for Lucy."

"Apparently," Daniel said savagely. "But I honestly hate her."

The two again walked along the length of the terrace as they spoke and at the end under the apple tree that bent over the far end, beyond the lighted kitchen window, Honor stopped. Daniel stood by her side, watching the red crown of light flaring up from the casino far down the lakeshore at Évian.

"We were just there last night," she said. "It seems such a long time ago. I do forget all about time here, don't you? It was fun last night, planning to go up to bed but then sitting in the living room and talking 'til all hours . . . ?"

"Tim and Sara are going to be married as soon as they can," Daniel said. "He told me so."

"He told me too," she said, "but I can't see that it matters to people like them. But it will be simpler when people like Lucy can't make her nasty insinuations."

"We're leaving tomorrow, Nor. I mean it."

"Ah," she said. "My masterful little brother. You just don't seem to be able to give me any reasons."

He sighed and told her harshly, "All right. The truth is, Nor, I've come to the conclusion that Sara brings out our weakest side."

She laughed, but with uncertainty. "Oh, you have, have you? What gives you that peculiar idea?"

"Look at us," he told her in a sharp voice. Now he broke off a twig from the apple tree and bit it softly, his lips touching its smooth leaf, before going on:

"Look at us! I know that I'm being lazy in not finishing my course at Grenoble as the family wants me to. I want to, too, but here I am, lotus-eating."

"Where does that hit me?"

"You're lotus-eating too."

"I'd hardly call it that."

"You're hiding here, Nor, if you want the plainer word. You know you've run away from Dijon. You didn't want to stay in Dijon because you've fallen in love with someone who's gone—at least you *think* you've fallen in love—so you come running home to Big Sister. Hide me, you're saying. Wrap me, please, in these nice soft layers of comfort and let me be lazy."

They were each silent for a few moments then Daniel went on:

"We think we're grown up, Nor, and free and really the only place where either of us feels happy is when we're here with Sara. What are you and I, I'd like to know, aside from two fine cases of arrested development. And we now have to prove we can stand alone and make our own lives independently."

"What real good will it do to hurt Sara's feelings and leave La Prairie now with the summer almost over? Don't you think it's a little late? And anyway I like it here."

Daniel seized her arm and then abruptly dropped it. "That's just it," he said. "We simply have to show Sara—Tim too—that we're strong and that we're free and that we don't just lie around all day. We have to act grown-up, Nor. We need to do this for ourselves."

"I still think you want to go to escape from something. Maybe you've got someone in a family way? Is it François?"

Dan turned away. "What's the use, Honor. You're getting stupider—do you know this?—as you age."

"Maybe," she agreed placidly but now her voice grew softer. "I am sorry, Dan. Wait a minute. I've been thinking a lot about Sara, too, wondering if I will ever be able to think and act in a way that feels free of her influence. Is this what you mean?"

Dan hesitated then said, his face serious and frowning, "That's exactly what I mean," stopping as if unwilling to go on, but now his voice quickened. "Yes, that's exactly it, that Sara dominates us both. This isn't her fault. It's simply the circumstance, the way she's made, as well. But we must learn to stand alone, apart from her. I'm leaving in the morning. I'll come back for a day or two, perhaps, before the boat sails."

His voice cracked, he cleared his throat, then hurried on: "You'd better come, Honor. We can have some fun. We'll have to travel third all the way unless you have much more money left than I have, but it will be fun. It will!"

"Well, don't try so hard to convince yourself, like we're having to have an operation or something. All right. I don't know that you're entirely right but maybe you are so, yes, I'll come. We'll tell Sara in the morning, then catch the noon train somewhere."

Honor was asking herself, But will this work? Will it do any good? I've escaped before, she thought, have made myself be rude to Sara, cruel to her, and ugly, and I've always come back. Will Daniel find that out or will he go on thinking that *this* time he'll be able to find his freedom? Women simply know more about subjection than men do.

Lights came on now in the living room, shining softly in the wide squares on the terrace.

"Look at Sara," Dan said. "She looks swell, doesn't she? You do, too, Nor. I meant to tell you. That's a nice-looking dress."

"Thanks," she told him dryly.

They stood watching as the tall woman walked dreamily about the long table, straightening silver, pulling at a flower, pushing in a chair. Daniel wondered why he so easily forgot what their sister looked like between the times when he could see her as sharply as he did now, when she was beautiful.

And Honor felt her own old self-depreciation seeping in: Sara looks so smart, she thought, so well groomed, how can I ever hope to even look decent beside her in this old green dress? Her hair's smooth, while mine's mussy. She'll talk wittily as I wonder why I even bother to open my mouth.

No, she thought. *Stop that!* I am a grown woman. I am strong. I've been in love. I know as much as my sister does and I'm as good-looking as she is and my dress is newer and even more lovely.

"My God, it's late," Daniel said. "Kelly will be in my room—he needs to borrow my razor. I need to see if Tim can give me new blades."

He took a few steps toward the lighted house, then turned back. "It's a bargain, then?" he asked, his voice a whisper, his face both stern and excited.

"Bargain," she said. "We'll tell her first thing in the morning. She probably won't even care. That's the worst thing about her but you never know. This time we'll show her." And Daniel laughed.

5

One night he called to the woman. She stumbled, full of sleep, into the circle of his light and saw his face had been smoothed still by the opiate but that his eyes were now full of a strong surprise.

He took her hand quickly. He knew his leg was gone forever, ashes now or pickled in a laboratory, and he could not even remember what it had looked like. Had it been hairy, freckled, smooth, brown, all those years it was with him? Had the toes been straight or bent with hard nails? Was there ever even a callous on that heel? Had it always been theoretical?

My foot, my foot, gone now! Never shall I know!

He kissed the woman lightly on her sleep-softened cheek and closed his eyes to hide the feeling of his remoteness, complete and irrevocable.

i

Honor stood for several minutes in the open window, watching her sister move deliberately around the table in the center of the room. She saw with a kind of affectionate amusement how completely absorbed the older woman was in such things as the position of a leaf under its flower in the low pewter bowl, the distance between a fork and a plate. Would she herself ever know that dreamy concentration on such unimportant things, she wondered? Perhaps being the mistress of a house changed a woman's feelings toward knives and sheets and laundry. So far, Honor admitted wryly, it was beyond her understanding how a person as quick and lovely as Sara could let herself become so. Being in love might help . . . but Honor felt quite certain that living with a man like her Jacob would never teach her the pleasant spell of possession of such things as linen and fine cutlery. She smiled.

"Hello," Sara said softly, as if she had heard. "I've seen you standing there. It looks nice, don't you think?"

She came over to the window and stood beside Honor, turned toward the lighted room.

"And you look lovely, little one."

Honor almost caught her breath when she felt Sara's arm slip lightly over her hips and rest there. She could sense warmth from it through the fabric of her thin dress and knew just where the wrist lifted, where the palm lay almost flat over the sharp ridge of her pelvis. It was queer to have Sara touch her. Sara, who for years had bathed her and knew her body intimately, and then suddenly to be grown up and to have never been touched and never looked at by her again. Sara had kissed her when she first arrived from America, it's true, and it was an almost violently loving kiss. But since then she seemed to deliberately avoid any physical contact with either Honor or with Daniel, or with anyone else for that matter. Had she ever even touched Tim in public?

Honor breathed quietly so the hand resting with such assuredness on her hip would stay there, unstartled.

"Thank you," she murmured. "You do, too, look lovely. That dress is like smoke and the table is beautiful."

Sara stood, still touching her—Honor could hardly believe it. Was this because of the party, that now certain barriers were down? She looked shyly at her, glancing sideways at the face so near her own. Sara was happy tonight. Honor knew this by the easy curves of her sister's small but voluptuously red mouth and the clear look of her brow, too slender under the wide height of her regal forehead. There was something gay and excited about Sara, in a misty way.

"Why are we having this party?" Honor asked, lips close to Sara's ear and her voice a near whisper. It was as if she were a little girl again.

Sara stared across the table into the long mirror and laughed. "Just *look* at us standing there, so tall."

Then she added, "The party? Oh, I don't know. I thought it might be fun but just look at the two of us in the mirror!"

Honor could not look, thinking oddly that if she did, she'd see not herself standing with her sister, but with Tim Garton. I'm in love with him, she thought, and it isn't wrong because I only love and don't want him to be anywhere but in this woman's life, that of my beloved sister.

She felt Sara step a quick pace away from her, and where the long warm hand had lain against her hip it was now cold under her dress. Honor shivered, then looked into the veiled eyes of Sara.

"Nor, will you get the sherry glasses and the decanter and the almonds and all the stuff and things and put them on the terrace?

It's time we started. Did you notice François's flowers? He grew them, he says, but of course he's a liar. Still I love him."

Sara was speaking amicably, impersonally.

Honor, moving carefully toward the terrace with the heavy tray in her arms was now listening to her sister's voice through the open windows and felt a flash of exasperation that was almost pain. It was cruel of Sara—yes, cruel—to wrap Honor in such a quick cloak of tenderness, then suddenly begin again treating her as if they were two well-bred strangers meeting at a tea. Who the hell did Sara think she was to lift Honor up then run off leaving her to fall down to ordinariness by herself? The only way to be, Honor told herself savagely, is completely cold to all. But she knew that the next time Sara showed one of her rare flashes of intimacy, no vows of coldness would be able to keep down the passionate gratitude within. Damn her, Honor said, as she put the tray down heavily on the iron table so roughly that all the glasses jingled. But soon she'd tell her that she and Daniel were leaving, that they were escaping from her and all her autocratic demands on their emotions. Then, she thought, she'll perhaps realize we're no longer children to be tormented, that we are human beings with feelings and dignity and so on.

Honor sighed knowing Sara would probably be polite and say nothing, do nothing to show she was hurt by their departure.

She ate several salty almonds, feeling hopeless, and tried not to think of that one dream in which she was screaming at and hitting her sister.

On the two steps down into the living room, Susan Harper stood watching Honor, thinking she'd never seen such a tall and beautiful girl as the one out there on the terrace in the afterlight. The mountains across the lake, blue-black, outlined like cut stone the fine boney silhouette of her long body and made the shadows under the girl's breasts and the sharp curves of her waist and haunches as clear as marble. Her dark hair and her skin seemed hard, too, and the silver leaves around the end of the skirt glinted in the light from the windows. Then the girl moved her shoulders in a human way and lit a cigarette.

Susan moved her own thin shoulders uneasily. She had never in her life worn such a beautiful dress as this. She knew that Nan Garton must have paid hundreds of dollars. She knew, too, that it had never before been worn, which made Sue a little uncomfortable. But when she moved and felt the cloudy silk folding effortlessly around her and looked down at herself shimmering there in all that delicate gold, she knew, too, that she somehow had a right to this dress.

Laughing softly, she drew her toes up away from the cold floor. Would anyone guess she was barefoot? Would Sara Porter disapprove if she knew?

Susan made herself as tall as she could and let a faintly scornful look come over her face as a shadow. When Sara turned from the window where she'd been looking out at Honor, she wouldn't be able to tell that Sue was still a little frightened of her. I'll be Mosca the Gadfly again, Sue decided. It had worked at lunch and at least I'm not sniffing. Sara Porter will like me and be glad when, later tonight or in the morning, I ask her advice about what I'm going to do. Of course, I do know already, but it will be best to talk all this over with an older woman. Then Joe will believe me when I tell him I must go home. He won't try to kiss me and make me change what I've decided.

Sue pulled herself tall and leveled her face with her chin tucked in, walking silently across the cool polished floor and over the softness of the rugs, lifting herself on each step so the great golden skirt swayed about her lavishly.

"Good evening," she said, as Sara turned quickly. She had been watching Honor. Her small mouth now drooped so it looked like she'd lost something and Sue saw that she looked wistful.

Now she stared for a minute at the girl who peered up at her, then Sara became warm and alive again, laughing excitedly. "Why, Susan, how lovely you are! Oh, that dress is *beautiful*!"

She put her arm lightly over Susan's shoulders and called, "Come look, Nor! Susan is the Golden Fairy! Oh, it's lovely. She's like in that book we used to have, do you remember?"

They all then laughed together and felt gay, suddenly, and when Sara poured the sherry they each touched the others' glasses as if the three of them had a great secret they were keeping from everyone else.

Nan Garton felt it as she stood in the window of the living room watching the three of them. It was their youth, she knew, and she cried out fiercely to herself, Their youth binds them together in possibility. But now I don't care, she thought. I can see clearly now and I know how very little such things as beautiful and firm rosy cheeks actually matter. I am now free from all that, she thought. I am free of Timothy and am no longer timid or afraid.

And now as she walked toward them she felt her entire body swimming easily in its own flesh. She had never before felt as quiet physically as she felt herself feeling tonight. She smiled at them and when their faces glowed as they looked toward her in the light coming from the living room, the pleasure and the love she saw filled her with calmness. Never again, she knew, would she care whether people looked at her with more admiration than they did others. Never again would she care whether they looked at her at all. This was a wonderful feeling. It felt like she was shedding an old and ugly skin.

Sara and Honor stood very straight in their long slender dresses and the golden sherry in their glasses glimmered with the same color as the threads in little Susan's dress. Nan was pleased—deeply, warmly—to see the lovely creatures. She felt benevolent, and the sight of a stranger in the dress she'd designed and had made then kept secret as something for her brother's pleasure was like honey to her soul. Susan Harper was a beautiful child. She glowed tonight like a golden moth in Nan's long guarded dress, and the older woman felt her skin prickly with sheer delight at watching. How her brother would love the sight of it, she knew, and she then flushed proudly at her own wishing this other woman well.

She walked out upon the crisp gravel listening to her own steps. She knew she looked well. Just before she'd come downstairs she'd stood for a moment longer before her glass and had seen the lovely person who looked back at her and knew she'd never looked better. It is because I am free now, she thought. I am no longer enchained to my own brother's dominance. I am, instead, now me.

Now, as she walked lightly toward the three girls she heard Sara calling to her with her breathless voice and saw the shining eyes of Susan and the dark smiling eyes of Honor and she thought, Why, they love me! They love me and I don't care. Soon I shall tell Timothy that I am free and everything will be just as it's meant to be.

She took a glass of sherry from Sara. It was brown and heavy under its even dryness, not at all the kind recommended to her by her wine man in Philadelphia. Was it correct? she wondered, then laughed into the glass as she'd almost choked. She touched glasses with each of the girls in turn.

She now heard herself as she talked to them, watching their faces in the soft light from the house, without knowing what she was saying, nor caring, as it all seemed interesting and merry.

When Dan and Football Joe stepped onto the terrace from their room, she watched as their faces lit with pleasure and didn't care that they either were or were not excited to see her as she stood with the younger women. Timothy was all that mattered.

But even if his coming was unimportant to Nan, to Daniel Tennant she was the most beautiful sight in the world as he stepped from the sill of his room. All that mattered to him was seeing Nan there in the faint light with the lake almost black behind her and her hair blowing softly around her small square face. Her eyes were wide and pale and they looked haunted. Her full skirts lifted, blue and a damask green, like weeds in a river tide. She held a round glass of sherry in one tiny delicious claw.

Dan looked at the others standing with her. Honor was tall and looked scornful but he knew that any man who was not her brother would find her beautiful. Little Susan tickled him almost physically, nearly made him laugh aloud, so much did he want to lift her up into the air and to whirl her around as they laughed and laughed. And Sara was beautiful even in her brother's eyes.

He frowned, knowing it was from her he and Honor would have to make their escape.

But it was Nan whose image really penetrated past his superficial sight, his outer vision, until he felt the lines of her inside his brain, and within his heart. She was delicate and mysterious, like a celestial monkey. He smiled then looked quickly at Joe.

Joe was staring at him. They each quickly dropped their eyes, with mutual irritation. Joe could hear Daniel clear his throat, pompously, as they walk toward the women and then was furious to hear himself do the same thing. What was he, a damned rubber stamp? Joe demanded of himself savagely. What would that girl standing there in her long green dress think of him?

He looked on her as he walked toward her. She was a clear one. She hated him. And he hated *her* with the fastidious little mouth so like Sara's, and her supercilious ways. He'd like to rip that dress off her and make her see herself as a woman, a real woman ready to love him. He could make her follow him around the world. He knew it. And he knew suddenly that he would follow her around the world. Hell, to either heaven or to hell. Joe almost groaned aloud.

Susan ran toward him. She looked smaller. Was it because his eyes were so full of the slim height of Honor Tennant? His girl looked prettier than he'd ever seen her before. Was that, perhaps, because his heart rocked with the beauty of the dark-haired snob? He felt his love's hand like a squirrel's upon his arm.

"Sue, darling," he said softly. "You look so beautiful!"

He looked down into her great black-rimmed eyes and realized that he did not know her at all. The woman who this morning had almost been his life was gone now, turned into mist. Would her heart break? When he told her that she must go? That she had to leave, that he had to be alone? He needed to think about Honor and about time and space.

"Where is Mr. Garton?" Susan winked faintly at Joe as she asked it, then turned to Daniel. The gravel hurt her feet. She stood cautiously on tiptoe as she looked at him. Then, as he stared down at her, she winked one eye outrageously at him. She felt very silly. She loved him, with his big nose and solemn eyebrows, yes, she loved dear Joe and her golden dress and the sherry and Sara Porter. She felt very silly, most definitely!

"Yes, where is Timothy?" Nan, watching the others saw her with new eyes, saw that Susan did not love Joe. She saw that Joe loved only her and that Honor loved only herself. She saw . . . yes, she *saw* that young Dan loved her but it did not matter. "Where is Timothy?" She asked, holding her glass steady as a stone. She wanted to see him and to know that he was near, so then when the time came she could tell him that he was no longer necessary to her.

Honor tried not to look in the mirror, because doing that every time she heard Timothy's name seemed weak and superstitious. She turned toward the lake. Far down toward Geneva the red and white lines of Évian hung on the water's edge. She thought deliberately of last night, of going into the casino there and nodding to the headwaiter and pretending not to notice the stares of the Chinese statesmen and their white-gowned German mistresses, and eating crayfish with her fingers. She was sure that if she concentrated on such things she would not think about seeing Timothy.

Everyone was talking. Joe Kelly had the softest voice you ever heard in a man. Dan's was ridiculously deep. He was saying things to Susan Harper. Honor smiled. Nan knew the sorts of things men like Daniel would say to girls like Susan.

". . . like a fish out of water, as I've always put it."

That was Tim Garton. How had he got here? Honor wondered, turning slowly on her silver heel, and looked at him as he stood talking to his sister. He wore a soft blue blazer and his hair was blue white in the light. He stood easily in his own skin. Yes, that was what Honor so loved about him, that he was so accustomed to living as if he had done it all several times before and was no longer ill at ease. She sighed, feeling without touching them the pins in her hair and the cloth binding her small waist and the line of silver leather around her ankles. She was irked by her body and longed to be impervious to it as Tim seemed to be to his.

"*Salud*," he said and touched his almost-empty glass to hers.

"*Salud*," she answered.

His green eyes were small and sat incredibly far back in his small head. She smiled automatically at him and then wondered why.

"Let's drink to tomorrow," he murmured.

She shivered and touched his glass again. What good was it to tell him that they were escaping and that they would be hurting Sara and wasting their own energy and money on something that would not help? She knew because she had done it before. She was sure Dan had as well. Then why bother again? Honor started to tell him.

"Dan," she said quickly. Then she stopped. His eyes were deep and excited and his lips curved and she saw that he looked very young. She was a woman and resignation surged in her. "To tomorrow."

Timothy laughed at her. "You sound like a woman both triumphant and full of resignation," he said.

Honor laughed. "Damn you, Tim Garton," she said and felt much better.

Sara had disappeared. François's back, respectful, with old trousers shining in a V between the sharp edges of his fresh white apron, stood in the kitchen door, where he listen to Sara's last instructions. A cigarette butt fumed on the step just outside the kitchen, where he had thrown it.

"But where is Lucy?" Nan knew, but she had to say it aloud, dutifully. It was a way of proving that she still thought of her old friend, still felt connected with her. She knew that Lucy was in her room, perhaps hiding just behind the heavy blue curtains listening to them all, torturing herself with their gaiety and their forgetfulness of her.

"Where is dear Lucy?" She asked again, mockingly fervent. They all stopped talking and Honor said, "Yes, where is she?" in a manner that sounded as tactless as if she'd just blurted out, "Oh God, I'd almost forgotten all about that fat old bore." Nan felt her lips tighten. Other people might be thoughtless, but she could never permit herself to be influenced by them. She felt filled with loyalty and affection now. She put her glass down and started toward the end of the terrace.

"I'll go find her," she said.

Lucy stood with dramatic suddenness in the main doorway. She wore a long black chiffon dress and her hair was piled up elaborately on the top of her head. It made her look handsome.

They all stood looking at her, thinking for the most part that night and a little makeup and perhaps some excitement were becoming to her. Timothy stepped to the table and started to pour her sherry. Honor said to herself, If she says, "*Hell-oh-ooh*!" in that horrible way of hers I'll scream. I will hit her. I cannot stand it.

"Hell-oh-ooh," Lucy called gaily. She tried not to pant as she stood looking at them. She had run down the stairs too fast. She'd held her head high and kept resolutely from her ears and from her heart the sound of Nan's voice as it had floated up to her where she'd stood behind the curtains in her little room.

"I'll go find her," Nan had said and Lucy knew that never would she be able to forget the complacent resignation that had echoed in her dear friend's voice. She'd clutched at the curtains feeling her world sway around her as she heard it and now knew that to Nan Garton—whose life was as dear to her as her own—she was a troublesome hysterical old nuisance. Then she had drawn herself up, feeling the comfort of a becoming dress and her best girdle. She'd hurried down the stairs as silently as her high party heels would allow her. She had stood for a minute looking out into the darkness, seeing the little group in the light at the end of the terrace, knowing that she'd been forgotten by all but her one dutiful friend.

"Oh, hell-oh-ooh!" she called. They looked glum. She would share them, make them at ease, no matter how her own heart bled. She saw their faces brighten. They were all there, she said resolutely to herself. These are bad people, except for my own darling Nan. It is she I must sacrifice myself to save. She stands there as defenseless as an innocent lamb with those two shameless visitors on either side of her. I shall force myself to be polite to them but no more. Good and evil. This is what I see. Nan . . . and facing her the insolent masterful devil who is her brother, trying to take her from me, and then that tall pathetic Honor, who longs to be natural and girlish with me and has to pretend to be sophisticated. Daniel, sweet young Daniel—it is perhaps not too late to save him at least from the corruption of this place, with all its loose women visiting and their panderers such as that horrible Joe Kelly. Daniel is sensitive. I can deal with him being moved by my real womanliness. And Sara, where is she? Where is her flat smirking face? And her smooth brown hair and her holier-than-thou complacency? Is she hiding? Planning some new way to make them a laugh at me? But I'll show them what good breeding stands for. I'll prove to them that a lady is not daunted.

She pulled in her stomach and walked slowly toward the table, her black skirts fluttering.

"Lucy," Nan called. "You had us all worried. Are you all right?"

Yes, yes . . . I am all right, Lucy thought, though my heart is broken and I am lonely unto death.

She smiled.

François, standing in the kitchen door, cleared his throat dramatically. They all looked at him.

"Sirs and ladies," he said in a low voice that commanded their attention as if he were on the stage of the Comédie-Française, "Permit me to drink to your very good health."

He raised a sherry glass somberly, looked at each of them in turn, then bowed to the invisible Sara and sipped once again. "The supper is served," he said.

ii

Timothy looked down the length of the carved table covered with coarse net and flowers and silver. At the end of the corridor of faces, Susan's, Daniel's, Lucy's to his right, with Honor and his Nan and Kelly facing them, he saw the body and the visage of his own dear love. He looked far down at her, past the flickering light of eight candles to where she sat. Even though she did not look at him, but bent her smooth head to the speech of the guests, he could see her and feel her, like a holy ghost, and she made him feel strong, indomitable.

"But are you sure you don't want your sherry?" He heard Sara ask it, and although he listened politely to Susan telling him about art galleries in Munich, he could hear every word at the other end of the table.

"Quite sure, my dear," Lucy said and tossed her head imperiously. "Quite. In fact, I have decided to go on the wagon."

Sara groaned. "But Lucy," she said, "how brave of you! But not tonight, surely. Leave it for tomorrow. Tonight is a party so you simply can't!"

Lucy laughed excitedly and turned over her wine glass. "Oh yes," she cried. "I have decided. No more liquor."

Joe leaned earnestly across the table. "But is it wise to stop so abruptly?" he asked in a soft away, as if genuinely concerned. He smiled at her.

Lucy felt her heart trip a little. This boy, in spite of his loose morals, was sensitive: he understood that she must protest, not at the drinking but the whole wretched scheme of things. She bent toward him. Then she glanced at Sara and saw in her cold green eyes such a vindictive gleam of mockery that her very blood stood still. What a hateful, hateful creature, she moaned inwardly. Oh, my poor Nan! That you should be subjected to the presence of this woman, just to stay near your brother! Lucy tried to smile into the warm small brown eyes of the boy across from her. "Must needs," Lucy said, being gaily noncommittal. "Needs must. When a woman reaches my age, you know . . . ?"

Joe interrupted her dutifully. Christ, he thought, I am such a clumsy boor. I hope I haven't been too late. These goddamned old women put me off, always giving me cues. It's like being examined for epigrams by the Rhodes board. I'll flatter her. I'll dish it out. Sara looks fagged, I'll smooth things over for her. He pulled his warmest, most innocent smile from his well-stocked bag of tricks and spread it tenderly across his endearingly ugly mug. That's what he thought, his smugly ugly mug, but it was oh so endearing . . .

"Lucy," he began and then stuttered in a shy way. "I . . . I mean . . . Mrs. Pendleton . . . You know, I never have quite got over being scared, since I got out of the orphanage, you know, of all these forks and things . . ."

He saw her lean impetuously across the table. Her breasts are dragging down, he thought coldly and looked piteously into her sympathetic eyes.

Timothy sighed. Joe Kelly, he saw, would go far. He was a good boy and would be an intelligent politician. What was this about Lucy's not drinking? Another bid for attention, he imagined. He saw Nan look sharply at her friend across the table.

"But, Lucy dear," Nan said clearly, "are you really on the wagon?"

For a few seconds there was silence. Honor put down the empty sherry glass that she had brought to the table and looked blankly at the two women who sat catacorner from each other, her face flat. Daniel stared at his older sister and noticed that her mouth was taut under its makeup.

"Of course," Joe Kelly heard, "we all know what it is to have such a thing forced upon us."

Lucy teetered self-consciously, like a whore, he thought, boasting of the clap before her uninitiated sisters.

"But Lucy," Honor said, "just for the party tonight!"

Lucy laughed again, her eyes shining.

Susan Harper spoke suddenly. Her eyes shone, too, and she knew she felt a little crazy, as if nothing mattered but getting all the unwilling attention away from this queer old woman who was in some wordless way trying to taunt Sara Porter.

"What does it matter?" Sue's voice was high and she laughed. "If Mrs. Pendleton wants to stop drinking—what does it matter? Why is it anyone else's earthly concern?"

Lucy looked at her. This child had been charming at first before it became clear what she really was, and even then she had seemed very girlish and sweet. She was different now. Perhaps Timothy and his woman had already influenced her by telling her lies. Lucy shrugged.

"Yes," she said lightly. "As Miss Harper says, what does it matter what I do?"

"But Lucy," Nan urged, "do drink just a little, won't you, just for tonight! Everything is so lovely and we all want you to have fun!"

(Oh hell, Timothy thought violently. Why does my Nan go on and on, placating, urging, smoothing? What difference can it make that this tortured woman have her way? She is bent on self-castigation. Nan, Nan . . . let her whip herself.)

"Oh no, never mind about me," Lucy said, smiling understandingly into the fervent brown eyes of the boy across from her then turning toward her hostess.

"Sara, my dear," she murmured graciously, "I think that your François has been trying to attract your attention now for several minutes."

Honor, too, had seen François patiently and discreetly hovering. What did he want, she wondered. Had the meal burned? She hoped not. She was hungry and felt careless and happy, ready to get a little drunk or to talk about dormice. She watched the servant, all the while talking as she was to Nan, whose conversation was queer and spasmodic tonight. Perhaps she feels a little silly, too, Honor thought. Perhaps she knows now that I have found the secret of her flowers. What will she say tomorrow when she learns that Dan and I have run away? Should we say good-bye to anyone?

François was whispering to Sara with his head down. She spoke softly to him. He disappeared and then, while they all talked not too self-consciously, he came back with a green bottle and poured pale golden wine rather tremblingly into each glass except for Lucy Pendleton's. They lifted their glasses solemnly as François stood at attention.

"To us," Timothy said and smiled down the whole table without looking to its end. "Better never lived."

François relaxed, scuttling toward the kitchen.

Sara then leaned forward. "He forgot his collar and tie," she explained clearly. "Poor man. This is a great day for him and he forgot his collar and tie. I told him to carry on and to simply fold a napkin around his throat."

"But of course," Nan cried.

"Why not?" Susan laughed, feeling sillier than ever. Mosca the Gadfly, she cried to herself. That's me and that's François too. She looked cautiously sideways at Dan Tennant who sat beside her.

Dan seemed quite unaware of her. His long nose and his queer birdlike profile loomed above her. She glanced quickly away. He was the darlingest, but definitely the *darlingest*, boy she'd ever seen. She was in love with Joe Kelly, however. No, she was in love with this boy Daniel or was it the silver-haired man who sat on her left? Oh, she thought, I so want to be young again waiting for Father to play with me and to comfort me. I want to be old and to not have all these problems.

François passed down the table and up toward Sara again with a fair napkin folded impeccably about his throat over his grimy shirt and under his white coat, and a platter of little cheesecakes balanced on one arm. They were hot and fragrant. The wine tasted good with them. The strangers gathered here together grew easier and began to talk almost merrily as they ate and drank.

The candles fluttered now as the valet, watching from the kitchen steps with his hot black eyes, walked softly to the windows and drew one curtain expertly across the first night breeze from Geneva. Timothy noticed this and lifted his glass. François bowed profoundly.

iii

"It's Chambertin . . . Gevrey-Chambertin, 1929," Sara said delightedly. She was like a proud child as Timothy walked without a sound around the table pouring wine slowly from a cradled dirty bottle. To Honor, watching him, it seemed as if he were doing a dance. Whatever he did was that way. She turned her eyes deliberately from him to smile at Joe Kelly.

They ate little roasted cold pigeons and dug into a magnificent aspic all atremble with carrots and radishes and slices of cucumber cut like stars and moons. François had made it, Sara said, and they looked admiringly at him as he pretended not to notice and slipped about the room. The wine was rich and ripe and slid warmly down their various throats in different ways.

Joe felt gay, reckless. This was the first decent food and drink since he dragged little Susan Harper into Germany. His stomach was accustomed now to harsh ersatz sausage and potatoes when they were boiled unto death. All this goodness was too much. Am I getting drunk, he wondered? He looked across the table at Mrs. Pendleton. She smiled at him, reassuringly. Dan Tennant, next to her, grinned slyly at him. Sue was next, sweet Sue, *his* Sue. She was busy with that wee pigeon wing. Poor kid, this summer has been more than she bargained for, I'd wager. She was hungry. She might be, for cold pigeon and red wine, but by God he'd satisfied her in other ways! He stirred manfully, smiling inside.

Tim at the end of the table looked at Joe and picked up his glass as he spoke. Tim knew what he was feeling, Joe was sure.

Joe looked past him, then drew his breath sharply. Honor Tennant sat there. He moved his chair and leaned forward. Tim's sister Nan sat next to him. She was a nice little woman in her way, unaffected for such a famous person, but histrionic probably, with her pale popping eyes and a manner too intense for him. He heard himself say something to her, sounding warm, as if it mattered, and then leaned farther around toward Honor.

Honor Tennant gracefully leaned over her plate, and against its Wedgewood birds and palm trees she pressed her knife into a brown-red breast. Aspic shimmered under the silver and on her own chest candlelight fell shimmering, as if she were china, as if she were a bird, as if she were a warm desire-filled woman. Joe turned his head slowly as if on a squeaking screw and smiled at Sara.

Damn Sara, he thought. Honor has a little mouth just like hers. But Honor is cold and snobbish. Damn Sara Porter. But Honor has none of Sara's ripeness. She needs a good man. Sara has one. Sara knows a lot and lets people alone. Honor still knows nothing. Joe stirred again, thinking of Honor and her ignorance.

The pigeon was good, tender and rich. Lucy ate delicately without picking up the bones, as Sara and the others did, even Nan. She savored each small bite. The aspic was good. Oh, she was so very hungry. Her eyes now watered in self-pity as she thought of her hunger and of how she would eat almost nothing all day, being the one moderate person here. She knew no one would notice, but she was resolute and resolved to say nothing, especially since she knew how the lack of sympathy for her very pointedly swearing off alcohol had gone. No one understood her, not even Nan. No one realized that she was doing it simply as a protest to save these young people from a wretched influence. How could anyone hope that Honor and young Daniel and even these two pathetic would-be moderns who were visiting at La Prairie would ever know the meaning of decency and moderation unless she showed them? Nan Garton, even Nan Garton, was lifting her glass and flourishing it under the very nose of the servant.

Lucy looked quickly at François then dropped her eyes. She must be careful. It was only too obvious that he was attracted to her. What was it about her that drew these men on, that brought the hateful look of . . . yes, *lust* into their eyes? François. Joe Kelly. Daniel . . .

Daniel was leaning toward her. His shoulder almost touched hers.

"Lucy," he said softly, "I didn't have a chance to tell you how lovely you look tonight."

Lucy looked at him sharply—had he read her thoughts? Was he mocking her, under the influence of his sister Sara? Was he like everyone else, against her? But as she saw his ingenious eyes, dark green and glowing far back under his heavy brows, she suddenly knew he loved her. How could she have doubted? It was the fault of this malice-ridden air about her. She shrugged quickly as if to shake such foulness from herself and smiled dazzlingly at him.

"Oh, my dear boy!" Lucy said, her voice going up and down the scale of well-poised graciousness. "You are so charming, really, to tell me! And did I ever tell *you* about the time the ambassador from Turkey . . ."

François stood at her right. He inserted the cradled bottle carefully under her elbow.

"No!" Lucy said sharply. She felt almost overwhelmed with irritation. She looked despairingly at Sara who returned her look blankly, then spoke with rapid undertone to the servant. How *can* they tease and insult and torture me, Lucy cried to herself. How can they go on drawing attention to me in this way, deliberately taunting me for being moderate and sensible?

She looked piteously around the table. Timothy was telling one of his stories. Only young Dan now looked at her. Lucy drew herself rigid inside her best girdle and laughed gaily as she went on, in an intimate undertone, about the Turkish ambassador.

iv

They next ate fruit soaked with kirsch in a bowl and little crisp biscuits made in the village for them and drank some champagne. Everything seemed to be easy. Timothy looked around at the faces that lined the table: they leaned this way or that, they spoke effortlessly, and their eyes were candid. Even poor Lucy Pendleton seemed temporarily at peace.

He lifted his glass slightly at François and nodded—François knew what he meant.

Nan knew too. She saw him looking about himself, looking pleased. Then she watched the servant who stood gazing into the long mirror behind Timothy. She saw him glance at the fragile intensity of the begonias brooding there beneath the glass, the flowers that he had carried down from the village, and she felt that he saw them more clearly than he did the people reflected up above them. She lifted her wine to her lips and felt her hand as steady as stone again, stronger than ever before in her life.

François filled her glass. His nails were grimy against the folded napkin around the bottle.

Honor, as his head bent almost level with hers to pour wine, stopped breathing, so strongly did François smell of garlic. She hated that smell. It made her choke. She remembered sitting next to a little girl in grade school and smelling that hideous smell. Now she tried to never breathe when she was close to people for fear it might sweep around her. Even when Jacob kissed her she held her breath for fear . . .

Lucy looked up. François stood at her side again, the champagne bottle cocked. Suddenly, instead of feeling the exasperation that had flooded her at his earlier attempts to pour her wine, she was filled with warmth and love. Poor man, she thought impetuously. Yes, poor man! He may be only a servant but he does know decency when he sees it. He was a valet to a prince once. He is struggling against terrible odds. He is a man. And he sees my bosom and is tormented. I know. I suffer for him. He is utterly shattered.

She smiled at him, conscious of her great heavy breast pulling down and out from her shoulder bones.

François started. He moved quickly behind her, his face discreetly puzzled. He bent over Daniel's shoulder. His hand trembled a little. Dan looked up at him as a little wine spilled.

"A light, please, François. But do forgive my asking Sara's man to light my cigarette for me. It is good training for him. It makes him think of another happier incarnation when he was an eunuch."

Susan laughed. She did not quite know what Daniel had said, nor why he'd said it, really, but felt it harmless and funny and silly. She watched François hold the candle closer to the tip of that boy's cigarette, then felt the marrow of her shoulder bones shudder as Daniel leaned in close to her and said, "You are the loveliest most unbelievable creature anywhere in the world."

His pupils were large and black. Susan looked straight into them and knew he was a little drunk and she wished she were too. She sipped at her cold wine and smiled at him. Tonight she would have fun. Tomorrow is time enough to say good-bye to all this and to Joe and to her own happiness.

V

Lucy took a quick sip from her cup of bitter coffee and shuddered slightly. "But I insist," she cried, her voice sharp under its tone of badinage.

"What is it?" Honor put down her cigarette and turned from Timothy and Susan. "What are you going on about, Lucy?"

Honor saw her sister's face freed suddenly from its mask of almost contemptuous impersonality and was now filled with apprehension. Was someone hurting Sara? Had something frightened her?

"What is it?" Honor's voice was alarmed.

Everyone stopped talking.

Sara dropped her hands. She smiled in a wry way.

"Nothing," she said.

"But it was!" Lucy cried. Her eyes were sparkling. "Darling Sara admired this silly little necklace of mine and so I have insisted that she accept it. I insist! That is all. Is that a crime?"

She laughed again and looked defiantly all around the table while her fingers pulled with controlled fury at the chain of Florentine gold that hung tightly around her ample neck.

Honor and Daniel each felt their blood freeze and dared not look at one another. All their old horror from their childhood rushed into them, remembering as they now did that Sara hated to have anything around her throat. Each was panic-stricken at the scene this might cause, almost to think of Lucy's—or anyone's—trying to put a necklace around their sister's neck. What would Sara do? Would she cry out, or faint? Would she suffer as they were suffering, those who knew her silent phobia, and were themselves now feeling choked and suffocated?

"It *is* a lovely necklace, but *lovely*!" Susan said brightly. She leaned across Dan, who was twirling his glass, his eyes downcast in his face masked by remoteness.

Lucy laughed shortly. "Well, I do think so!" she announced, before turning again toward Sara who sat calmly, her face now very much resembling her brother's.

"I do insist," Lucy said again. "This chain will be perfectly beautiful on you, Sara dear, and I've been wondering all summer what to give you as a little memento of all our gay good times here. You can wear it with anything. You'll wear it *always*."

Sara looked about the table then at Lucy. "Thank you," she said. "Thank you, Lucy."

Timothy saw that she was looking at him. He stood up.

"You're a generous darling, Lucy," he said. "It's a lovely gift. And now let's have some brandy on the terrace." He walked quickly around the table. These Tennants under all their flat-faced calm really were too damned finicky, he thought. He put his hand lightly on Lucy's arm.

"Are you sure you won't have a little nip with me?" he asked her softly. "You look very tired tonight, my dear Lucy. You are too sensitive . . ."

Lucy felt herself being drawn toward the terrace. Damn Timothy Garten, she thought. Then she laughed. He was sly. He was fascinating. But she was the one who really knew the power of love. She would keep Nan from him if it was the last action of her own tortured body.

"No brandy," she cried gaily. "Old as I am, I don't need that to get myself a good time. Come on, all you young people."

She felt for the chain that lay at her throat. What was it that she'd stirred by her overly generous offer to that Sara? She shrugged then pulled furiously at the cigarette as Timothy held the candle to light it for her.

vi

Nan lingered in the room after the others had gone out on the terrace. It was quiet there. The candles were low, and lines made by the heavy net across the dark table zigzagged here and there, pulled by a wine glass or a coffee cup. The flowers looked brighter than when she'd picked them.

She lifted her cup to drink her half-cold bitter coffee.

She could see herself in the mirror. It was like an illustration from some storybook, perhaps *The Princess and the Goblin*, perhaps some other book where the tiny delicate girl stood in the palace candlelight with stars and darkness behind her through the great window. Nan looked small and ageless. She smiled at her own bland romanticism.

To François, who stood suddenly in the kitchen door, she said carefully and in schoolgirl French, "The dinner was excellent. It was beautifully served."

He bowed and then laughed a little with his eyes twinkling. "Did Madame notice?"

Nan shook her head. She didn't know what he was talking about and didn't really care but she acted as if she were listening.

"My collar," François said as he leaned down precariously from the step and clutched his napkin-wrapped throat. "Did not Madame see that from the first course at the beginning of the banquet I was completely nude about the neck?"

Nan shook her head at him again and smiled as he cackled delightedly.

"So much the better," he said. "So much the better! If I may be permitted, it seems to me that all went very well. Even the aspic . . ."

Nan started. She must say something about the aspic, of course, but what a bother it was to try to make people happy. She murmured graciously and more or less grammatically in French and left him bowing and teetering in the doorway.

Outside, the terrace seemed empty at first. Then she saw that Honor and Football Joe and his little love stood by the table at the far end, talking with Sara. They were all smoking and the lights from their cigarettes were level with the lights from far down the lake as if the people, their warm bodies, were part of the night, all but invisible but for that little fire.

Dan stepped from the shadows near the house.

"May I get you a chair or scarf or a cigarette or something?" he spoke with nonchalance as if he were world-weary. Nan smiled secretly, then at him. She was pleased not to be forced to walk out alone in the company of the others. In spite of her new freedom she still liked the reassurance of attention.

She took his arm lightly.

"It's warm now," she said in a low voice. "Will you sit with me there in the deck chairs?" She heard her voice making this sound provocative. I really am a bitch, she thought for the second time that day with an undoubted feeling of complacency. Yes, a bitch. What a pity that I've discovered this so late in life!

Daniel resisted the impulse to take her in his arms, to kiss the politely charming smile from her lips, to carry her far away down toward the brook and into the night. He held her chair for her carefully then sat on the gravel by her side.

"May I get you some brandy?"

"Brandy is too strong. I tried to like it but I just can't. My husband used to give me one sip from his glass. I felt like a taster for the Borgia, rather. I was never poisoned but I simply hated it."

They were whispering to each other. From the group at the end of the terrace came the sound of easy laughter. A soft breeze brought the sound of the bell clangor from the village to them.

"Curfew," Nan murmured. "Dan, where is Timothy?"

Daniel held the match cupped for her with his hands. When did he suddenly become enslaved to the will of any beautiful creature, not dominated by Timothy but his dominator? It was a queer thought, leaving him to wonder which was she? Could I rule her? he asked himself before he could stop the question that shouldn't have been put into words. Well, could you dominate Sue Harper, Tennant? Of course. She may be Kelly's girl but I could have her. He felt self-confident and warm and when the match burned at his palm he dropped it with a comforting oath.

"Excuse me," he said. "Tim's walking up the path with Lucy up there toward the gate."

"Oh dear."

"What? Why, Nan? Are you afraid Lucy is making a scene? Or should I have said that?"

"Oh yes, Dan. You know that this summer has been rather difficult. Poor Lucy . . . there's no use talking about it. But really she's not well. She's so different here. At home she's the most thoughtful loving person. A little overwhelming at times perhaps, but so loving. But here . . . I'm afraid she's really made it hard for Sara."

Nan did not want to talk about Lucy with this boy. She felt disloyal. Dan Tennant was too perspicacious.

He picked up some gravel in one long hand and jiggled it with a tiny rattling noise. Nan could smell smoke from his cigarette and the faint clean odor of pine soap on his skin. Why had she opened such a conversation? How could she discuss one of her dear friends with this child? Was Lucy right? Did Nan really make herself cheap? Was she throwing herself at Dan's head?

He leaned very close to her. She could see his strange eyes twinkling far back between their short thick lashes. And in each pupil a red crown from the casino at Évian was reflected like a tiny flame.

"Fortunate they," he quoted solemnly, "who though once only and then but far away have heard her massive sandal set on stone . . ."

Nan clapped her hands over her mouth and tried not to laugh that she heard Lucy's ponderous footsteps. Daniel was impudent.

She felt cross to think that she had believed him sensitive, sentient. He was an impertinent schoolboy. She laughed in spite of herself, then half-rose from her seat, repentantly, crying as she did so, "Lucy, darling! Come sit here with us, please!"

Lucy came slowly across to them. Her black dress fluttered majestically about her. She felt handsome and dignified. When Daniel stood beside her as she settled herself into the chair next to Nan, she smiled understandingly at him. She seemed to hear Sara's deceitful breathy voice once more saying at the supper table, "How lovely you look tonight, Lucy!" And then she was looking once again into the young man's eyes, knowing that it was really he who saw not with Sara's sly superficiality but deeply, as only a young man could. She thrilled again, to the core of her body, knowing that, even if it was hopeless, this lad loved her under his charming speechlessness.

"Thank you, Dan," she said softly.

"Not at all, Lucy. May I get you some brandy, your cigarettes, a shawl, or something?"

Lucy laughed gaily. "Nan! Did you hear this young rascal? A shawl! Not yet, my dear boy! In a few more years perhaps, but not tonight, certainly!"

Daniel stuttered uncomfortably and hurried to the kitchen.

François was putting dirty plates in neat piles on the drain board. Sara stood beside him with a bottle of cognac in one hand and a little glass in the other.

"Here now," she was saying. "This is ordered, François. Monsieur would wish it. Leave the dishes. Drink this . . . you must be tired. Drink it and then you go on up the hill."

"Oh, Madam," he protested, giggling self-consciously. "François is never tired but if Madame insists . . . if Monsieur Garton would wish it . . ."

He turned, his hand outstretched toward the little glass, then whipped to attention as he saw Daniel.

"Is there something I can do for Monsieur?" His eyes were shining.

Sara sighed. "Get out," she said softly to Dan in English. "Do not lead him on, for God's sake. He's longing to stay here until midnight, thinking valiantly over these dishes. I want him to go home."

"Trust me." Dan said to François in his most insouciant French, "To your health, old fellow. No, nothing tonight. But in the morning I probably will need your help."

François nodded, bowed. Daniel bowed. Sara said good night and walked down the steps into the living room.

"Whatever for?" Her voice sounded puzzled as she handed the bottle of cognac absently to her brother.

"Oh, nothing much. I thought I might get him to help pack for me, you know? As a rehearsal, as we will be leaving one of these days soon." Dan felt he sounded foolish.

"You're a nut," Sara said. "After all these years of going back to school, you don't really need a valet to pack your two suitcases, do you? And anyway," she went on in a quiet voice, "don't let's talk about your leaving. I hate it. Don't talk about it until just the night before you have to go. That's soon enough."

Daniel cleared his throat. "All right."

The table stood pushed toward the end of the room. The green rugs were rolled up. Candles flickered along the top of the bookcases and cast strange shadows into the room and into the other room in the mirror. Timothy stepped soundlessly from the hall and started the gramophone.

As the music of the German tango swooped firmly into the air, Daniel stood miserably waiting for something to happen. He knew he should ask Sara to dance with him, but perhaps Tim would first. He hated to dance with Sara more than anything he knew. She danced well in a strangely languourous way that excited him so he trembled. She was cold, impersonal, and in some fashion almost lascivious when she danced with him and he hated it.

"Dance with me, Dan," Sara told him.

"What'll I do with this bottle?" Dan looked quickly at Timothy who stood with his head down listening intently to the music.

Sara laughed at him then lifted her arms swaying in her filmy gray dress looking like smoke before him. He put the bottle on the table and folded his left arm against her back. He could feel sweat clammy on his palms.

vii

It was late. Lucy, watching from the big chair in the corner, wished she were upstairs quietly reading in bed. But Nan had said, so long ago in the morning, that she felt Lucy should stay with the others and feel herself a part of things. Very well! Lucy wriggled, hid a yawn. She would show Nan how undeserved a criticism she had made.

She wondered how human beings could dance as hard and as wildly as the people who were whirling there before her. It was not age that made her know when enough was enough and to refuse any more of the men's urgings. She felt as young as any of them and was surely fresher looking than some she could mention. Honor's face was frankly gaunt and her magnificent dark eyes flowed feverishly far back in her head. She looked excited and a little crazy as she danced. Little Susan's freshness had grown bright and brittle over the evening so she now looked more the tart she really was under all her seeming decency and even Dan, the youngest of them, was pale and tired in spite of his obvious gaiety.

Sara . . . it was hard to tell about her, except that she moved ever more dreamily and looked paler and more remote as she danced on and on.

Nan Garton was the only one who seemed much less than exhausted. Lucy twisted her mouth bitterly as she watched her friend. Had Nan forgotten all the behavior of a well-bred woman that she could hang this girlishly on the arm of a stranger, such an unprincipled stranger as Joe Kelly? What would Nan's mother think if she could see her? What was her loving brother Timothy doing to allow his sister to make such a fool of herself?

It was liquor that was making fools of all of them. That was the truth of it. They were all drunk, drunk! Lucy felt sick with self-righteous horror, as one who has newly renounced alcohol can feel. She shuddered with profound disgust to watch other less abstemious people dance and laugh around her.

She felt terribly lonely. Suddenly it became plain to her that she was almost certainly dying of some mysterious disease. Memories of whispered conversations between old women when she was a child thronged into her aching head. Cancer. Madness. The bloody flux. Madness. Oh, how the poor dearie suffered before God whisked her off. The agony. Lucy's eyes dazzled with hot tears. Nan would miss her but then it would be too late.

Lucy stood up and went into the kitchen, miserably sure that nobody would even notice. She was hungry. Poor Sara's sad attempt at a feast had been almost laughable, Lucy thought triumphantly, not at all the kind of meal to give to healthy growing youngsters like the Tennants. Things had been well cooked and well served by François in spite of Sara's shiftlessness in letting him appear practically undressed. But the affectation of it all! Cold pigeons! What they all needed was a good roast of beef with plenty of creamy hot mashed potatoes and gravy. It may not be Continental and sophisticated and precious, she thought savagely, but . . .

Empty champagne bottles lay in the sink. Dirty dishes were piled there. Lucy's lip curled.

Softly she opened the cooling cupboard. There was a bowl of mayonnaise with a glass plate set over it. She tiptoed to the bread-box, took out a handful of rather leathery toast sticks, and carried them to the cupboard where she stood ravenously dipping them into the thick rich yellow sauce and eating them in big untidy bites.

viii

Honor ran from the room, then stopped and stood breathing quickly in the darkness outside, her head full of music. She laughed to think that for once she had forgotten to move slowly in a manner better suited to her stateliness.

"Oh, Joe," she said, "that was fun."

He stood with the lights behind him so, when she turned, she saw only the black outline of his enormous shoulders and the thick wedge-shaped ears against his skull.

"Why are you staring at me?" he asked. Even without music playing his voice was almost too soft to hear.

"Am I staring? I was thinking that I had planned not to call you Joe. I don't believe in calling people by their given names until I get to know them."

"But you know me now."

Honor laughed again, turning toward the lake beyond. At the edge of the terrace daisies in a long line glowed like faces.

"Do I?" she asked.

"Yes, Honor," Joe said, sounding impatient. "Goddamn it, you know me better than anyone."

"Do I?"

He stood close to her but without touching her at all and Honor was too conscious of him suddenly. She surprised herself by wondering if she could breathe calmly.

"You should always wear silver," Joe then went on in a conversational way. She started, felt annoyed with him. She smiled teasingly.

"Like George Sand? Have you ever read *Mare Nostrum*? It's by Blasco Ibáñez or one of those boys. George Sand was in it, I think. She wore a silver dagger in her hair, as I remember."

"If you're Sand, who is your Chopin?"

Honor suddenly hated this impassive large man with his thuggish face and purring voice. What business is it of yours? she wondered. Who are you? she'd have liked to suddenly scream at him. How dare you ask me such a question?

"Must I have a Chopin?" She spoke lightly, scornfully. "No dagger, no lover. I am the cat that walks by itself. Let's get more champagne. Let's dance again."

"You stay here."

He took her hand, pulled her close, then seemed to fling her hand away, as if it hurt him.

"I saw you there tonight," he said, his voice so quiet she, in spite of herself, leaned nearer. She rubbed her wrist where he'd held it. The man was a boor and a brute.

"I don't know what you're talking about," she remarked. She wished there were more light so he could see the look of disdain on her face, her lifted eyebrow, her eyes bright with anger.

"I saw you there. I wasn't asleep when you stood there at the table with François looking down at the flowers set before the mirror. You carried flowers in you hand, in a bowl, and you were wearing a long white thing like a winding sheet. You were so beautiful. I said then as I watched you from under my half-closed lids that if you saw me you'd think I was sleeping. I said then that as long as you're alive I will hunt you, that you, Honor Tennant, will be my wife."

Honor laughed. How dare this conceited bully talk to her like that?

"You're such a romantic, Mr. Kelly."

"You're damn right about that, my girl. I am a romantic. I am common. I'm an orphan. We will marry. I'll give you a silver dagger and I will be your lover. I don't need you yet as I've already got you here inside me." He held her by the wrist.

"I've never heard anything so foolish," she said. She was terribly disturbed.

"Let go of me, Joe. You're hurting me. You are completely crazy."

She moved away from him, walking slowly toward the dark in which sat the fountain. Joe was there moving along beside her.

"Don't think I'm leading out into the darkness for another little thrill," she said. "I don't need any kissing."

"You won't get any," he said. "I don't want any of *your* kissing, at least not tonight. But please realize I love you, Honor. I love you more than you have the brains or the guts to yet know. I'll wait for you."

They stood beside the fountain without saying more. Some little lettuces lay there floating in the cool water, which would crisp them for tomorrow. The leaves broke the steady rhythm of the water into spatterings as they drifted under the path of its stream.

What about Sue? Honor wanted to ask. And I'm going away tomorrow and what, anyway, would my sister have to say about tonight?

ix

Susan sat on the terrace atop a cold iron table. She felt very happy. She had not sniffed once since before dinner, years ago. She was a little drunk, which was delightful. She swung her legs back and forth under her skirts, feeling with voluptuous delight the clouds of gauze and gold that scraped delicately against her skin.

She'd danced in her white walking shoes that no one knew about aside from Honor. She'd danced with Daniel. He was too tall. He danced stiffly. He was definitely the most darling boy in the world.

Timothy had danced with her, too, and she knew now she would never again dance as well. He moved to the music as naturally as he walked, perfectly. He was charming, exciting. He was everything.

As Joe was dancing with her, she had not let herself think—in feeling his arms around her and spinning to the music in the candlelight—that she would soon be thousands of miles from him, alone and loveless. Would it break his heart? Dear Joe! She almost moaned at the thought of hurting him, he was so defenseless. But now she was determined, now, that leave she must. She would tell him in the morning.

Lucy was a nice woman who'd talked to her. She was nice but she seemed not to have much fun. Earlier in the evening Sue had had the feeling that Lucy hated everyone, particularly Sara, also Joe and Sue herself. All this was because Lucy so believed in sins of the flesh. I may believe this, too, she thought, but not like Mrs. Pendleton. This isn't her fault, really. It's just how old people are. How terrible it must be to grow old!

And Nan Garton and she had sat together talking as naturally as if Sue were not almost swooning with shyness and delight, as if Nan were not one of the most famous and certainly the most lovely of people in the entire world. Could that really have happened? When she went back to school and told them, would anyone believe her? Yes, yes! She would have this dress! "Keep it," Nan Garton had said. "Please keep the dress, Susan. It was so obviously made for you. When you wear it you can think of me." Susan laughed, knowing she'd never wear it again but that she'd have it for her children and grandchildren and she'd show it to them and tell them about this night and how she'd talked with the exquisite Anne Garton Temple.

Sue picked up the glass that sat beside her on the iron table and emptied it. I'll never grow old in the pathetic way Mrs. Pendleton has, she said, as a toast to herself. I will have children and grandchildren and I'll show them this dress and tell them about my triumphs.

She looked through the open windows into the room. Someone had put out new candles in the pewter holders and the light inside was brighter now than it had been all night. Timothy was dancing, his face rapt. Sara Porter, in his arms, had her head bowed, as if she were almost asleep. It was a slow dance and they moved effortlessly, like one body. That's the way I want to be, Susan thought.

She liked watching Daniel too. He was in love with Nan, it was obvious in the way he danced with her. He'd put on the "Valse Triste" record and he moved, with Nan held lightly in his arms, into the shadowy corner of the room. He held Nan rigidly away from his body, his face as pale as death. As Sue watched his long thin limbs moving in an almost painfully graceful rhythm, she pitied him. The poor boy is suffering, she thought, and she felt a little like crying.

X

Timothy stopped the record before another waltz had really begun and stood by the gramophone as a fugue called and frolicked in the air.

Lucy had come unnoticed from the kitchen. She now stood by the table where Sue sat swinging her legs. Honor walked from the darkness near the fountain, Joe Kelly silent and enormous just behind her. Nan stood with young Daniel in the doorway, each laughing a little and still breathing fast from their last dance. All rested as the music surged around them. It was played on an organ and reminded them of church.

"This sounds so good to me," Nan said, "after the other."

"It's the end of the evening," Sara said. "Let's have one last drink, shall we? For a bonne bouche? Giuliano! You're the one who will be fresh as you haven't been dancing. Dash down to the cellar, will you? For the bottle there in the icebox? It'll be cold enough now."

"Why do you call Joe that?" Susan asked. She'd blurted this out. She sounded to her own ears like she was being impertinent.

Sara laughed. In the light from the flickering candles standing far away from her across both the terrace and the width of the room her face was as white as a moth's wings and just as mysterious.

Because the man's her lover, Lucy thought contemptuously. Or he once was, very obviously. How very crude of poor little Susan to ask, how cruel for him to have brought her here. So typical of Sara to have invited one of her discarded lovers, asking him to bring his present mistress, to the house where she was nothing but a *kept woman*! Oh, Nan! Nan! I must get you away from the corruption of their influence.

Nan heard the music, heard Sue's question, heard her own passionate heart as it beat firmly and steadily within her. She was uplifted by the wine and by those moments when her body was being held closely by Dan and by Football Joe and by Timothy too. Nan felt powerful, longing only to tell her dear brother that she at last loved him and all the world truly, as she was now free of the obsession. Giuliano? What did it matter? An affectation or affection? What did any of this mean, all these syllables and phrases? No matter now. I am free of all this. Good-bye, Timothy.

Dan and Honor looked at one another in the near dark, each seeing the other carefully. They heard how Sara was binding the younger man to her with her tiny silken web of romantic thread that was strange, lovely, exciting. It will hold him, they knew, causing him to listen for his name being said by her, her singling him out, this the same queer mesh she weaves around everyone, including the two of us.

Joe came across to them with a bottle clumsily wrapped in a crumpled towel. He was thumbing up the cork.

"Why is it?" Honor asked abruptly. "You'll tell us why Sara calls you Giuliano, won't you, Joe?"

He held the bottle that was carefully pointed out toward the emptiness where the lake was. His face was blank.

"I don't know," Joe said. "Why do you?" he asked Sara. His voice was softer than ever and more full of wonderment as he spoke to her.

Sara laughed. "Oh, I don't know. Maybe because it's fun? And now let's have one last glass. I'll hold Tim's for him until he comes."

Except for Lucy, they all held out their glasses and Joe filled them carefully.

"God," Daniel suddenly exclaimed. "I didn't know Tim could dance like that!"

In the room the man alone was whirling lightly in front of the great mirror, watching his own movements with what seemed like speculative laughter in his eyes. He rose on his toes and swooped and swung around to the music that now pounded the air, moving faster and faster, and now his feet began to twinkle on the shining floor and as the watchers stood in the darkness looking in at him and at his image doubled in the glass, they could hardly follow the intricate pattern of tappings he was making in counterpoint to the fugue. Faster now and more wildly, he spun and leaped.

There was the sound of glasses breaking and all their eyes swung to where Sara stood watching, the two glasses she'd held lying in shards now on the gravel and her hands at her throat.

"Stop!"

Her voice was a harsh scream, as shrill and shocking as a peacock's.

"Stop!" she cried again.

Timothy, now panting, stood and looked at her as the music, too, ended with a major resolution, as if in relief.

"I'm sorry," Sara said. "Please excuse me."

"It's late," Tim told her gently, looking at her in a puzzled way.

"My throat hurt," she told him. "As if something . . . ?"

"Well, let's all just have this drink and then go on to bed, shall we? I'll have a sip of Nan's."

"And you'll drink from mine," Honor told Sara, her sister's strange cry still echoing in her ears.

They drank to one another, then stood for a few more minutes talking softly of the night and the smell of jasmine in the air, and each thought vaguely of tomorrow. Then they said good night and Timothy left to take Susan and Joe Kelly up the hill to the village in the little car, the others going to their rooms without more words.

When he got back the house was silent. Tim blew out the candles and the night flooded into the room. He ran quickly up the stairs. Sara would be waiting for him.

6

He ran quickly up the stairs. At the first landing he stopped. He waited, a strange expression on his fine, goat-like face, and—as his left leg seemed to yawn—then he leaned his forehead against the cool plastered wall.

Too Terrible to Bear

M.F.K. FISHER AS NOVELIST

An Afterword by Jane Vandenburgh

In the last days of summer a stylish expat couple are welcoming guests to La Prairie, a glorious five-hundred-year-old Swiss estate perched in a meadow high above an alpine lake, surrounded by vineyards. Sara Porter and Tim Garton have removed themselves to Europe to avoid, in part, the approbation of small-minded American society. Though they are clearly spiritually bound, each is still legally married to somebody else.

The year is 1938.

Although the ambiance of their beautiful farmhouse—fountain on the terrace gurgling musically, daisies hanging heavily on their stalks—contributes to the feeling of timelessness, the writer is specific about the date. It is August 31 and the concrete manner in which the story is repeatedly anchored alerts the reader that this is not the summertime idyll it might first appear.

La Prairie functions as an island of beauty and calm seemingly exempt from temporal reality. Here Tim and Sara and their guests talk and drink and eat the magnificent food we'd expect in a book by M.F.K. Fisher, even as twin disasters—one personal, the other historic—bear down on them. As they sit at the long table in the shade of an ancient apple tree, the countries surrounding neutral Switzerland are all moving ever closer to war.

In this powerful and evocative story, the coming war in Europe is the dark backdrop against which all foreground action is set. As storms gather all around them, Sara and Tim live simply and—with little by way of household help—grow flowers and fruit and vegetables, placing this bounty on the table for the pleasure of their guests.

Those who've come to La Prairie are the artistic, the beautiful, the fortunate: Honor Tennant and her brother Daniel, American college students studying languages in Europe. There, too, is Tim's sister, Ann Garton Temple, called "Nan" by her friends, an internationally famous poet travelling with her friend Lucy Pendleton, a painter. They're joined by Sara's old friend Joe Kelly. Orphaned as a child, Joe became a college football star and is now at Oxford as a Rhodes scholar. He and his girl from the States have spent the summer tramping around Europe, a lark that would pass today without comment but might then have ruined this coed's reputation.

We're carried along in the lightest of veins, as if all this story wants to be is a comedy of manners, yet at the edges cold reality begins to dawn: Joe Kelly and Sue Harper have just hitchhiked in from Munich where they've witnessed throngs of starving Jewish refugees. Joe, who's known privation, is sympathetic while Sue, seeing a begging child, cloaks herself in cynicism and looks away. No one here has any real sense of the dimensions of the advancing horror. How can they? In 1938 the word "holocaust" was not yet spelled with a capital *H* and no one could yet imagine the enormity of the coming evil.

Tim and Sara and their guests cannot yet grasp that all existence lies at a perilous edge in those final days of August and that they're about to be exiled from the paradise of La Prairie. They—and we—simply cannot know what disaster will look like when it arrives, only that it surely will.

~

THE DARK CHORD with which the book begins is mysteriously struck at strategic intervals. Written lyrically, as if from the midst of an opium dream, these passages tell of an anonymous man's agony at being suddenly stricken with a nameless condition that, progressing quickly, will cost him his leg. The lines appear without explanation or attribution and serve as section openers and to explicate the title.

One of the great strengths of this book is the manner in which the two almost inconceivable horrors—one intimate, the other global in scope—are kept tactfully at bay as Fisher's characters seek, as an anodyne, to concentrate solely on the beauty of their peaceful lives in which all grievous hardship can still be ignored or denied. In painting this story with the deep contrasts of chiaroscuro, Fisher has managed to write of personal losses so profound she might have otherwise been stunned into silence. The implacable sadness here is only glancingly alluded to, as if, faced directly, the pain would have proved unbearable.

M.F.K. Fisher worked always from autobiographical impulse, inventively depicting the places she lived and traveled to, where she shopped, those she sat with to eat her glorious meals, writing self-revealingly of the details of her own life long before anyone thought to call this kind of personal history "memoir." She so effortlessly captured a specific time and place, working quickly and assuredly, that her storytelling strikes the contemporary ear as conversational and intimate, as if she's maybe confiding in (maybe only) you. If she were a painter we might say she worked *en plein air.*

She was urged to write a novel by many people, including Dillwyn Parrish, the man who would—as soon as each was free to marry—become her second husband. Working from life as unapologetically as she did in her essays, Fisher gave little effort over to artful disguise. Each character here is readily identifiable—the houseman François being, in real life, a villager named François, Fisher's part-time help in the kitchen who was also the town undertaker. Her sister Norah, named "Honor" here, is affectionately called "Nor." And Dillwyn Parrish was famously known to his intimates by the nickname "Tim."

Whose life am I to remember, as Fisher was known to say,
if not my own?

In 1938 M.F.K. Fisher and Dillwyn Parrish were living at Le Paquis, a farm outside the Swiss village of Vevey on which La Prairie is vividly based. The real-life events of late summer directly underlie the story told in *The Theoretical Foot*, as they relate Dillwyn Parrish's swift descent into the agony of Buerger's disease, a circulatory condition causing blood clots in the extremities and resulting in gangrene. His first attack of thrombophlebitis came in the earliest days of September of that year, directly following a night of revelry in which he'd enchanted their houseguests with the grace of his dancing.

As is described in the six hallucinatory passages, Parrish's left leg above the knee was lost to amputation within two weeks of that first attack. The pain in his phantom limb was so excruciating it could be mediated only by the powerful opiate analgeticum, available in Europe but not in the US. When their dwindling finances and the advancing chaos of the Second World War forced them to sell their Swiss estate, the two set about amassing as much of the drug as possible before returning to California. They bought land in rural Hemet, Riverside County, and—in what may have been wry comment on the lushness of the life they'd left in Europe—they called the place in Hemet "Bareacres." They moved into the caretaker's cottage and set about doing renovations, and here Fisher finished the book she'd started at Le Paquis.

Throughout her life M.F.K. Fisher resisted writing fiction. While she was a quick study on sights, sounds, and tastes—all the authentic texture of the sensual world she so easily inhabited—she may have felt she simply didn't resonate on the particular frequency that allowed the thoughts and feelings of others to be readily known to her. In *The Theoretical Foot* she seems to have almost not understood what to do with the autobiographical impulse and so takes the comic tack of subverting it. Sara Porter, as the writer's stand-in, occupies this story's center serving as its dynamic hub, each of the other characters then radiating directly outward from her. As vital as she is to the souls of the others—each indeed seems to even define himself or herself in relationship to Sara—she is herself seen only in their points of view so her own interior life remains mysterious, all but unknown to us.

And the others *do* seem to think about Sara continually, with Honor and Daniel and Tim's sister Nan, and Joe and Sue each wondering who and what Sara *really* is—as warm and charming as she seems or mean, snobbish, aloof? The terrible Lucy Pendleton, as Sara's foil, reveals herself as a self-deluded hypocrite who entertains salacious fantasies even as she sets herself up to judge the other woman's morals.

Fisher always described Dillwyn Parrish as the one true love of her life. The story's mechanism demonstrates how this works in that in the novel Sara, the Fisher character, is known intimately only by Tim.

~

After their return to Riverside County, the two were finally married in the county clerk's office in May of 1939. Struggling with the inevitability of further amputations and the fact that the one efficacious drug was in short supply, Dillwyn Parrish shot himself in August of 1941. Fisher's brother David Kennedy, upon whom the character Daniel Tennant is closely based, hung himself in his parents' barn in Whittier, California, in July of the following year. There is no evidence in the pages of its typescript that Fisher ever so much as looked at *The Theoretical Foot* again.

But the book we have in hand was finished, so why, with all its beauty and thematic power, wasn't it published while M.F.K. Fisher was alive, maybe brought out later when her fame was in its ascendency? Much of that complicated story is lost to time but surely both the layerings of her personal tragedies and family pressure played a part.

Dillwyn Parrish, as illustrator, had collaborated with his sister Anne on a series of children's books and the two were exceptionally close. Her books for adults, escapist romances, sold well in a bleak Depression mileau in which even sophisticated literary people were starved for the easy wit of light entertainment. Her bestsellers had made Anne Parrish rich enough that she could help her brother buy the Swiss estate, which they'd originally conceived of as an artists' retreat. It was to Le Paquis that M.F.K. Fisher and her husband, Al Fisher, had come as guests.

The household in Hemet was supported in part by Anne Parrish's generosity. Motivated by her success, Dillwyn Parrish and M.F.K. Fisher collaborated on a novel, a comedy of manners in the same light vein as his sister's books. Their own concerned a group of travelers gathered in a pension on Mont Pèlerin high above Lake Geneva. *Touch and Go* was published in 1939 under the pseudononym Victoria Berne. Though they'd hoped to make heaps of money, sales were disappointing.

If Fisher had thought to write another lightly witty, pleasant, and pleasing story in *The Theoretical Foot*—as its weightless tone does sometimes suggest—her more truthful and biting nature immediately got the better of her. The book's intial scene has Joe Kelly and Sue Harper—"naked as they were born" as Fisher was fond of saying—having just had sex. They then blow off their meeting with Sara Porter in order to fall back into bed and make love again.

It was during the 1930s, we remember, that James Joyce's *Ulysses* had been embargoed, its import into the US banned by customs officials who had deemed the book obscene. *The Theoretical Foot*—written by a woman and depicting smart, stylish, educated, in all ways enviable women who clearly enjoy their own sexuality—would have been published into times that held that any woman "living in sin" relinquished all claim to respectiblity. Men in these same circumstances would have been seemingly exempt from at least the virulence of such criticism, of course.

What would have ruffled the feathers of the Lucy Pendletons of the world is that neither Sue Harper nor Sara Porter is made to suffer. Neither becomes pregnant and is then cast off, neither drinks arsenic or succumbs to alcoholism or, alone and abandoned, goes mad and throws herself beneath the wheels of a train.

And Lucy Pendleton is portrayed as the very embodiment of those who judge others on grounds of impropriety, snidely condemning her hostess while going ahead to enjoy the wonderful food served at her hosts' table. Lucy will not deign to pick up the tiny game bird served at dinner using her fingers, as the others all do, as she's deemed this unmannerly, behavior she is righteously superior to. She then sneaks into the kitchen to secretly gorge on bread dipped in mayonnaise.

This is the book Dillwyn Parrish's sister read in manuscript directly after Fisher's having finished it. If her sister-in-law strenuously objected to her own portrayal in the famous literary personnage of Ann Garton Temple, she was even more offended on behalf of her friend Mary, who'd been a guest at Le Paquis, and who appears as the Lucy Pendleton character. Anne Parrish called the book hurtful, writing in a letter to Fisher dated 3 February 1940, she wished she hadn't read it, saying: "I feel as though I had overheard confidences not meant for me, eavesdropping unwillingly on you and Dillwyn talking together." And Fisher had, in fact, done little to cover her traces in that she'd named the brother and sister in her story "Tim" and "Ann," then had Lucy go on and on about the incestuous valence of their relationship.

Anne Parrish stressed that in her view the book simply shouldn't be brought out, but added, "[The] time may come when you feel that you do want to publish something with so much force and so much beauty, after so much work. If [so], I think you should use still another pseudonym. Not for my sake, not even for Mary's . . . but to spare yourself and Dillwyn embarrassment."

Fisher's friends, Lawrence Clark Powell and his wife Fay Powell, had been given the book in manuscript at the same time. Each was enormously pleased by it, liking it almost without reservation, their letters and that of Anne Parrish's arriving at Bareacres almost concurrently. Having received their words of praise, Fisher wrote saying these "were as manna to me, since only the day before they came I learned that it will be impossible to publish the thing and furthermore that I had wrought irrevocable damage to one of the few friendships that I care about. I was shocked and terribly surprised. But Tim has always said that I am basically naïve and I suppose that was proof that he's correct. Anyway . . . it did me good to learn that you both thought the book had its good points. I'll put it away and start soon on another one."

Indeed, a year or so after Dillwyn's death, Fisher, needing money, did submit the book to her publisher Duell, Sloan and Pearce. It was rejected for reasons unknown but may well have had to do with its full-frontal attitude toward women's sexuality. And though another writer might have thought to rewrite the book in order to deal with her sister-in-law's objections, Fisher didn't do so.

Though there's no indication she ever became anxious to see this book in print, neither did Fisher suppress it. Having put the manuscript away, she seemingly cleared it from conscious memory as she struggled to recover from the numbingly painful events of those years, its pages lying somewhere untouched until late in the 1970s. Henry Volkening, her longtime agent, had died and she was now represented by Robert Lescher who was newly energetic on her behalf. Fisher obliged Lescher's enthusiasm by sending him everything she had, including the typescript of this book.

Mary Frances Kennedy Fisher simply didn't consider herself a novelist. When urged by her third husband Donald Friede to write the novel that became *Not Now but Now*, Fisher told him: "But I am not a novelist. I've been reading novels all my life, and I don't want to write one." It seems to have slipped her mind that once—and not so very long before—she *had* written one, a love story as tragic as it is beautiful, capturing the historic and incandescent moment she'd spent with the one person she ever completely adored, the man she'd marry and would then almost immediately lose. Lost, too, would be their almost implausibly idyllic life in what now seems not just another country, but another world, the one time and place, as Fisher would later say, she was ever entirely happy.

She'd typed the title page to read:

The Theoretical Foot

A Novel by M.F.K. Parrish